Three irresistible,
least-likely-to-marry knights...

Edmund de Graves.
Revered, powerful, golden.

Rafe Bracton.
Wordly, charming, dangerous.

Campion de Burgh.
Elegant, mature, formidable.

**miraculously find brides—
just in time for Christmas!**

Welcome to Harlequin Historical—where history and fantasy collide! If you want compelling, emotional stories by some of the best writers in the field, look no further.

In addition to our four monthly selections, we are delighted to bring you this special Christmas Collection, led by bestselling and award-winning author **Jo Beverley**, with "The Wise Virgin." *Publishers Weekly* has described her work as **"romance at its best."**

Critics have called award-winning author **Margaret Moore** **"a master storyteller."** "The Vagabond Knight" marks her twentieth title for Harlequin. She also writes for Avon Books.

The popular **Deborah Simmons**, known for her sexy Medievals and Regencies for Harlequin, gives us "The Unexpected Guest." Reviewers claim Simmons **"guarantees a page-turner."**

Have a wonderful holiday, and happy reading!

The Editors,
Harlequin Books

Jo Beverley
Margaret Moore
Deborah Simmons

The Brides of Christmas

HARLEQUIN®

TORONTO • NEW YORK • LONDON
AMSTERDAM • PARIS • SYDNEY • HAMBURG
STOCKHOLM • ATHENS • TOKYO • MILAN • MADRID
PRAGUE • WARSAW • BUDAPEST • AUCKLAND

If you purchased this book without a cover you should be aware that this book is stolen property. It was reported as "unsold and destroyed" to the publisher, and neither the author nor the publisher has received any payment for this "stripped book."

ISBN 0-373-83417-9

THE BRIDES OF CHRISTMAS

Copyright © 1999 by Harlequin Books S.A.

The publisher acknowledges the copyright holders of the individual works as follows:

THE WISE VIRGIN
Copyright © 1999 by Jo Beverley Publications, Inc.

THE VAGABOND KNIGHT
Copyright © 1999 by Margaret Wilkins

THE UNEXPECTED GUEST
Copyright © 1999 by Deborah Siegenthal

All rights reserved. Except for use in any review, the reproduction or utilization of this work in whole or in part in any form by any electronic, mechanical or other means, now known or hereafter invented, including xerography, photocopying and recording, or in any information storage or retrieval system, is forbidden without the written permission of the publisher, Harlequin Enterprises Limited, 225 Duncan Mill Road, Don Mills, Ontario, Canada M3B 3K9.

All characters in this book have no existence outside the imagination of the author and have no relation whatsoever to anyone bearing the same name or names. They are not even distantly inspired by any individual known or unknown to the author, and all incidents are pure invention.

This edition published by arrangement with Harlequin Books S.A.

® and TM are trademarks of the publisher. Trademarks indicated with ® are registered in the United States Patent and Trademark Office, the Canadian Trade Marks Office and in other countries.

Visit us at www.romance.net

Printed in U.S.A.

Table of Contents

JO BEVERLEY was born, raised and educated in England, and holds a degree in English history, so it comes naturally to write historical romances set in her native land in her three chosen periods: Medieval, Georgian and Regency. Her twenty novels have gained her numerous awards, including four RITAs from the Romance Writers of America and two Career Achievement awards from *Romantic Times Magazine.* She is a member of the Romance Writers of America Hall of Fame.

In a review of her first book, Rave Reviews declared, "The sky's the limit for this extraordinary talent!" and the reviewer has been proved correct. Her November 1998 novel, *Forbidden Magic,* spent five weeks on the *USA Today* bestsellers list, and appeared on the extended *New York Times* bestsellers list. In a review of her May 1998 medieval release, *Lord of Midnight, Publishers Weekly* described her as "arguably today's most skillful writer of intelligent historical romance."

Jo lives in British Columbia, Canada, with her husband and two sons.

If you enjoyed "The Wise Virgin," look for her recent books, mentioned above, and *Secrets of the Night,* a Georgian historical from Topaz, 0-451-40889-6, published in July 1999. A new Georgian romance will be published in May 2000. Jo enjoys receiving letters from readers. Please write to her c/o The Alice Orr Agency, 305 Madison Avenue, Suite 1166, New York, NY 10165. A self-addressed stamped envelope is appreciated for a reply.

The Wise Virgin
Jo Beverley

Prologue

"They've stolen the Blessed Virgin Mary!"

The serfs of Woldingham gaped after the horsemen thundering away down the road into the winter woods, their captive's cries fading on the frosty night breeze. Then, like a flock of starlings in the field, they scattered. Most ran for their simple thatch-roof houses, hoping not to be connected with the disaster. The really cautious gathered their families and took to the woods themselves.

After all, who else but the de Graves would commit such a crime? And when the Lord of Woldingham clashed with his old enemy, no one was overcareful where the arrows and even the sword blades fell.

Soon only the village priest and headman were left on the moonlit road leading up to the castle, if one didn't count the abandoned donkey stolidly waiting, head down. Even Joseph had thrown off his borrowed cloak and scuttled away. The two men looked at each other in silent commiseration, then they set off at a run toward the castle that loomed nearby. Despite narrow hall windows blazing with festive light, and bonfires in the bailey, it was an ominous shadow against the starry sky.

Someone had to tell Henry de Montelan, Lord of Woldingham, that his daughter had been seized by his bitterest enemy.

At Christmastide, too.

The gates stood open, waiting for the traditional procession to bring the holy couple up to the castle seeking shelter on Christmas Eve. Unlike the wickedness shown in the Bible, the Lord of Woldingham would offer the shelter of his keep to Mary and Joseph, leading them into the luxury of his solar chamber. The play was a tradition dating back generations, to the last de Montelan to go on Crusade, a tradition closely linked to the blood feud between Woldingham and the nearby castle of Mountgrave.

The two guards stared at the hurrying men, then peered behind for sight of the procession. The priest, Father Hubert, and the headman, Cob Williamson, told of the disaster as they rushed through. The guards came to full alert.

Trouble.

And at Christmastide, too.

The two men threaded their way through the crowded bailey, calling their news but not stopping to answer alarmed questions. Tipsy cooks stopped basting the carcasses roasting on spits, and the sweating baker cursed, then called his assistants to clear tables of bread into baskets and out of the way.

There'd be armed men and horses through here soon.

And at Christmastide, too.

The noisy celebration in the great hall spilled golden light out of the arrow slits and billowed jollity from the open, expectant door of the keep. The two men labored up the outer stairs then stopped to catch their breath. Within the hall, huge fires leaped to drive away the winter chill, spraying sparks as logs settled, blending smoke with the torches flaming on the walls. Around the room, the ladies and gentleman of Woldingham made merry along with guests, household knights and senior servants. A tumult of children—striplings to babes—romped under and around the tables, tangled with a pack of dogs.

Slowly they were noticed, and an expectant silence settled.

Lord Henry de Montelan rose, massive, gracious and rosy with good cheer. "Here at last, eh? Well, say your piece!"

The headman looked at the Father Hubert and the priest accepted his role. He stepped forward. "Lord Henry, a terrible thing has happened."

The silence darkened. "What?" demanded Lord Henry, coming down off the dais toward them. His four stalwart sons rose, dazed but alert. A hound growled.

"What has happened? Where is the holy couple? Where is my daughter?"

The priest fell to his knees. "The de Graves have stolen her, my lord."

After a deadly moment a man howled. Sir Gamel, fiercest of Lord Henry's sons, leaped over the table in front of him in one bound, his teeth bared. "My sword! My sword! I'll gut them all. To horse! Revenge!" He stormed toward the door, brothers not far behind.

Lord Henry stopped him with a hand, perhaps the only man in England able to do it. Though Lord Henry's color stayed high, it was not a sign of good cheer anymore. "Aye, my son, we'll have revenge, and blood and guts aplenty, but we'll not run into a trap. Horses!" he bellowed, and the men in the hall burst into action. "Armor! Weapons! Gamel, Lambert, and Reyner—you hunt them down and bring Nicolette home safe. *Safe,* remember. Harry," he said to his eldest son, "you and I will stay here. In case."

Stalwart Harry agreed, but with a scowl of disappointment.

"At Christmastide?" young Reyner asked, sixteen but nearly as big as his brothers. "They'd steal the Virgin on Christmas Eve?"

"Nothing," growled his father, "is too wicked for the de Graves."

In moments the noise of the castle changed to martial tone, and the lord, his oldest son, and his master-at-arms were huddled in military conference. Father

Hubert and Cob silently congratulated themselves on coming out of it whole and slipped away down the steps. Since no one seemed to be in a mood for feasting, a hunk of roast pork and some loaves went with them. A bit of a feast for the poor villagers.

"A fine state of affairs," mumbled Cob around a piece of juicy meat.

"At Christmastide. At a holy pageant! Godless men. Godless!"

"It's to be hoped the poor Lady Nicolette comes to no harm, Father. For everyone's sakes."

"Indeed, indeed." Then the priest slid a look at his friend. "But do you know, Cob, I could have sworn I saw Lady Nicolette up in the gallery over the hall, peeping out."

The headman stopped. "What? Nay, Father, you must be mistaken. How could that be?"

"Well now, what if some other gentle lady played the part of the Virgin? I thought it a little strange that Lady Nicolette did not speak to me and kept herself so huddled in her cloak."

Cob swallowed the meat in one gulp. "But it's *tradition*, Father. A holy tradition. The youngest virgin of marriageable years in the lord's family plays the part of the Blessed Virgin. And by—"

"—being welcomed into the hall of Woldingham, instead of turned away to lie in a stable, brings God's blessings to everyone in the coming year. Yes, yes. It makes you think, doesn't it?"

"It makes you bloody afeard, it does! What's to

become of us all with the tradition mucked about like that?''

"And what's to become of those involved when it all comes out?'' the priest muttered.

He wasn't thinking about the peasants, or even the feuding men, but about the young women involved in this perilous deception.

And the possible reasons for it.

Father Hubert crossed himself and started to pray.

Chapter One

The huge padded belly finally had a benefit, Joan of Hawes decided as she bounced across the horse, face down, in front of her captor. It cushioned the worst of this. She'd given up screaming and yelling. All that had achieved was a sore throat. Her captor was treating her as if she were a roll of fleeces, ignoring her—other than one strong hand in her belt that stopped her falling off, accidentally or on purpose.

Despite fury and fear, she was grateful for that firm grip. They were racing down a woodland track at a gallop, and she'd no mind to die over this. But who had snatched her off the donkey, and why? And why now, when it would cause such terrible trouble?

Suddenly the rider pulled the horse to a head-tossing, stamping stop, and hoisted her up just like a bundle. Before she could shriek, he turned her, and put her down sitting sideways in front of him on the horse. By the time her dizzy head had settled, they were off again and she'd only caught a glimpse of a

dark-hooded form. Now, however, she could see other
riders around. Strange riders, flowing dark, fast and
fiendishly quiet through the winter-bare, frosty wood.

Earlier, they'd swooped down on the village in silence, like black hawks from the sky....

"Sweet Mary, save me," she whispered. Had she
been seized by the forces of darkness?

She twisted to try to see if her captor had a human
face, but saw only darkness. A shiver of unholy terror
passed through her, but then common sense returned.
He was hot like a man, and smelled like a man—
sweat, wool and horse. Now she saw that his hood
hung forward to shadow his face, and his skin was
darkened in some way. A common raider of some
sort.

Then she understood more. This galloping horse
had no saddle, and the man she was squashed against
wore no mail. The bridle and reins were rope. Not
unearthly devils, then, but men without jingle of bell,
harness or mail. All the horses were dark, too. No
wonder they'd appeared as if out of nowhere.

It was—it had to be—the de Graves, her uncle's
bitterest enemies, taking this opportunity to ruin the
de Montelan's most sacred ceremony. All the same,
she couldn't help admiring the planning and execu-
tion. She did so love a job well done.

But why, oh why, did they have to choose *this* year
to make mischief, when it was going to cause such
terrible trouble? Her cousin Nicolette had been sup-

posed to play the Virgin, and no one must know that she and Joan had changed places.

Perhaps they'd let her go soon. They'd succeeded in disrupting the ceremony, and had no need to keep her. If so, could she get back to the castle before Nicolette was discovered there? Probably. If he put her down now.

"Sirrah," she said.

When he ignored her, she shouted it. "Sirrah!"

He paid no attention, intent on the dark road and speed. Speed taking them farther and farther from Woldingham. Joan eased her arm forward and jabbed back as hard as she could with her elbow.

The horse misstepped, and her captor grunted slightly, but he only said, "Stop that."

Then they were off again, and she knew—knowing men—that there'd be no stopping until he decided it was right to stop. May the devil rot his toes. She thought of throwing herself off the horse, but wasn't feeling suicidal. Just frightened and irritated.

What foolish mischief this was. But then, the whole bloodthirsty feud between the de Graves and the de Montelans was foolish. It had cost lives over the generations, and disrupted the whole countryside hereabouts, and all because of a piece of cloth carried to Jerusalem back in the First Crusade.

In the weeks since Joan had arrived at Woldingham to be companion to her cousin Nicolette, she'd learned all about the wicked, dishonorable de Graves family. They were supposedly guilty of everything from stealing that banner to putting the evil eye on the Woldingham sheep last August. The stories might be true, but she wasn't convinced, mainly because of the current head of the de Graves family.

Not that she'd met the famous Edmund de Graves, of course, but all England had heard of the Golden Lion—beautiful as Saint Michael, brave as Saint George, protector of the weak, defender of the right, dire vengeance on all who did evil…. Legends were told of him, and troubadours sung his praises.

The Golden Lion was son of the famous Silver Lion—Remi de Graves, mighty warrior and advisor to the king. Lord Edmund had been trained from boyhood by the best tutors and warriors, including the almost mythical Almar de Font, a renowned hero in his own right. At sixteen, the Golden Lion had carried the prize at a glittering tourney. At seventeen he had fought brilliantly in the war against France. At eighteen he had singlehandedly cleared out a nest of outlaws, who were terrorizing the area around one of his estates.

It was possibly true that generations ago a de Graves had cheated a de Montelan out of the banner, but the Golden Lion could have nothing to do with wicked rivalry and revenge today.

Could he?

So, was she *not* in the hands of the de Graves?

The horse was pulled to a halt again, pressing her even harder against her captor. Whoever he was, he was a superb rider. This was a fiery destrier, heat and muscles seething beneath her, and her captor was controlling the beast with just legs and a piece of rope.

"Husha, husha, Thor," her captor murmured, leaning forward to pat and soothe the horse's arched neck. His massive chest almost crushed Joan and she squeaked a protest.

He straightened. "My apologies, Lady."

"Now, sirrah," she said, ready to argue for release, but he told her to wait and turned to the other dark riders gathering around, breath puffing white in the cold air.

To her irritation, Joan found herself waiting. She studied the half-dozen hooded men, seeking a clue as to where they came from. They wore no badge, and were almost silent shadows against the moon-silvered woodland, with horse-breathing and hoof-shuffling as the only sounds.

"All's well," her captor said, and without comment the others spun to ride off, scattering.

They really scattered, too, going in different directions, avoiding paths and melting into the woodland. This efficiency did hint at the hand of the great Lord Edmund, but she wouldn't believe he would stoop to something so petty.

It must be some of his men indulging in a prank. She'd heard that the men-at-arms and retainers of the two families were the ones most keen to make trouble. The main point here was to get free and get back to Woldingham.

"You are from the de Graves?" she whispered, as

he turned his horse into the woods, in a different direction again to that taken by the others.

He leaned over her again, but this time to protect her from the prickly holly branch he pushed aside. "Of course. You are safe, Lady, never fear."

Safe. It seemed a strange thing to say, and he was wrong. Joan had never felt less safe in her life, and it had nothing to do with him. She and Nicolette had planned to switch back once the Holy Family was in the castle, but the more time that passed, the more likely it was that Nicolette would be found. Uncle Henry would think they had played a childish trick, and would be furious. If he found out *why,* though.... Joan couldn't even imagine the rage and violence that would result then.

She had to get back.

"Let me go," she said urgently. "You've achieved your purpose."

"Have I?"

"Of course—"

He put a large, callused hand over her mouth, and she heard what he'd heard—the distant howls of her uncle's hounds.

"Sounds carry on still winter air," he breathed into her ear. "Don't try to speak."

He removed his hand and they moved on, the pace slow now because of the unpredictable ground. *Don't speak?* How was she to hammer sense into his head if she couldn't speak? All the same, Joan sagged into silence. *What point in arguing?* How was she to get back to her uncle's castle undetected with hounds on their trail?

The thought of Nicolette; however, made her try again. Perhaps the hounds wouldn't be interested in her trail. "Put me down," she whispered, "Then you can get away."

"We are getting away," he whispered back, with a hint of humor.

"You're alone. You can't fight them. And the hounds—"

"Have many tracks to follow. You find it hard to hold your tongue, don't you, Lady Nicolette?"

Before Joan could decide whether to tell him she wasn't Nicolette, he said, "And here is the well-planned water, to hide our trail."

It was a shallow stream, gurgling noisily over rocks. The horse splashed into and along it, guided by its rider with only subtle shifts of his muscular body.

Clever yet again. "What do you want with me?" she whispered. "Why are you keeping me?"

"Can't you imagine?"

Imagine? Their plan was to disrupt the ceremony. What else?

Then a horrible thought occurred to her.

What if the plan went further than that? What if the plan was to stir the smoldering feud into a hellish fire? There were some at Woldingham who wanted all out war, including her cousin Gamel. What if there were similar men at Mountgrave Castle? Men who wanted to pour oil in the fire.

Disrupting the pageant would be a mere splash of oil. Kidnapping only a cupful. But rape...rape of Lord Henry's only daughter would be a whole barrelful. It would start a conflagration quenched only by the blood of a whole family.

And if only Cousin Joan was available, well, a jug of oil would make a violent enough flame.

Joan sent an urgent, silent prayer to Mary, protector of all virgins, and tried desperately to think of a way to escape.

Fight him off? Ridiculous.

Jump off the horse and run? She'd be caught in a moment.

Push him off the horse and escape on it?

A trained war horse wouldn't be taken, and she might as well try to push the hills alongside the stream as push this man off this horse!

Helplessness started an uncontrollable shivering, and a whirling panic in her mind.

"Cold?" he said. "We'll be in a shelter soon."

"Where? What? Where are you taking me?" Her voice turned shrill, and with a curse, he clasped his hand over her mouth again.

"To a cave," he said, sounding irritated. "It's prepared for a lady's comfort. Now, stay silent until we reach there, woman."

Since he kept his hand over her mouth, she didn't have a choice. However, Joan's fear shrank a little.

Thrown back against him as the horse picked its way up what was probably a sheep track of some sort, she considered his irritated tone. Could a man intent on rape and murder really speak like that?

How could she know? With a bundle of brothers, she knew men quite well, but she knew nothing of how they behaved in war, or in a bloody feud. At the thought of her brothers and her family, tears smarted in her eyes.

In trouble again. That's what they'd say if she lived to face them. Her brothers would rush to kill her defiler, but that wouldn't do much good after the fact. They'd all think it was her own fault, and as usual, they'd be right.

When Joan had arrived at Woldingham, wrapped in furs and hoping for new adventures, she'd found her cousin Nicolette a feeble, weepy sort of person. She'd been summoned, apparently, because of that— to be a companion and raise her spirits. Her aunt Ellen had informed her that Nicolette suffered from a case of a lovesickness—that she was even having to be guarded from running away with the man. She was not to be encouraged in her folly.

"Your parents report you to be a young woman of sense, Joan, and not given to foolish fancies."

Joan had not been feeling particularly sensible at that moment as she was temporarily staggered by the opulence of Woldingham—by the size, the number of retainers and the glittering treasures everywhere she looked. She'd mumbled meek agreement—she had promised her mother she'd behave—but ventured a question. "Whom does Cousin Nicolette love, Aunt?"

"It doesn't matter. He is completely impossible. Completely."

Joan couldn't imagine how Nicolette could be so silly as to imagine herself in love with a landless knight or a troubadour, and she was happy to help her recover. She herself was firmly of the belief that love could be guided toward sensible, suitable targets.

Nicolette had seemed to welcome companionship and distraction, and soon became a lively, charming friend—even if she did sometimes relapse into sighing, unhappy moments. Joan had enjoyed the wealth and comfort of Woldingham, and the rich selection of handsome, eligible young men paying suit to Nicolette.

She'd already decided an older, sensible man would suit her better as a husband, but she had no objection to flattering flirtation with toothsome gallants.

Even though Nicolette was clearly not tempted by any of her gallant swains, Joan had expected the excitement of Christmas to banish all sighs for a while. The closer it drew; however, the more distracted and melancholy Nicolette became. Her loving parents fretted, but never gave the slightest sign of bending.

The man must truly be impossible.

Then one day, Nicolette fainted. After she'd been

carried into the luxurious bedchamber they shared and left to rest, Joan gave her a piece of her mind. "Nicolette, this is foolish beyond measure. No man is worth starving and fainting over!"

"Yes, he is," her cousin said mutinously, but then tears glistened in her eyes. "But it's not that exactly...I'm so afraid..."

"Afraid? Of what?"

"The...the play."

"The Holy Family one? On Christmas Eve?"

Nicolette nodded.

"What is there about that to make you ill? You've played the Virgin for three years, haven't you?"

"Since I started my courses, yes. The youngest virgin of marriageable age..."

"So?"

Nicolette's eyes searched the private room as if someone might be lurking, then she whispered, "I'm not."

"Not what?"

"A *virgin*."

Joan gaped. It was so outrageous she'd not believed it.

Except that it instantly explained so much.

"What's worse," Nicolette added, covering her face with trembling hands, "I'm with child! What am I going to do?" She looked up, wild-eyed. "Don't tell Father and Mother!"

"Of course not." Joan, however, felt ready to lose her breakfast herself. "Why? How...? I assume," she snapped in outrage and terror, "you weren't visited by the Archangel Gabriel! Were you raped?" It seemed the only explanation.

Nicolette sat up. "Of course not. I love him!"

Joan stared. Mooning over Sir Nobody, or a charming troubadour was one thing. Giving her body to him...? "When?"

"At the Martinmas Fair. I didn't plan it. I swear it. It just happened. We stole a few moments. We were so unhappy, and...oh, if only Father would relent! But I never thought until recently that I might have conceived."

Would Uncle Henry soften when he learned of the child? She knew the answer without asking. Nicolette's parents doted on her, but that meant that if they'd refused the match so firmly the man must be truly unsuitable. A baby would change nothing.

Except that it changed everything.

She shuddered at the thought of the reaction when Nicolette had to confess. Would the baby save her from blows? From being thrown into the foulest dungeon? Would her parents' love survive the shock and shame?

Whatever the immediate reaction, Nicolette would end up in a convent until she bore her child, and it would be either strangled or given to serfs to raise. After that, she would either stay behind walls or be married off to whatever man would take money to overlook her flaw.

Joan gathered her weeping cousin into her arms,

though she had no real comfort to offer. The growing child could not be hidden forever. It was all just a question of time.

When her cousin had collected herself a bit, Joan gave what little comfort she could. "Don't worry about the play. Nothing shows. No one will know."

Nicolette stared at her. "Joan, God will know! I can't represent the Blessed Virgin! It will bring a curse on us all."

"Your baby will bring a curse on all soon enough. What difference does a play make?"

"All the difference in the world!" Nicolette put her hands to her stomach. "I know I carry disaster, but that means I cannot add to it. Ever since the de Graves stole the Bethlehem Banner—" she hiccuped on new tears "—ever since then, Woldingham's well-being comes of the Holy Family play."

Joan hoped she was as good a Christian as any, but she had little belief in God paying attention to plays. The reenactment had a lot more to do with human rivalry than with piety.

The grand de Graves and de Montelan families had many estates and moved between them, but they both celebrated Christmastide here in the area. The de Graves displayed the banner that had been carried into Bethlehem during the Crusade. In direct reaction, the de Montelans welcomed the Holy Family into their home, proving their superiority to the rest of mankind. Both families were thumbing their noses at one another rather than engaging in an act of piety.

"You're going to have to do it for me," Nicolette said, jerking Joan out of her thoughts.

"What?"

"Play the Virgin."

"I can't do that!"

"You have to. You *are* a virgin, aren't you?"

"Of course, I am!"

"Well then. I looked at the family records, and I think you are the youngest virgin of marriageable age anyway."

Joan considered what she knew. Her mother was Lord Henry's sister. Of three brothers, two were unmarried, and one had only sons. She had four older married sisters and five brothers. It did seem likely.

"But I can't pass as you."

"Yes, you can. To preserve the illusion of the Holy Family, you'll slip out of the castle secretly."

"With no guards?"

"The guards will just see you down to the village, then return. They won't notice anything. You'll be enveloped in a head-cloth and cloak, with a big cushion for the pregnancy. Besides, it's not their place to speak with you. And remember, when you appear in the hall no one here is supposed to recognize you, either, so you stay well swathed."

Joan had to admit that it seemed possible. "But what of you? You can't be seen. And won't anyone notice that I'm not at the celebrations?"

Nicolette leaned back, frowning over it. "Your

courses!'' she suddenly said. "You suffer so much from them.''

"That's true,'' Joan agreed. She always had terrible pains and, for at least one day a month, had to take to her bed with soothing potions and warm stones to hug.

"You'll have your pains on Christmas Eve.''

"My courses are not due until a week later.''

"I don't suppose anyone will be counting. And I'll pretend to be you.''

"That won't work. Your mother fussed over me the last time.''

"You'll make it clear you don't want fussing, and then she'll be so involved with the Christmas Eve festivities that she'll not have time. I'll huddle down in the bed and moan if anyone comes.''

"I can see a hundred ways for this to go wrong!''

"So can I, but we have to try. Please, Joan. I won't commit sacrilege.''

In the end, Joan had sighed and agreed. "But the problem still remains, Nicolette. What are you going to do?''

For a moment she thought her cousin wouldn't answer, but then she whispered, "I've been in touch with *him*. I've told him about the child. He's going to find a way.''

It was a solution, but a terrible one. "Run away? Leave your family?''

"I have no choice.''

"Oh, Nicolette!'' Joan leaned forward to embrace

her cousin, tears stinging her eyes. It was tempting to berate her again for the string of follies that had led to this suffering, but she knew her cousin must recognize every single one. Now, in this dire situation, what choice was there? It would be hard enough to evade the guard around Nicolette and steal her away. Then Nicolette would be cut off from her family forever, and everyone at Woldingham would be cast into misery. And for what? For that phantasm called love, that wildness called lust.

The best Joan could pray for was that in this dreadful situation, Lord Henry would bend and decide that accepting an unworthy husband was better than losing his daughter forever. After a month at Woldingham, she had doubts. Though just, Lord Henry was relentlessly stern. The innocent were not punished, but the guilty were not spared. He seemed to regard any flexibility or hesitation as if it were a deadly plague.

And, she thought, clasped in the enemy's arms, here she was. Guilty of deception, and possibly sacrilege. What's more, Nicolette was stuck in the castle, presumably still huddling and groaning; the play and feast were both ruined; and the de Montelans were out in furious pursuit of the de Graves, murder on their minds.

Chapter Two

The horse halted, and she glared up at the man. "You," she said, "have made a stupid mess of everything."

"This mess is none of my making," he said shortly, sliding off the horse. He reached up and lifted her down as if she weighed nothing, which certainly wasn't true. She was instantly reminded that she was the prisoner of a very strong and ruthless man who might have evil intentions.

"Come into the warm," he said, leading her toward an ominous opening in the hillside. "Perhaps it will improve your mood."

A curtain had been hung at the cave opening, probably to hide the light, for inside, the space was lit by three dish-shaped oil lamps. There must be an opening above, for the smoke wasn't choking them. It was a little warmer, but not much.

Hay and water stood ready for the horse, and he cared for the beast first. Joan hadn't been aware of how much warmth she'd drawn from his body during the ride, but now she shivered. Perhaps also with fear. A fire was laid ready, so she lit it from one of the lamps and held her hands to it as she looked around. Two fine wooden chests, three jugs and thick furs spread over a ledge of rock.

To make a bed? She swallowed, trying to decide if she were better off trying to pretend to be Nicolette. Then she shook her head. Even neighbors who were deep and ancient enemies couldn't help but meet. This man doubtless knew Nicolette by sight, and no one who knew them would confuse them.

Nicolette was slender, with fine hair the pale gold of rich cream. Joan was well-curved with curly hair closer in color to honey. The huge bolster that faked her ripe pregnancy was proving useful in hiding the shape difference, but that couldn't outweigh the rest when he had a chance to really look at her.

With a final pat of the horse's neck, he came over to her.

"Please, Lady Nicolette, take a seat," he said, gesturing to the furs.

Joan stayed facing the fire, putting off the moment. "Who are you, and what do you want with me?"

"I'm sorry," he said, sounding sincere. "I thought you truly would have guessed, Nicolette. Beneath dark cloth and grime lies Lord Edmund de Graves, and you are now safe in my care."

Joan turned slowly, dizzy with shock.

Golden hair, and beneath the soot on his skin, a

face handsome enough for the Archangel Michael. His skill with the horse. The very quality of that horse. His effortless air of command.

The Golden Lion.

And he'd rescued Nicolette. Why?

Because, of course, he was her lover!

She took the few steps backward to the ledge and sat with a thump. What man would be attractive enough to turn her cousin's wits, and yet the most unsuitable husband in the world for Nicolette of Woldingham?

Lord Edmund de Graves.

"Don't be afraid," he said, pulling off his leather jerkin, revealing a rich green tunic beneath. "We're safe here. In a little while, the first hunt will have died down and we can make our way to Mountgrave."

He dipped a cloth into a bucket of water and scrubbed his face clean. Joan just sat there, stunned and bitterly disappointed. She supposed he was going to be as bitterly disappointed any minute now. Dense of him not to have realized he had the wrong lady, but after a lifetime with her dense brothers she wasn't completely surprised.

At least she needn't fear rape. Instead of pure relief, however, she ached with regrets. Regrets for a tarnished hero. Edmund de Grave—the sort of man to ruin a maid in some corner of the Martinmas fair.

He turned to her. "Please, my lady. We are safe. Make yourself more comfortable."

There was no point putting it off. Joan unwound the enveloping head-cloth.

The smile disappeared. "So. Who are you?"

"Joan of Hawes, cousin to Lady Nicolette."

He sank cross-legged beside the fire, in a breathtakingly elegant movement that seemed unconscious. "Then we have a problem, my lady."

Fighting tears, Joan stood and loosened the low girdle that held her paunch in place. With a wriggle, she made it fall to the ground so she could kick it away.

Well-shaped lips twitched. "Such a casual way with offspring."

"I'm sure many women wish pregnancies could be ended so easily."

"True enough. Why were you playing the part, Lady Joan?"

"You know that, my lord," Joan snapped, sitting down again, and gathering her cloak around her.

"Ah," he said, eyes widening slightly, "the virginity of the Blessed Mary. Truly, I should have thought of that."

"Indeed you should!"

His brows rose a little at her tone. They were lovely brows—golden and smoothly curved. His hair was lovely, too, waving down to his shoulders.

What a deception.

What a waste.

What a temptation, even so.

This was doubtless a lesson planned by heaven to

reinforce her belief that a woman who chose a husband by looks was a fool.

Suppressing a sigh at a bitter lesson learned, she rose. "Now will you return me to Woldingham before folly turns to tragedy?"

He didn't move. "If I had a magic wand, I doubtless would, Lady Joan. As it is, we still must evade the first fury of the hunt. We'll have to rest here for a while." He swiveled, reaching for a jug and two cups, then poured wine for them both. He held one out, and Joan took it, noting that the cup was heavy silver, richly worked. When she sipped, she found rich mead. Even as a fugitive in a cave, Edmund de Graves did not live simply.

That part of the myth was true. The splendor of Mountgrave was part of the myth.

And part of the bitterness between the families, since the de Montelans attributed the de Graves' extreme wealth to their possession of the banner.

Joan wanted to insist that they leave but knew he was right. This area would be full of Woldingham men by now, men who would kill first and think later. The Golden Lion was reputed to be a warrior of almost miraculous skill and strength, but even if that were true, he couldn't defeat ten or twenty—especially unarmed.

Then she saw his armor and sword in the corner near the horse, dull steel and glittering gold, glinting in the firelight. Even armored, however, he couldn't get her safely undetected back to Woldingham yet.

Which blew away any hope of returning before Nicolette was discovered and their actions were known to all.

With a sigh she leaned back on the luxurious make-shift bench.

"Where is Lady Nicolette?" he asked.

"In bed, pretending to be me and unwell."

"Can she remain there undetected for long?"

At least he was as clever as described. No need to lay it all out for him. "Perhaps for a while, my lord. If no one suspects."

"Lady Nicolette is deeply loved by her family. No one will visit her to make sure she is comfortable?"

"You forget. It's not Nicolette. It's me. I'm a mere cousin."

"But a guest. It seems neglectful."

She really didn't want to discuss her private matters with the Golden Lion, but she said, "I have very painful courses, my lord. I've had one bout since arriving at Woldingham. Lady Ellen knows there is nothing to do for me but leave me alone for a while. And she will be busy."

"Ah, and by great good fortune, your courses came now? You are bearing up bravely."

Heat rushed into her cheeks. "They are some days off yet, my lord. We could only hope that Lady Ellen is not paying close attention to such matters."

He shrugged and sipped his wine. "How could you have hoped to pull off the deception to the end?"

She told him of the concealment on the way to the

village. "Then, if everything had gone as planned, Joseph and I would have been escorted to the solar, and the feast would have begun. We would have put aside our cloaks and slipped out to join in the celebration. Nicolette would have appeared, of course, not me. I'd have taken her place in the bed. The deception would not have had to last for long. In an hour or so, I was going to have a miraculous recovery and join the company." Rather wistfully, she added, "I was looking forward to it."

"Poor lady," he said, with a hint of a smile. "We had no choice, however. Other than tonight, Lord Henry has kept his daughter under close guard, and I want no more bloodshed between us."

She thought of the howling hounds and gave him a look.

"There's been no bloodshed yet, and will not be if I can help it," he said.

"That's another reason you won't try to get me back to Woldingham now."

"Exactly. If your family managed to kill me, it would not promote peace."

"This whole adventure will not promote peace!"

"I know it all too well. How long can Lady Nicolette maintain the deception?"

Joan abandoned any thought of making him see how stupid it had been to seduce Nicolette to begin with. "It's impossible to say, my lord. Will Lady Ellen be distracted by the seizure of her daughter, or will she think to come to me with the story? I hope the former. It is possible that I'll be ignored until tomorrow. Can you return me before then?''

''Perhaps. It was never part of the plan. What will happen to Lady Nicolette if she is discovered?''

Joan shrugged. ''She can't reveal the real reason, so she'll have to claim it was a girlish trick. Lord Henry will punish her for sure.''

''How severely? You have destroyed Lord Henry's holy play. Perhaps committed sacrilege, or even treason.''

Joan didn't need the worst put into words. ''Lord Henry loves his daughter deeply.''

''But I don't suppose he loves you that deeply. Perhaps it would be better not to return you to Woldingham at all.''

''I will not leave Nicolette to face him alone.'' The noble statement was interrupted by a noisy rumble— from an empty stomach.

Lord Edmund's brows rose, but he stood to pick up a wooden box and put it open on the ledge beside her. ''Pork, bread and a cake of dried fruits. Not a feast, but something.''

He took none, and returned to his seat by the fire. Joan would have liked to match him in nobly ignoring the food, but she was famished. ''Woldingham fasts on Christmas Eve,'' she said. ''I've only had dry bread and water all day.''

''Whereas I have eaten fish and other foods. Please, my lady, eat. It is for you. While you eat, we can decide what to do.''

Joan tried to control her hunger in front of him, and took only dainty nibbles of pork and bread. "You have to return me to Woldingham, my lord, in case there's a chance to preserve the deception."

"If the deception has been discovered, however, it will go hard with you."

"I don't suppose he'll kill me. Or Nicolette," she added, suddenly struck by his lack of concern over his beloved. "Of course, when he finds out about the child..."

"I am aware of that danger, Lady Joan. This was all an attempt to bring Lady Nicolette to safety."

She opened her mouth to berate him for getting Nicolette with child, but she managed to control herself. "How long before we can attempt the return?"

He looked at the box. "With your appetite, not long."

With heating cheeks, she realized that, morsel by morsel, she'd eaten most of it. "I'm hungry."

"It's as well I'm not." Did his lips twitch again? Was he *laughing* at her? Joan was taking a hearty dislike to the Golden Lion.

Deliberately she picked up the last of the fruit and took a big bite. "*When* can we return me to Woldingham, Lord Edmund?"

"At dawn, perhaps. The serious hunt should have petered out by then. Your safe return will still leave Lady Nicolette imprisoned, however. Can you think of a way to help her reach Mountgrave?"

Joan was about to declare that she wouldn't do that

even if she could, when logic intervened. This was the father of Nicolette's child, the man her cousin loved, and at last he seemed to be putting her welfare first. Nicolette would want to be with him, and would be infinitely safer with him than with her family once her belly started to show.

"Why should I help you?" she asked, hoping to find out more about his intentions. Did he plan to marry her cousin? How could he, without the blessing of her family, with Lord Henry doubtless howling his outrage to the king?

He sipped from his cup. "Wouldn't she like to be reunited with her lover?"

"I'm not sure. It will cause such grief and trouble."

"The cursed feud has been causing grief and trouble for generations. Her belly will cause more. Will Lord Henry soften when he knows she's with child?"

He clearly knew the answer. Joan put down the fruit, her appetite truly gone. "This is such folly. Why must the enmity between you and Lord Henry run so deep?"

"It runs dry on my side, I assure you, despite the deaths over the years."

Joan remembered hearing that Lord Edmund had asked for a truce. "But he will not bend?"

"He's not completely inflexible. I think, deep inside, Lord Henry tires of this madness as much as I do. But this matter has turned it all back into chaos."

"As it was bound to!" Patience snapping, Joan

leaped to her feet. "'Fore God, Lord Edmund, how could you have been so foolish?"

Ignoring his sharp movement, she carried on. "Seeing you, I can begin to understand why Nicolette was swept beyond wisdom, but you have more years and experience. You are the Golden Lion! You should have had strength for both." She turned to pace the confines of the cave, and her thoughts continued to spill out. "Ah, you men are impossible! You think with your—"

He grabbed her skirt and jerked her toward him. Short of toppling onto the fire, she had no choice but to go. "Stop that!" At the last moment, she fell down on her behind rather than go any closer, but he seized her waist and drew her implacably onto his lap.

"Seeing me?" he said, a strange glint in his angry eyes. "Lust after me yourself, do you, Lady Joan?"

May the clever man get warts, and she deserved them herself for revealing her folly.

Joan turned her face away. "I merely accept your appeal, my lord. To a susceptible young woman."

"And you, of course, though young, are not susceptible."

"Not at all." Hastily she added, "And please don't feel you need to prove otherwise—"

He cinched her closer, tight against his broad chest, forcing her to face him, to face teeth bared in a furious smile. "How well you know foolish men, Lady Joan. We can't resist a challenge, can we? Are you sure you were fit to play the Blessed Virgin?"

A hand slid up to settle beneath her breast. Only beneath. A subtle threat, but he could probably feel the frantic pounding of her heart. Why, oh, why hadn't she followed her mother's advice and learned to hold her tongue with men?

"My lord," she said, trying the soothing tone she'd use with a snarling dog, "you don't really have any interest in me, and you dishonor Nicolette by this behavior."

"But we men are impossible." Confining her with one strong arm, he seized her long plaits in the other hand. "And we think with our rods. That was what you were about to say, wasn't it, my foolish virgin?" He began to wrap her hair around his fist, drawing her head inexorably back, then back farther. She squeaked a protest, but it did no good. She ended up stretched like a bow, waiting helplessly for the attacking kiss.

Only then, his eyes on hers, did his lips slowly lower.

At the last moment, they slid away, down to her extended, vulnerable neck. A choked sound escaped her as he ran his hot lips up and down her throat, teasing skin, nerves, tendons and the pounding blood vessels beneath.

It was nothing.

It was terrifying.

"Don't. Please…" Her plea escaped as a whisper.

He ignored it and pressed his teeth into the side of her neck—not hurting, but showing ruthlessly how vulnerable she was. How he, like a ferocious animal, could sever skin and flesh to kill.

That wasn't, however, why she was so panicked. What terrified her was the ridiculous excitement bursting into flame within her. She'd never been handled like this by a man before—never. And her astonishing reaction was a breathless dizziness that was equal parts bizarre, irrational pleasure and blind terror at feeling this way.

He raised his head to look at her with dark, angry eyes. "Still think you are a good judge of men, Lady Joan?"

She could only stare, knowing her eyes must be white around the edges, feeling her heart thunder close to bursting.

"You thought me safe, and I am not. You thought I would take your sharp tongue without retaliation, which I will not. And then you thought worse. You impugned my honor."

With a sharp tug on her trapped hair, he said, "This has not been my idea of a perfect Christmas Eve. This enterprise was embarrassing to think about, tedious to arrange, and dangerous to carry through. It springs from stupidity, weakness and rigid minds. And now, by the thorns, it was all for nothing. I have the wrong woman, and she's a sharp-tongued bitch who wants to lecture me about wisdom and strength. Don't believe the legend of the Golden Lion, Lady Joan. I'm just a man, with all the faults of men. Perhaps I raped

Nicolette. She is after all, the precious daughter of my enemy.''

Joan found the power to shake her head as far as she was able.

''No? As I said, don't believe the legend.''

Consciously or not, he'd relaxed his grip a little. Swallowing, she said, ''Nicolette said it wasn't rape. She wouldn't lie about it.''

''Will she stick to that story when her family's fury falls on her head?''

''She won't lie.''

''Even though she has been such a foolish virgin?''

His cynical disdain was stinging places that had no right to care. ''She was clearly a very foolish virgin to give herself to you.''

Anger flashed and his teeth showed like fangs, but then, like light shifting, it became a true grin, and his expression gentled. ''Ah, Joan, but you're beautiful when you're angry.''

Before Joan could react to that ridiculous statement, his lips descended on hers at last, his strong arm holding her close against him, too close for struggle or escape. She tried to writhe, but even that was scarcely possible, and her bound hair meant she could not free her lips from the overwhelming assault.

She must have stopped struggling, because his left hand was now stroking her side. He started to rock a little, and his lips freed hers to murmur, ''My honey, my pretty one, my sweet, fiery Joan. Give me your lips, give me your soft sighs. Melt to me. I'll never hurt you.''

He kissed her again, and she couldn't stop her lips softening a little, soothed by his gentle, foolish murmurs.

Foolish.

Scarce believable. But...

Edmund de Graves. And her...

He kissed her cheeks, her eyelids, then her lips again. ''Open to me, sweetheart. Let me taste you fully.''

She wanted to taste him, just this once. She let the Golden Lion meld their lips, let him taste her mouth. Tasted his heat, felt his hand on her breast, rubbing the astonishingly sensitive peak.

Her head swirled as with a fever, but she knew this was madness. She must stop him. This was what he'd done to Nicolette, and look at where that had led!

Just a little more, though? A little more before fighting him off...

He suddenly lay back, their lips still joined, so she sprawled on top. Both hands seized her thighs, spreading them over him. He set her lips free, but stayed close, breath warm against her cheek. ''I hunger for you, Joan. Let me feel more of you, just a little more.''

He was big and hot, as if power glowed out of him and into her. She hungered, too. Dazed by him, by her effect on him, she cradled his strong face in her hands, loving that intimate contact. ''A little, then...''

She wouldn't go too far, but she could enjoy a little more.

He pulled her skirts free so she was naked against his tunic. Murmuring soothing nothings, he eased up his own clothes. She stiffened then. No, she mustn't.

But it was only his belly he exposed to her. Her skin lay against his hot, hard flesh, so she felt each of his deep breaths in her most intimate place. Poised for flight, she still thought, *Not yet. Not quite yet. This is too extraordinary, too wonderful.*

He slid his powerful, callused hands up her legs, beneath her skirts, to grip her hips, to hold her pressed to him. "So hot and wet against me." He shifted his torso, moving under her, against her. "Beautiful lady. Give yourself to me."

Joan swayed, fevered, feeling almost as if she breathed through her secret places, breathed in him— his heat, his power, his vibrant essence. His eyes trapped her wits, gazing at her, into her, dark with desire.

For her.

No.

It was *Nicolette* he loved. Nicolette!

"No." She clawed first at one confining hand, then the other, making no impression through the cloth of her garments. "We can't! Let me *go!*"

His hands swooped free to ruthlessly trap her wrists. Oh, what a foolish maiden she had been. And yet, even then, she wanted. Perhaps, even, she wanted him to force her, to override her sense and honor and force her into pleasure.

If not for Nicolette.

Poor Nicolette, betrayed...

Helpless, Joan went still, tears escaping. "Don't," she whispered.

Suddenly Lord Edmund let her go, flinging her hands away. Thrusting off, she toppled free and scrabbled away from him, away to the far side of the cave. When she looked, he was rearranging his clothes.

He met her eyes calmly. "Let that be a lesson, Lady Joan, not to be so disdainful of weak, susceptible women."

After a shocked, agonized moment, she picked up a rock and hurled it at him.

He ducked, and it cracked against the far wall. "Don't do that again." It wasn't a request.

"You're vile! How could you do that when you love Nicolette?"

"I don't give a hen's hoof for Nicolette of Woldingham."

"But—oh!" She wished she had the courage to throw another rock at the heartless brute. "She loves you!"

"No, she doesn't. She loves my brother Gerald. I look forward to introducing you two. He, at least, deserves the sharp edge of your tongue."

"Your—" She let out a shriek of pure frustration. "You should have told me!"

"You should not have impugned my honor with your vile assumptions."

Joan covered her trembling lips with her hands as she finally accepted what a fool he'd made of her. Deliberately. Effortlessly. And she'd crumpled.

And even now, under shock and anguished embarrassment, under the certainty that she would hate Edmund de Graves till the day she died, a little glow warmed her at the thought that at least he wasn't Nicolette's lover.

Fool, she told herself. Fool. Even if free, he was not for Joan of Hawes, and she wouldn't have him if presented on a golden platter by a choir of six-winged angels!

He'd found his cup and was filling it with more mead. "I hope you've learned your lesson, Saint Joan. Seduction's an easy enough matter, especially for a man with a pleasing form. You women," he added, glancing at her, "are all too possible."

Joan actually curled her fingers around another loose rock, a lovely fist-sized one, but she knew when a threat was real. This was a man who'd take instant retaliation. She miserably accepted that she was frightened of him as she'd previously been of no man—that she'd met a will and an edge equal to her own. She'd rather die, however, than let him know. She turned her back in frosty disapproval.

He chuckled and moved. Her skin prickled with wariness, but the next she knew, he was through the curtain and out of the cave.

First came relief, then fear. Would he abandon her here?

His horse was still here, however, placidly munching hay. Despite his lesson, she did know men quite well. She had five brothers. No man would leave such a horse for long, nor his armor.

Private for a moment, she hugged herself and even let a few tears escape. Some of them came from fear about this whole situation, but mostly they came from shame. She hated him, but she hated herself more for being such easy prey, for that foolish, newly found part of herself that had wanted to believe his trickster lies.

That she was beautiful when she was angry.

That she could stir instant passion in a man like Edmund de Graves.

More than anything, however, the tears were a sign of her frustrated fury. Oh, but she wanted the last little while back, and a chance to behave differently. To win. Now she could think of all kinds of clever ways she could have turned the tables and made him look the fool.

She rubbed tears away. She couldn't turn back time, and a wise woman learned lessons so generously offered. Aye, she thought, sitting up and straightening her garments, she'd even be grateful to him for it. No man in the future would cozen her like that, and it did indeed make her more sympathetic toward her cousin. No wonder Nicolette had succumbed—and she had also been in love.

But not with him, a silly gleeful part of her noted. With his brother!

There, it was a warning against love, too! Joan had already decided that love was a folly, and that young men—especially handsome ones—were more trouble than they were worth. She planned to marry an older man, a placid one who would be happy to have a managing wife and who wouldn't want too much attention in bed.

Recent memories flared, saying that bed attention might not be all bad, but she stamped them out. It had been a lesson. Nothing more than a lesson.

She rested her chin on her raised knees and contemplated the glowing fire, trying to settle her mind to serious matters. How could everyone get out of this with a whole skin?

By sweet Saint Margaret, mother of the Virgin, it would be hard. Despite the dangers, she had to get back into Woldingham, and quickly. If Nicolette had not been discovered, and if Joan could sneak back in undetected, they could pretend that Nicolette had been the victim all along and had escaped.

That wouldn't solve Nicolette's true problem, but it would get them through Christmastide.

Lord Edmund didn't want to try to return her to Woldingham now, and Joan could see his reasons, but she felt they must try, and soon. In fact, it would be easier and safer if she attempted it alone. The worst that could happen would be that she'd be "rescued" by the men of Woldingham.

Despite the excellent sense of it, she knew Lord Edmund would not agree. It would offend his manly honor to let her go off alone. Perhaps if she put to him sweetly and gently...

She sighed. She wasn't sure she was able to be sweet and gentle, even under this dire need. For the first time it stung a little. She knew she was too fond of speaking her own mind and making her own decisions. Her parents had seized on the invitation to Woldingham with glee, and not just because it was an honor to visit their grand relations. They'd hoped that Lord Henry's firm rule and Lady Ellen's gracious elegance might teach her better ways, ways more likely to find her a husband.

They had also hoped she would benefit from the example of the sweet-natured, soft-spoken Nicolette.

Lord Edmund was right. Despite liking her cousin, she had looked down on her for her gentle ways, and for letting a man trick her into giving him her maidenhead, no matter how much she might love.

Love. A weakness, not an inevitable part of human existence.

Lust, she admitted, was a part of God's plan, designed for procreation, and she'd just been given a short, sharp lesson in the power of lust. She really should thank him. She'd be forewarned and forearmed another time.

Another time.

With Lord Edmund?

She suddenly blew out a breath. What kind of

thoughts were these? They were certainly unsuited to the moment. If she didn't find a way out of this predicament, she'd likely end up in a convent as punishment, with lust a matter that need no longer trouble her.

What was needed here was a sound plan, and she had it. All she had to do was convince the ever-noble Golden Lion to let her make her way through the winter woods alone.

She sat up straight. If he'd gone any distance, perhaps she could just slip away. Before she lost courage, she stood, gathered her cloak around her, and went to ease out through the curtain.

Chapter Three

She almost walked into him, a dark silhouette against a starry sky. He turned at a sound. No chance at all of slipping away. Why had she expected it?

So, she had to persuade him, but Joan paused, caught by the scene before her eyes.

From their hillside, the land lay before them like a black cloth embroidered with fire. To her right and in the distance glowed Mountgrave. To her left, and closer, lay Woldingham, with lights in the keep and bailey. Perhaps they were continuing some semblance of the feast. People had to eat.

Between the two castles, the dark was scattered with smaller lights from peasant cottages in tiny hamlets, and in the middle, a bonfire of some sort. Above, like a high arched roof, the sky flickered with silver stars, God's protective mantle, with the Christmas star the most brilliant of all.

The star of the Prince of Peace.

"A wonder of God's work, is it not?" the man said quietly from beside her.

"God's beauty above, man's folly below. What of the lives of all the ordinary people down there, my lord, disrupted by a quarrel?"

She heard what might be a growl. "It is more than a quarrel, Lady Joan, and is no fault of the de Graves. We want only peace."

"Have you offered to return the Bethlehem Banner?"

"Return?" He turned to her, stiff with outrage, and they faced each other in the dim light like the warring castles. "The Bethlehem Banner never belonged to the de Montelans."

"They tell another story. They say a de Montelan carried it into Bethlehem. But does it matter?" She spread her hands, gesturing at the scene below. "Lord Edmund, someone is going to have to bend."

"Lady Joan, you are naive. To bend is to be defeated."

At that moment, the bell at the monastery of Colthorpe began to ring, counting the hour of terce. Midnight.

Joan sighed. "So Christ is born again to bring peace and brotherly love to the world. It is as well," she added pointedly, "that God's patience is infinite."

"It is not becoming of a lady to preach."

"It is not becoming of a Christian to refuse to turn

the other cheek. Or to refuse to forgive your enemies.''

He stabbed a furious finger toward Woldingham. "Go preach to your uncle, woman!''

"I tried!''

"And you still have your skin? You cannot have preached very hard.''

Joan gave a wry smile, though Lord Edmund probably couldn't see it in the dark. "It was in the days before Christmas. Lord Henry takes the season seriously.''

"But not seriously enough to end a pointless feud.''

"How, when you will not bend? I'd hoped, from your reputation, that you were a better man—'' She caught herself, scolding like a shrew again.

She'd become used to thinking of herself as honest and forthright, someone who did not dress up her opinions in silk, and who would not be intimidated. Now, here, talking of Christian forbearance and humility, she began to think that perhaps her mother was right about more than tactics. Perhaps it simply wasn't very Christian to be so blunt.

"I'm sorry,'' she said carefully. "The feud is no concern of mine, except that it explains why the de Montelans will never allow Nicolette to marry your brother. For now, we had better discuss what to do next.''

"Apart from beat you?'' But then he shook his head. "Lady Joan, you are an unnatural, undisciplined woman, but I'll leave you to your uncle. He deserves such a cross to bear. As for our actions, I have decided that at dawn I will take you to safety in Mountgrave.''

''Mountgrave!'' She paused and moderated her tone. ''My lord, for Nicolette's sake, you must return me to Woldingham.''

''The possibility of her remaining undetected, and my returning you undetected, is just too small. The area still crawls with your uncle's men.'' He gestured, and she saw tiny, moving lights here and there. Parties from Woldingham, still hunting.

''I see lights near Mountgrave, too. Will they be your men?''

''No. My men have instructions to stay safely within the walls. I am trying to accomplish this without bloodshed. Just before dawn, my forces will ride out to clear a way to Mountgrave, so we should be safe.''

''But you're casting Nicolette to the wolves! If I went alone, now, to Woldingham, I might make it in time.''

He turned to her. ''You jest!''

''About such a serious matter? Lord Edmund, I know it offends—'' She bit that off. ''I know it would be hard for you to let me make my way there unescorted, but it is the way most likely to bring everyone off safe.''

''Impossible. By stealing you away, Lady Joan, I

have made myself responsible for your safety. I cannot allow you to take such risks.''

''I don't see why you have any right to prevent me!''

''Because you are a woman, and I am a man.''

''Very well! If you insist on being so noble, my lord, escort me to Woldingham at dawn instead of to Mountgrave.''

''I cannot risk making myself another martyr, and stirring deeper enmity. Your uncle's men will be forced back from Mountgrave, but they will keep both watch and search near Woldingham. Also, my men can come to our aid on my land, but not on Lord Henry's.''

Joan tucked her chilly hands up the sleeves of her gown. ''But what of Nicolette?''

''And what of you, in the end?'' he said. ''You tried to help your cousin, Lady Joan, and do not deserve to suffer from it.'' He suddenly moved, turning toward the cave and putting a hand to her back to steer her in that direction. ''Come into the warmth and let us see if we can find a miracle.''

Joan went, hoping he hadn't noticed her start at his touch. This power he had over women was most unfair.

As they sat on the ground, safely separated by the low fire, she raised a question that had been scratching at the back of her mind. ''Tell me something, Lord Edmund. Where is your brother? Should he not be here with Nicolette rather than you?''

"Indeed, he should." He put another piece of wood on the fire, and it crackled into flame. Concern in his eyes, he said, "I don't know where he is.

"He was supposed to be in this role," he continued, "but he disappeared yesterday. Out on some business that went against my orders. I chose to go through with my plan. I pray he's returned to Mountgrave by now, and is keeping his hot head."

She suddenly had a terrible suspicion. "Did you tell him what you were arranging?"

He jerked to look at her. "Are you a witch, woman?"

"Are you a fool? Why didn't you *tell* him?"

"I do not need to tell my younger brother everything I plan. And he deserved to sweat for his stupidity!" He suddenly leaned forward, almost too close to the flames. "How did you guess? What do you know?"

Her mouth dried, but not from fear. Because she had bad news for him. "Lord Edmund, I'm very much afraid that Lord Henry has your brother in his dungeon."

"What?" He surged to his feet, and for a moment, she almost feared for her neck, but then he controlled himself and sank down again across the fire from her, not relaxed at all. "Speak."

Joan took a breath. "This morning, in the midst of all the preparations for the feast, some guards brought a prisoner to Woldingham. I didn't get a clear look at him. Perhaps it isn't your brother. And yet, he didn't look like a peasant, despite simple clothes. My uncle had him put into the dungeon, saying that he'd have no unpleasantness at Christmastide, but he seemed extraordinarily pleased about something, and he doubled the guards. I didn't think much about it, being more concerned with my own problems, but now, I fear it is your brother, caught while attempting some rescue of Nicolette.''

"May the imps of hell torment him," Lord Edmund said.

"Lord Henry?"

"My brother."

"You should have told him. Of course he thought you didn't care—"

"A stick will do, Lady Joan. There is no need for the flail." He rested his head for a moment on tense hands. "So, we have two to get out now."

"And me to return." She held chilled hands to the fire, wondering whether Lord Henry's resolve about the peace of Christmas would hold when he thought his daughter was in the hands of his prisoner's family. Gerald de Graves might be under torture even now.

She looked at Lord Edmund. Despite arrogance, he clearly loved his brother, and was also one to take the burdens of the world on his shoulders.

"If I could return secretly, my lord, perhaps I could free your brother. Then he could escape and maybe even take Nicolette, as well."

"I thought you said that Lord Henry had him under double guard?"

"But it is Christmastide."

"If even one of my guards could be tricked or overcome by a woman, Christmastide or not, I'd have his neck. And unless I underestimate Lord Henry, he will have put his best men to guard a de Graves. He finally has the key."

"Oh." She felt stupid for not seeing it. "He'll offer your brother's life for the Bethlehem Banner?"

"And if you did manage to steal that chance for victory, your life wouldn't be worth a pin."

"He couldn't know."

"Once considered, who else?"

After a moment, she said, "Nicolette. If I managed to return undetected, Lord Henry would think Nicolette had been the Virgin, not me. If she then disappeared with your brother, he'd think she'd returned to free him. If they got away, all would be well."

It sounded hopeful to her, but he shook his head. "First, no one woman—or even two—is going to free a de Graves from Lord Henry's dungeon, especially without being recognized. Are you willing to kill the guards? Second, from what I know of Lady Nicolette, even her doting father would not believe her capable of attempting it. No, I'm sure he'd have to realize that you are the key to the whole thing."

Joan couldn't help but feel rather flattered by that.

"If I keep you," he continued, "I have an equal piece to offer for my brother's life."

"I'm not Lord Henry's beloved daughter."

"You're a relative under his protection. He could hardly refuse."

He was right. "That saves your brother *and* your precious banner, but leaves Nicolette and me exposed! You have to let me try to get back into Woldingham. Now, in fact. I promise to try to get your brother and Nicolette out."

"It's impossible."

"Lord Edmund, you are the most inflexible man I have ever met!"

"You are hardly bending in the wind of reason, Lady Joan."

"Because I'm right."

He leaned forward. "I cannot risk the banner my family has protected for generations."

"I will not risk my cousin's skin, without at least trying!" She'd doubtless have thrust her chin right up to him if not for the fire. As it was, the heat was flaring at her jaw.

"You are my hostage, Lady Joan, my means to save my brother. You will remain with me. If the two of you had not engaged in a foolish deception, all would have been well."

"No, it wouldn't, because my uncle would still have your foolish brother. And if you'd told him—"

"Stop flaying me! I have a family disaster on my hands, which is now going to make a feud I have been trying to end even deeper. I asked for none of this."

"Nor did I ask to be tossed over a horse, dragged to a cave, and...and assaulted!"

His tense face suddenly relaxed. "Yes, you did."

"What?" she spluttered.

"Ask to be assaulted. At least you asked for more. Begged, in fact."

She reached for a rock but then restrained herself. "Very wise."

He smirked. It was definitely a smirk.

She picked up the fist-sized rock and threw it. Since she was daring the devil, she did her best to hit him with it, and throwing things hard and accurately was one of her skills. If he hadn't flung up an arm to defend his head, she might have knocked him out. Then she could have escaped.

At contact, he hissed with pain, but he was already lunging for her.

The fire was between them, but it didn't stop him. Probably he was through it so fast it had no chance to catch him. She scuttled back but had no escape. And anyway, mad impulse past, she was fixed in terrified paralysis.

He seized her around the waist and swung her over his raised knee. Through three layers of sturdy cloth, his strong hand stung, but she thanked heaven for those three layers of cloth.

He stopped much sooner than she'd dared to hope, and straightened her to face him, kneeling.

"No screams?" he asked.

"Over that?" she asked, with a bit of bravado, for

she'd felt the swats. "You're not howling and you'll have a bruise."

"Did you not consider," he asked, looking as if he'd like to spank her some more, "the wisdom of injuring the weapon arm of a man who might be your protector?"

"I was aiming for your head. You probably don't need that to—"

The flare of rage in his eyes silenced her. "I'm sorry," she said quickly, and meant it, though she did hope he didn't think his hand had cowed her. "But if you're going to beat me for my unruly tongue, Lord Edmund, your hand will wear out."

"I might consider it a noble sacrifice for mankind. And, Lady Joan, I punished you not for saucy words but for a dangerous physical attack."

"You shouldn't have taunted me!"

"You can't return word attack in kind?"

That halted her for a moment, but then she said, "Your original attack was physical."

He let her go and stood. "Ah yes, I suppose it was."

His look suggested that he understood how devastating his original physical attack had been, and how that had led to this. All she could do was meet his eyes as if he were a man who stirred not a single lustful thought in her.

As if he weren't as beautiful as a warrior angel.

As if his rare smiles didn't make her want to be foolish.

As if her innards didn't tremble every time he touched her.

Her eyes almost stung with the effort of staring blankly at him, but she did it.

After a moment he shook his head as if she were a mystery to him. Good. Very good. "Lady Joan, why are you at Woldingham?"

She was still kneeling as if at a shrine. She hastily scrambled to her feet, taking the opportunity to straighten her clothes, the excuse to look down. "To change my ways and find a husband," she admitted.

"The men being driven away by your daggerlike tongue?"

She couldn't help but smile at him. "Is it as lethal as that?"

He burst out laughing. "Lord save the world. I think your father should put you in a convent that has a vow of silence."

"I'd break out. I'm not just a tongue, you know."

"No, you have a brain behind it, which is why your tongue is lethal. Tell me, why do you attack when you must know you'll be punished?"

She'd never really considered that before. "I can't seem to resist it. People are so infuriatingly stupid sometimes."

He smiled, turning away as if trying to hide it. "Yes, they are, aren't they?" He looked back at her and a connection of some sort made her heart do a silly little somersault. Immediately she guarded herself. Oh no, my lord, that won't work twice.

"Very well," he said, sober again. "Truce. We're engaged in matters too serious for this. Don't throw any more rocks when I offend you, and I won't retaliate for the things you say to me."

"Are you sure that's wise?" she asked. "I'm not sure I've ever unleashed my tongue."

"I think I can bear it. The question is, what can you bear? You were right to point out that if I use you as hostage for my brother, Lord Henry will have to know about the deception. You will suffer for it."

"So will Nicolette."

"She deserves some punishment. Perhaps I should return you to your own home, though you'll doubtless face punishment there, too."

Did he perhaps care about her safety? That tempted Joan to smile. "My parents wearied of punishing me years ago."

"It would have been better if they had persisted."

She cast him a reproachful glance and his lips twitched. "Unprovoked attack. I do beg your pardon, my lady."

"They will be disappointed," she admitted. "They continue to hope, you see, as if time might turn me sweet and pliant, make my hair silky and my figure willowy."

This time it was a definite smile. Lord save her, he had dimples. "Lady Joan, there is nothing at all wrong with your figure."

"Lord Edmund," she said, her thumping heart betraying her words, "I am immune to that sort of attack now."

"It's simple truth, Lady. Men's tastes vary as much as women's, and I like a woman of substance, one I'm not afraid of breaking."

"Oh." She realized she was running her hands over her generously curved body, and his eyes were following her hand.

More acting?

She told herself so. Whichever, she stilled her hands and clasped them modestly before her. "I think I must balance the scales by complimenting you back. You doubtless know it all too well, but you are a very handsome man."

"More curse than blessing. Women make fools of themselves over me, and if they are married women, they create enemies."

Make fools of themselves. Oh, if there were words to armor a maiden to a man's charms—even this feast of a man—those were they. Whether given deliberately or not, she silently thanked him.

"Now we are equal again," she said, turning to pace as she spoke, and glad to break the taut connection between them. "Can we return to plans? Returning me to Hawes would ensure my safety, but Nicolette and your brother would still be in peril. Nicolette has no safe explanation for the switch, and your brother will die unless you return the banner to Wol—"

"Not return," he interrupted sharply. "It was never theirs."

Joan flung up her hands. "How can an apparently reasonable man be so...so unreasoned! Sir Remi de Graves and Sir Henry de Montelan—I'm surprised you aren't called Remi, my lord—"

"My older brother, who died when twelve."

Joan rolled her eyes. Two families trapped in an ancient quarrel. "Sir Remi and Sir Henry went on crusade together, cousins and brothers in arms. They carried with them a banner they hoped to bear victoriously into Jerusalem and into the place of Christ's birth in Bethlehem."

"A banner made by my ancestor's mother and sisters!"

"But carried by both, yes?" When he didn't deny it, she went on, "Unless the de Montelans lie, Sir Remi was wounded in the taking of Jerusalem, and Sir Henry alone rode with it to Bethlehem to complete their vow."

"Remi was wounded in saving Sir Henry's life. His blood stains the banner to this day!"

"No one denies that. But why do not the de Montelans have a right to the banner half the year, as they claim?"

"Because, Lady Joan, they would not return it."

"Are you not judging them by yourselves?"

She watched his hands clench into fists then, with effort, relax. "Are you saying," he asked grimly, "that if I gave the banner to Lord Henry now, he'd return it in a six-month?"

"No. But he has many a six-month to make up for. Lord Edmund, someone has to bend!"

"It will not be me. I will not betray the generations that have gone before."

"I see. You're afraid of them, and of what people will say."

His fists clenched again. "Take back those words, Lady Joan. I fear only God."

Joan wished she hadn't said it, largely because she could see it hurt him in ways she'd not expected or intended. She was past the point of return now, however. "I cannot take them back, my lord, unless you prove them not to be true."

He whirled away, looking up. "What sins have I committed, Lord, that you punish me with this woman? Her tongue flays me, yet my honor says I cannot strike back! My body burns—"

Though trembling with physical fear, Joan caught those chopped-short words.

Oh.

My body burns. One thing was sure—that had come deep from within. It had been no trick.

Of course, she told herself, there was nothing deep and meaningful about it. But it was undeniably satisfying to think that at this moment, the Golden Lion burned for her.

He turned to look at her, almost sheepishly. "Lust," he said.

She nodded. "You're probably used to it. It's new to me."

"You've never lusted?"

"Not like this."

He ran a hand through his hair, looking away. "We should not even be aware of these things at such a time. When so many important matters hang in the balance."

"It's not easy to stop, though, is it?"

His eyes rested darkly on hers. Flickered over her. Back. "No, it's not easy to stop."

What would happen if she touched him? She'd probably end up like Nicolette. At the moment, it didn't seem to matter. "Does your lust make it hard for you to think straight?"

"I would have thought that was obvious!" He turned abruptly to seize the jug of mead and fill the two cups. Some splashed on the floor. He passed one to her and unsteady hands brushed, sending sparks up her. Their eyes held as they drank.

Broke free.

She wanted to ask many questions, the main one being, did this happen to him all the time with woman after woman, or was there anything special about it? Just a little bit special? Something about her?

Another one was, if she tried really hard, tried to become more gentle and sweet natured, to guard her tongue, would there be any hope...?

Oh, indeed, she was a foolish virgin. He wasn't

trying to trick her again, but she was doing it all by herself!

"The first idea was better," he said, sitting on the rocky shelf covered with furs, as far as possible from her and the heat of the fire. "You will be my hostage to bargain for Gerald."

Matching his cool tone, Joan said, "I think it would be better for me to attempt to return to Woldingham, now."

"The woods will still be crawling with men."

"I'm one small woman."

"And hounds."

She'd forgotten the hounds.

"If I use you as hostage, I can make it clear that the raid was simply to gain a prisoner to balance my brother. Yes, Lord Henry will be angry at you and Nicolette for switching places, but if he does not punish during Christmastide, perhaps his rage will fade. If not, we still have twelve days to think of some other solution."

The thought of Lord Henry's massive hounds on the hunt had definitely sapped Joan's courage for a lonely trek, but she said, "Your plan means Nicolette will have to face them alone. She'll be so afraid."

"Unlike you?"

"I'm with you, and she's with Uncle Henry."

His brows rose. "As you've seen, I have no scruples about meting out punishment at Christmastide."

She almost said that she didn't fear him, but he'd probably take it the wrong way. She would mean that she didn't fear terrible punishment from him unless she did something truly terrible, in which case she'd deserve it.

What if he did something terrible?

"What are you thinking now, you wretched woman?" But the smile in his eyes took any offense from it.

She surrendered to honesty. "I was wondering whether you'd let me punish you if you did something stupid or wrong."

"No."

"Why not?"

"Why should I?"

"Strength," she complained with a huffed-out breath. "It's most unfair."

"Woman was put on the earth to be governed by men, and man was given the strength necessary for the task."

"So," she mused in deliberate wickedness, "if you were weakened by injury…"

"I'd stay well out of your reach! Very well, Lady Joan," he said, "I take your point and will make you another bargain. If ever, during our brief adventure, I give in to temptation and strike you again, I will let you pay me back in even measure." Before she could quibble, he added, "And you may compensate for strength and size by using a tool—stick, rock, what you will."

"Even your sword?" she asked, eyeing the magnificently scabbarded weapon lying near his mail.

"If you think that just."

She pulled a face at him. "I have to be just? That takes the fun out of it."

He laughed, a natural open laugh despite the perilous nature of their problems.

Something deeper stirred inside her. Here was the first man she'd found that she could talk to without watching every word, who seemed able—after a fashion—to accept her blunt speech, and even give as good as he got.

Sad that it would only be a "brief adventure."

Enough of that. She resolutely turned her mind back to plans. "If you exchange me for your brother, nothing will have changed."

"True. It will be worse, in fact. I'll still have to rescue Lady Nicolette or Gerald will rush into danger again. And all hope of peace will be over."

He sighed and leaned back against the wall. "The irony is that Lord Henry was moving a little. I've been negotiating with him for nearly a year, with only moderate success, but recently he became much more open to suggestions. Two things happened simultaneously, just weeks ago. Gerald confessed his folly and told me Lady Nicolette was carrying his child, and Lord Henry proposed peace, sealed by a marriage, the matter of the banner to be sorted out later. It was almost complete capitulation."

"Nicolette and Gerald? But then—"

"Of course not," he said, looking at her. "Nicolette and me."

"Oh." Joan could see what a disaster that had been, but she was struggling with the thought that even Lord Henry had tried to bend. He surely couldn't have known which de Graves Nicolette loved, so he'd assumed the most likely and tried to obtain him for his daughter.

"Without Gerald's news, I would have accepted. As it was, all I could do was propose a marriage to my brother, which Lord Henry quite rightly took as an insult. If I'd been given any time to plan at all," he added with irritation, "I would have married again myself and thus been unavailable."

"You've been married?" Ridiculous to be hurt.

He looked at her strangely. "I'm twenty-five years old and destined to be Lord of Mountgrave since I was ten. Of course I've been married. It was arranged when I was thirteen. An excellent alliance, but my wife died of a flux two years ago."

"I'm sorry."

He shrugged. "I've been busy with warfare and attendance on the king since I was sixteen, so I never saw her for more than a week in a six-month. I'd say 'poor Catherine,' except that she was perfectly content in the situation."

"I can understand that," Joan said, struck by the charms of such an arrangement. Her parents, and the neighboring families she knew well, did not spend much time apart. With grand families, however...

Then she looked at him, blushing. "I wasn't referring to you, my lord!'' Then she wished she'd not even hinted at marriage between them.

''You think you could tolerate my presence for a little longer than that?''

''Of course! I mean…'' She collected herself from the embarrassing mire. ''I merely thought that I might seek out a similar husband. One much engaged with national affairs.''

''A husband who will leave you in sovereignty over your world?''

''You have to see, Lord Edmund, how ill suited I am to day-by-day compliance.''

He leaned back, studying her. ''But—and remember you agreed not to throw rocks at me—you seemed to enjoy a man's physical attentions.''

Her blush was an answer. ''But I doubt many men could make them as pleasant to me as you did.''

He smiled, and looked away for a moment almost bashfully. Truly, at times, Lord Edmund was a tantalizing mystery, and it was his faults and frailties that fascinated her more than his obvious charms.

If only…

Don't be foolish, Joan.

He patted the fur beside him. ''Come sit over here. It doesn't suit me to talk across the cave like warring factions.'' When she hesitated, he added, ''You have my word. I won't hurt you.''

Chapter Four

"I know," she said, walking over. "You seem to have forgotten that I might have reason not to want to sit."

"I didn't think I'd been so harsh."

"You weren't," she admitted as she sat. She looked at his arm, hidden by his sleeve. "What of you?"

He pushed up the sleeve and, with a wince, she saw a dark red bruise near his elbow.

"Nothing that will impede my fighting," he assured her, flexing the muscular arm. But then he held it out to her. "Perhaps you should kiss it better."

She looked him in the eye. "Oh no. Then you might think you should kiss *my* hurts better."

Dimples flickered. "If you wish, my lady."

She stared into his eyes. "Don't."

As if he understood, his expression turned wry and he lowered his arm, leaning back against the wall. "So, my wise virgin, what are we to do?"

She grasped the assumption that they were talking about the feud, Nicolette and his brother. "I do admire your desire for peace."

"Even if I cannot bring myself to do what is necessary to create it, and surrender the banner?" His brows rose. "Silence? I pray I haven't cowed you."

"I'm practicing tact and tongue control, since I fear this will all end with me imprisoned in a convent."

"A terrible waste."

"Perhaps in time I'll become an abbess, able to flay the male world with impunity."

"A waste."

"My cleverness and administrative abilities would be put to full use."

"A waste," he insisted.

"A waste of what, my lord?"

"Of a great deal of heat and fire." He held out a hand. "Come here."

Though her body longed to leap at him, Joan made herself eye that tempting hand. "I've learned my lessons well."

"I have more to teach."

Joan swallowed. "I don't deny you have an effect on me, Lord Edmund, but two Woldingham maids carrying de Graves babies will hardly improve matters."

"I won't get you with child."

"Many a man says that."

That anger sparked in his eyes again, anger because

she was doubting his honor. She didn't. Truly. And yet, she didn't trust any man in matters like this.

"Swear it to me," she demanded.

Frostily, totally without dimples, he said, "I swear on my immortal soul, Joan of Hawes, that I will not get you with child this night."

"Good." But she sighed. By obtaining the oath, she'd destroyed any chance of needing it.

But then his hand stretched out again, and her pulse started a nervous beat. "This is hardly the time—"

"This might be the only time. The feud is now likely to be cast in iron. Would even your tolerant parents allow marriage between us, to the great offense of Lord Henry?"

"*Marriage?* You can't expect me to fall for a trick like—"

"Joan!"

She covered her unruly mouth with her hand. "Oh, I'm sorry. I truly didn't mean... But—" she hardly dared put it into words "—are you saying you might want to *marry me?* Why?"

He captured her hand and tugged her closer. "Poor Joan. Have you been so unvalued?"

"N-no. I've had men interested, but none who interested me. But you..."

Dimples flickered. "Awed by the great Edmund de Graves? I'd have thought you'd learned better by now."

"I've learned nothing but good of you."

She was against his broad, warm chest.

"You see my faults as virtues. What more can any man want?" A hand slid beneath her plaits, rough hot against her neck. "I like you, Joan, as I've liked no woman before. I like your courage and your calm head. Now I've grown accustomed, I even like your sharp tongue, for it is wielded by a clever brain." He tilted her head up toward him. "Can you imagine how wearying it is to be surrounded by people who reverence every word I say. I'd welcome a truth sayer." His other hand found her thigh and stroked upward, over cloth. "And my body likes your body—very well, indeed."

"My body likes yours very well, too. But is this wise? We have plans to make."

"The plans are made. I'll bring you through this unscathed if I can, so at dawn I will take you safely to Woldingham."

Complete reversal. "But—"

He slid her off the bench, to stand between his legs. "We have a night to pass before dawn, and I have plans for that, too."

"But your brother!"

"I'll find some other way." He pulled her close and his head came to rest between her breasts.

She held him off. "What of the danger to you?"

"It is nothing beside the danger to you."

"This is folly. Take me to Mountgrave and bargain me for your brother. At least Nicolette and I will not lose our lives."

"Trapped in a convent? Close to death for you,

Joan. Let me prove it. Prove that it would be a waste.'' His hands merely flexed on her hips, but she swayed, and her body, her inner body, ached.

''All women feel this way, but many become nuns, and happily so.''

''All women do not feel this way. Some, though excellent wives and mothers, are cool. My Catherine was. She was a dutiful bed partner, but if she could have started a child with a hug she would have preferred it.''

Joan found that impossible to believe. Her hands rested on his shoulders, close to his bare neck. With her thumbs, she tilted his chin up. ''Are you sure of that?''

''Yes, for we spoke of it. Though not as sharp as you, Catherine didn't hesitate to speak her mind. She was some years older than I, and experienced. Twenty when we finally wed, and two years a widow. I was just fifteen. She knew her needs and how to demand them, and did not mind if I took other women for more vigorous sex-play.''

Joan frowned, and his brows rose as he continued, ''Are you saying that when you wed your busy man, you will expect him to be virtuous when he's away?''

''I'd hoped he would not be much interested in sex at all.''

''That would be a waste of another kind. Even if your matings are few, Joan, you should want them to be fiery.'' He pulled her closer. ''Do you deny the fire in you?''

Hot almost to sweating, she could only shake her head.

"And I burn. Do you think I burn for every lovely young woman I meet?"

"Yes."

He laughed. "Very well. A little, yes. But not like this, Joan. On my honor."

He looked completely honest, but her stern common sense was not dead. "It's only the night, and the cave, and the fear."

"I'm not afraid."

"You're probably never afraid."

"Any man fears when there is reason to. He does not let it rule him. But I do not borrow fear, and nor should you. What tomorrow brings, we will deal with tomorrow. Now is now and, yes, it's the night and the cave. But it's also you." He rubbed his face against her, and his mouth brushed—once, twice—across her nipples. "I never thought I'd like a woman with a sharp tongue, still less one who hurled rocks at my head. But you are like pepper to my senses—burning but delicious."

Looking down, she could see her brazen nipples pushing at the cloth. She watched as he repeated, "Delicious," and put teeth gently to first one, then the other.

Conquered, she let her weak knees give way so she knelt, supported by her arms on his thighs. "You shouldn't encourage me. I'm sure my tongue can get worse and worse."

''Then I will teach it other tricks.'' He captured her head and kissed her, engaging her tongue in another kind of battle.

When it ended, she clung to him, dazed. ''You could blunt a tongue entirely that way.''

He smiled, stroking her hair. ''That's what I thought. But there are other ways.'' Sitting straighter, he dragged his tunic and shirt over his head, presenting a stunning, firelit torso, a sculpture of muscle. ''Explore me with your clever tongue, Joan.''

She reached for him, but he captured her hands, holding them on his thighs. ''Just your tongue.''

Her tongue stirred hungrily in her mouth as she studied him, already savoring the warmth, texture and taste. Broad chest, small, flat nipples, a trace of hair low down the middle, around his navel and lower...

His navel, just above the drawstring of his braies.

Slowly she leaned forward to circle it with her tongue, closing her eyes the better to savor the heat, the taste of sweat and salt, the texture of smooth skin and ticklish hair. She dipped her tongue into it and felt his ridged belly muscles shudder.

Oh, she liked that.

Deep inside, her body pulsed insistently in response.

She wavered for a moment, fearful of her own hunger. Of conquest and consequences. But then she remembered his oath, and she knew the Golden Lion would keep it.

Putting her mouth to his navel, she kissed it, feeling

his hands tighten on hers, feeling her own hands clench on his thighs. She took her mouth away to blow on his wet skin, smiling at his shiver. Glancing up, she saw that he was leaning back, his eyes shut, lost in sensations she was creating.

Smile widening, she trailed her tongue lower, easing beneath the tied top of his braies. She felt him move and looked up a little nervously, wondering if she'd gone too far.

His eyes were open, meeting hers, heavy lidded. "If I wasn't feeling kind, I'd dare you to go further."

"I'm sure you know I can't resist a dare."

"I thought you were a very sensible virgin."

"You swore an oath, and I'm a very curious virgin. I've never seen…" To her annoyance, words escaped her then. "I can feel that you are… I mean…"

"Yes, I am." He released her hands and untied the cord that held his woolen garment up, then leaned back, leaving her to do as she wished.

With a bubble of excited anticipation and a wave of hot embarrassment, Joan lowered his braies.

Oh, my. She'd heard enough jokes and whispered stories to know what to expect, but she supposed most women saw this coming at them with intent. Presented to her like this, he was beautiful and she wanted to taste him.

"Tell me if I hurt you," she whispered, before touching her tongue to the tip of his rigid shaft.

She thought he laughed, though it might have been a groan. He was hard as rock, but like a rock warmed by the fireside then covered in silk. A musky smell teased at her, warm, comforting in some way....

Reason said other men were made much the same way, but she couldn't imagine feeling like this about another man.

He'd been right when he'd said her family would never permit such a marriage, even to the great Edmund de Graves. It would offend family loyalty too deeply.

What was to become of her?

Fighting away tears, she ran her tongue up and down him. When she brushed the ridge near the tip he jerked. She noted that and returned to tease.

"Does doing this disqualify me from the convent?" she wondered, contemplating the glistening, vulnerable tip.

"You don't have to tell them." He did sound breathless.

Arms resting on his tense thighs, she looked up. "What's going to happen if I keep doing this?"

"I'll spill my seed. You won't get pregnant unless I spill it in you."

"Do you like what I'm doing?"

His eyes crinkled. "No. But I liked what you were doing."

With a laugh, she said, "Tell me what you'd like even more. Give my sharp tongue power over you, Edmund de Graves."

"Don't say sharp to a man at a moment like this!" But he was teasing, and he suggested things. With a smile, she did them, aware with dazzled astonishment of him falling apart, exquisitely, trustingly vulnerable here at this moment with her.

When his breathing steadied and he opened his eyes, she said, "You're right. I'm not suited to a convent. This is too much power to give up."

He laughed and pulled her up for a ravishing kiss. Before she knew it, his hand was under her skirts, his mouth was at her cloth-covered breasts. When she arched and cried out, astonished by building sensations, he stilled his clever fingers and raised his skillful mouth. "The power goes both ways, Joan. Do you want me to stop now, before you turn to mindless wax in my hands?"

She shook her head. "Serve me. Give me what I want."

He laughed at her parry and obeyed, and who was to say who was the victor, who the vanquished at the end?

They lay together on the fur-covered ledge, and for Joan, at least, it was a time of strange adjustment. He'd taught her a lesson earlier about lust, but this had been a more potent one. The lesson she had learned here was that lust had a beauty of its own, and that she didn't want to live without it.

She wasn't prepared to say that she could only experience the beauty with this man, but she felt quite sure such harmony of desire was rare.

Yet to have him was almost impossible.

Their marriage was no more impossible than Nicolette and his brother, a part of her argued, and that would have to be, despite the enmity.

She couldn't give him up.

She couldn't!

She rose up on her elbow to trace his lips with her finger. "I want to marry you."

Those lips twitched. "I'm good, aren't I?"

She punched him on the shoulder for cocky arrogance. Justified, though.

He turned serious and caressed her face, brushing wild escaping curls off her cheeks. "I'd like to marry you, too, but I don't see how. Duty comes first. I'm determined to end this feud. At the very least, I cannot make matters worse and steal you away, too."

"If your brother and Nicolette are to be together—"

He laid fingers on her lips. "Gerald is not me. He is not the Lord of Mountgrave. He can move to one of my other estates and be out of sight. He won't have to constantly deal with Lord Henry over local and national matters."

"Lord Henry will never forget or forgive the loss of his beloved daughter, even if they move to Spain!"

He closed his eyes. "I know it. But our marriage would be daily salt in the wounds."

Joan straightened, frowning. "Then there's only one way. We have to end the feud."

"Willingly. Point the way."

"There's always a way."

"I wish I had your faith." He captured her and drew her down to him. "As it is, all we have is now."

She didn't give up—there generally was a way if a person was determined enough—but certainly going around and around it now would be a waste of time.

Of precious time.

She slid out of his hands and off the ledge to remove his loose braies, taking deep pleasure in his long, muscular legs, only realizing then that she was down to her linen shift.

Yes, he was good.

When he was naked, she said, "Turn over. I want to explore your back."

He merely lay there. "Make me."

The resulting fight was a different kind of education to Joan, and equally enjoyable. She was like a child next to his strength, but he managed his power with control and was surprisingly vulnerable to tickles, so she ended up straddling his back, massaging his muscles, each flex of her spread thighs against him stirring her aching hunger.

Oh yes, she was hungry for him.

Famished.

Thank heavens, his oath could be trusted.

And curse it.

She thought he'd fallen asleep, but when she carefully eased off him, he turned and snared her, to stroke and suckle her into wild pleasure again. In fairness, she could only do the same for him, when they lay together talking, but carefully—not of anything connected to their troubles—till at last, they slept.

When she awoke, a glimmer of light around the curtain warning of dawn, she felt more starving than sated.

If he'd planned to teach her that she was a lusty woman, he had undoubtedly succeeded. She leaned up to feast upon him with tear-stinging eyes. Two of the lamps had spluttered out during the night, but by the dying flame of the third she could see bristles on his square chin. She ran her fingers tenderly over the roughness.

His eyes flicked open, smiling, but she thought she detected the same sadness behind them as ached in her. "We must return you to Woldingham, Joan."

"What of your brother?"

"Lord Henry won't murder him. I'll negotiate something."

"You'll exchange the banner for him?" With sudden hope, she realized that would end the feud.

He rolled on his back, arm over eyes. "How can I?"

"It's a piece of cloth. He's your *brother!*"

The concealing arm fell away. "It's my family's honor through four generations. Blood has been lost over it many times."

"And clearly more will be." She was determined not to scream at him, especially about things he must know perfectly well.

"I swore an oath," he said. "All the men of our

family do at the time they become knights. An oath never to give up the banner to the de Montelans.''

She shook her head. "And *they* swear an oath never to cease the fight to regain it. What madness it all is. All the same, when I'm back in Woldingham, I'll set your brother free. Somehow.''

He gripped her shoulder. "I forbid it.''

"If Uncle Henry won't kill your brother, he won't kill me.''

His hand tightened. "He might not stop much short. Joan, for my sake, take no risks. The thought of you suffering weakens me.''

She pulled free of his hand and stood. "The thought of you suffering weakens me, but I don't suppose it will stop you from fighting.''

He sat straight up. "You are an unnatural woman!''

"So? I thought you liked that about me.''

A wry smile chased away his frown. "My training is to control and protect you, Joan. It is the way of the world for men to fight and women to stay safe.''

"Then why are you worried about what Uncle Henry will do to me?''

"It is also the way of the world for men to punish. You will not,'' he said, "try to rescue my brother.''

"I'll not take unnecessary risks.''

He gripped her arm. "You will take *no* risks!''

"And if your brother escapes,'' she continued, despite a scurrying heart, "he'd better take Nicolette with him.''

"Joan!''

Though quivering, she met his angry eyes. "You can't control me, Edmund. I will do what I think best."

"You will put your foolish head in a noose."

"*Why* do you assume you are cleverer and more sensible than I am?" She tore free again and put distance between them. "I assure you, I no more want to be caught by Uncle Henry than you want that. I'll take no foolish risks. But if I see a chance to get them away safely, I will take it."

He pressed his hands to his face, then lowered them. "Promise me one thing."

"What?" she asked warily.

"If you get Gerald and Nicolette out of Woldingham, go with them. Do not stay to face your uncle's wrath. I'll see you safe back to your family."

"I'll try."

"Promise!"

"I promise to try!"

He glared at her. "If it's you or her, you'll stay to face the punishment."

"Isn't that what you would do?"

"That has nothing to do with it." Edmund stood to pull on his braies and knot the cord. He turned his back to do it.

Joan began to dress, too, not nearly as miserable as she ought to be. She'd enjoyed that battle of wills as much as she'd enjoyed their wrestling earlier, and she loved his obvious concern.

He was right. She was an unnatural woman.

She'd kept her shift through the night, but her other clothes were strewn around. As she collected them and put them on, she watched him dress, savoring his beauty.

He was hers. Deep inside, she knew it, even though she knew their happiness might be impossible. Such a little time for so strong a bond, and yet it was there, tugging at her, already like a painful scar.

She knew he felt the same. That's why he was going to try to return her to Woldingham. It would put him in danger, and, even successful, would leave him in a weak position. *He* might have faith that Uncle Henry wouldn't torture his brother to death, but she wasn't entirely sure.

Joan pulled her tunic down over her head. "I think you should take me back to Mountgrave and arrange the exchange."

He turned to look at her. "That wasn't your plan."

"I've changed my mind. Your brother risks death."

"If it comes to that, I'll doubtless give up the banner for him. For his safety, and his marriage to Nicolette."

Joan should have felt enormous relief at that tidy solution to everything, but his anguish over it was obvious.

"Break your oath?" she whispered.

He sat to pull on low boots. "If he starts sending me my brother in pieces, what choice do I have?"

Joan put her hand to her mouth, sickeningly certain her uncle was capable of it. "But then—"

"Don't argue," he said curtly. "You'll waste time and tongue." He suddenly strode over and seized her, kissed her, putting her tongue to alternate use.

When he released her, she staggered, watching him go toward his armor, go toward becoming the Golden Lion, who was not for her. To the man who would risk his word and honor to give her the greatest chance of safety.

"This doesn't make sense!" she exclaimed.

He whirled. "Joan, you are the only innocent in all of this!"

"Innocent?"

"Gerald and Nicolette have committed sins both of stupidity and immorality. I pushed through this plan without truly thinking things through, and without involving my brother fully in it. This disaster is my fault."

Joan opened her mouth to argue, but he swept on. "You tried to help your cousin, and your plan was sound. If I'd not interfered, you'd be in no danger. Therefore you, at least, should come off safe. My honor demands it."

And there, she saw she was up against a wall as high and strong as those around both castles.

She went to help him into his armor, another thing she'd done for her brothers now and then. "My honor demands that I try to help you and my cousin."

He ignored her, and did without her help as much as possible.

As he put on iron embellished with gold, the change was completed. Her midnight friend and lover transformed into the Golden Lion, a creature of myth and glory—of another sphere.

Marriage? Had that really been whispered in the night? It just proved how foolish nighttime whispers were. Even if there was no enmity between their families, such a great lord was not for her. He might as well be the Archangel Michael as far as she was concerned.

It had, after all, just been the night and the cave, but she wouldn't have missed it for her chance of heaven.

And she still thought they ought to go to Mountgrave and exchange her for his brother.

Chapter Five

As misty gray heralded dawn, they made their way down the steep hill toward flatter, more fertile ground. She was perched up behind Edmund on his big horse this time, hand in his belt. He only had padded cloth between himself and the horse, and the rope bridle, so they still moved quietly, except for the subdued rattle of armor. His sword was in its scabbard, but he carried his big shield on his arm, since he couldn't sling it on his back and had no saddle to hook it to. She couldn't help worrying that the weight must tire even him over time. She worried, too, that his right arm might have stiffened by now from her wound.

She smiled at her own ridiculous tendency to fuss over him like a mother with a delicate child. This was the Golden Lion, undefeated in tourney for many years.

For a while they moved through a misty world still silent as night, but then pink touched the sky and the first bird began to call. As the pearly light spread in the sky, Joan kept her ears alert for sounds of danger, as she was sure he was doing, but it was as if the hunt had ceased.

Here, at least.

She didn't know this countryside well, but she assumed that the deer paths he chose led to Woldingham, and if there were enemies about, that's where they'd be found.

Foolish man.

As when she'd been first captured, she thought of slipping off the horse to escape. It would be easier now since she rode behind him, but just as pointless. He'd capture her in seconds. Instead, she wrapped her arms around his mailed chest, hating the harshness between her and his flesh.

In the end, danger came abruptly, catching them in the worst possible place. Thor had just scrambled up the steep bank of a stream when four horsemen galloped along a nearby path.

Edmund immediately stilled the horse, and the men almost missed them. Then one glanced to the side and hauled his horse up, crying the alert.

To run was hopeless. To stand was surely to die!

"Get off and head for Woldingham. To our left and as the crow flies." Edmund dropped the reins and drew his sword.

"No—"

"Obey me, Joan."

The Golden Lion had spoken, and after a heart-breaking moment, Joan slid off the horse. He couldn't fight with her on his back—but she wasn't running away.

She ducked into the cover of some evergreen growth and wove as quickly and silently as possible to somewhere else. Anywhere else. Yells and the clash of metal made her jump, and she peeped out from behind a big tree, to see a mess of men, horses and swords.

They'd kill him!

She only just stopped herself from running out in a futile effort to help.

Then Thor kicked backward and a horse went down, squealing, the rider tossed off and, at least, dazed. Immediately, he reared, startling another horse into shying away. Praise heaven, none of the attackers was on a warhorse. A mighty swipe of Edmund's sword unseated another rider.

Joan expected blood to gush, and when it didn't she realized the Golden Lion was trying not to kill. "Noble fool," she muttered, but she understood. Any new death would widen the rift between the families.

The two remaining horsemen were hovering, not quite so keen to get close. The one who'd been thrown was staggering up, however, sword in hand. Edmund could probably ride away, but he was trying to guard her flight. Should she go?

Then one of the horsemen turned to where she'd run into the bushes and called, "Lady Nicolette! Come out! It's safe."

A strange definition of safe, but she was thrilled

that they still thought Nicolette was the stolen Virgin. If she sneaked back into Woldingham...

Then it occurred to her that these men could have been out all night. If Nicolette had been discovered, they would not know.

She hovered, uncertain, her mind momentarily wiped of all ability to make decisions, and before her, the men seemed motionless, too, no one knowing quite what to do.

Then, the man on the ground charged, his sword pointed. "He's murdered her! He's murdered the Lady Nicolette!"

As if goaded, the other two charged, and Edmund whirled in the middle, miraculously countering three blades, but blood suddenly gushed from his right arm. He still swung the sword, but for how long? She could not possibly run away and abandon him.

Urgent breath burning her throat, she ran back to the stream, heedless now of noise or secrecy, and gathered half-a-dozen fist-sized stones in her folded-up tunic. Then, with them bouncing bruisingly against her thighs, she ran back as close to the fight as she dared.

Just two on one now, and only one mounted, but Edmund was weakening, and the man on foot was creeping up on him. She fished out a rock, prayed, and hurled it as hard as she could at his helmeted head. The clang must have been enough to deafen him, and he wavered, then turned instinctively to face the new enemy.

Joan was behind another tree by then, watching Edmund ignore a perfect opportunity to run the man through. The moment let him wound the other man in the sword arm, however, disarming him. Then Edmund kicked him out of his saddle to the ground.

She hurled another rock at the man looking for her. She missed his head but by luck caught him on the sword hand. He howled and dropped the weapon. *Concentrate. Concentrate.* Her next rock found its exact mark in the middle of his forehead, and down he went.

The unseated man had remounted, but held his horse back, seeming not to like the odds anymore, but the first thrown one was staggering back to his feet. Joan hurled a rock at his legs. By luck, it took him on the knee, and with a howl, he collapsed down, hugging it.

When she looked back, the other man was unseated again, and when Thor reared up over him, he took to his heels. Edmund seized the nearest available horse. "Come on, my disorderly lady."

He was right. She was here in the open, hurling stones at her rescuers. She'd ruined all chance of a sneaky return. She scrambled up onto the big, nervous horse, and as soon as she was in the saddle, they raced off, one other loose horse driven before them. Edmund called, "Grip the mane!" and kept hold of her reins.

She obeyed, but screamed, "I can ride!"

He slowed for a moment, looking at her, then

tossed her the reins. Side by side, they hurtled down a cart track, the free horse charging ahead. She dearly hoped they went in the right direction.

She *could* ride, but she'd never done that much flat-out galloping and the stirrups were far too long for her feet. She gripped as best she could with her legs, giving thanks that the saddle was high front and back, and took a firm hold of the pommel, as well.

She said a silent prayer of thanks, however, when Edmund slowed their pace, for she needed to catch her breath. Not for long, though, for their attackers might have regrouped, or the fleeing one might have found reinforcements.

When the warhorse came to a dead halt, she glanced a query at Edmund and saw him sway and almost fall. Bright blood poured from his leg. Thor must have stopped on his own, sensing his rider's weakness.

How much blood had he lost? How long could he keep conscious?

"Edmund!" she said sharply. "Look at me!"

His head turned, but she wasn't sure his eyes were focused.

Joan crossed herself. "Blessed Mary, help us." Careful ears caught no hint of pursuit, but she couldn't trust to a smooth journey. She wasn't even sure they were going in the right direction.

"Edmund, is this the right way?"

He shook his head slightly and looked around. "Yes. Not far now to Mountgrave." A spark of anger lit his eyes. "You should have done as you were told, and gone to Woldingham. You heard what that man said. Called you Nicolette."

She tersely made her point about them being out of touch. "And anyway, it's an issue no longer. They saw me. You might as well use me as a hostage. If you can stay on long enough to get home. Can you get on this horse? The saddle will help."

He eyed it, and shook his head. "Better to stay on Thor. You get up behind to help."

Joan much preferred a saddle, and she wasn't quite sure how to get up on the big horse without Edmund lifting her there, but she slid off her mount. With relief, she saw a hump of ground ahead and led Thor there. Blood still flowed down Edmund's leg, so she used her head-cloth to make a hasty bandage. More seemed to be coming from higher, though, from under his mail. No time to find that wound, or to treat his right arm.

From the hillock, and with some wincing help from Edmund's left arm, she managed to scramble up astride and behind. She heard him murmuring to the big horse, and having seen Thor in battle, she could only be grateful.

She could feel the horse's tension, however, a kind of seething need to act, probably because of the smell of blood. She looked down and saw too much of it on the earth and grass below.

They had to get to safety.

She kicked the horse's sides—far higher than it was

accustomed to, she was sure, for her short legs were spread over the top of his mighty back. Nothing happened.

She glanced frantically behind. "Edmund, get him to move!"

Edmund jerked as if he'd been slipping into unconsciousness, but he said something and shifted his body slightly, and Thor began to walk. She wanted to scream for speed, but that would toss them off.

She twisted to stare down the road behind. All was quiet. As they made their way slowly, she strained for sounds. Then she heard it. Pounding hooves. Out of sight as yet.

"They're coming. We have to go faster!"

He was clutching the mane, half-collapsed forward now. He couldn't stay on at any speed. If he didn't, she couldn't. She virtually perched on top of the huge beast and wasn't used to riding bareback, even at the best of times.

"I'll get off," she said, but he said, "No!"

He collapsed down, arms around Thor's neck. "Mount me, and take the reins."

Spurred by a raucous cry that meant their pursuers had caught sight of them, she scrambled forward so she was astride his waist. He choked a cry, and she almost retreated, but she looked back and saw the enemy. Five men with death on their minds.

She leaned forward to grab the reins, and screamed, "Go, Thor! Go!"

By a miracle, the mighty horse lunged into action,

iron-shod hooves chipping frosty ground beneath, each pounding beat rattling her bones and threatening to shake both riders free. But it was almost as if the horse worked to keep his riders on, and she had only to grip with her legs and try to keep everything balanced.

Then she felt Edmund begin to slide. His left leg must have been painful or even numb, and his right arm hung useless. She shifted, trying to counter his slide. Thor stumbled, out of balance. An arrow whistled past, making her yelp in fear. A few inches left and it would have been in her back!

Perhaps that was why it was the only one.

Then Thor squealed and bucked. The whistle seemed to come later, so Joan only realized the horse had been hit by an arrow as she and Edmund began to slide off. She grabbed for the mane and fought it, and the brave horse stilled, shuddering, trying to help.

The hunting cries were almost at their back now.

They were taken.

Then, ahead, a true hunting horn.

Precariously balanced, she looked up and saw Mountgrave on its hill and an army pouring out. Too far. Too late.

But when she risked a twisting glance, she saw the five men behind had halted, staring at the rescuing force in frustration. One had a bow, and he nocked another arrow, aiming right for her. Another man pushed the arrow to one side, but he looked into Joan's eyes and promised retribution.

The men whirled and raced away down the path, back to safety, back to Woldingham with a tale of treachery.

Joan eased off Edmund's unconscious body and burst into tears.

The next little while passed in a daze, as release from immediate terror turned her almost faint. She was lifted onto another horse and carried back to the castle at a walk, faintly aware of somber concern all around, and not for her.

A reverent, whispering concern for Edmund de Graves. Dear Blessed Mary, was he *dying?* What terrible wound had caused all that blood? What harm had she done by sitting on top of him?

When they clattered into the castle, they were swarmed by another small army, this time of servants, some quick to help, others there to stare at their lord with distraught eyes. Joan, still carried in her rider's arms, saw Edmund being carefully eased off Thor's back.

He was silent and immediately submerged in a sea of caring bodies. He could be nobly suppressing pain. Or still unconscious. Or dead.

No, not dead. They'd be wailing if he were dead.

"Lord Edmund," she said to the man holding her. Older, with intelligent, experienced eyes. "I must go to him."

Did those eyes see too much? "No need, Lady. He will be well cared for."

"But…" Joan forced herself into silence. Her feeling that she should be by his side was nonsense.

"I am Almar de Font, Lady. And you, I think, are *not* Lady Nicolette de Montelan."

"Joan of Hawes. Lady Nicolette's cousin." Then she added helplessly, "*The* Almar de Font?"

His lips twitched. "If there were another, my lady, I'd be forced to fight him for possession of the name." He turned and called something to the people around, and in moments she was carefully handed down and assisted, with fussing care, to stand.

He swung off and stood beside her. "All a man truly owns, my lady, is his honorable name."

Joan looked around at the massive, mighty walls and keep, at hordes of prosperous servants, dozens of fine horses, a small army of well-trained men. Edmund owned a great deal more than his name, but she wondered how much pleasure he gained from it.

She let herself be guided into the keep, feeling as if she'd arrived in a mythical land. Almar de Font was perhaps more famous than the Golden Lion.

He had enjoyed many heroic adventures of his own, but fifteen years ago, he had settled to being the mentor and trainer of his friend and lord's two remaining sons. The name Almar de Font *meant* honor, honor to the death, and she was bitterly sure that he would never let his lord and student bend his honor enough to give the banner to the de Montelans.

Not even to save Sir Gerald's life.

"Lady Joan!" She suddenly found herself enveloped in silk and perfumes, all part of a babbling woman. In a moment it began to make sense.

"So brave! So saintly! Come. Come."

Joan was given no choice, but carried on silk and perfume to a small but exquisite chamber hung with tapestries and warmed by two extravagant braziers. By then she had sorted out that her captor was Lady Letitia, Edmund's sister, and that the army was a bevy of maidservants, each one dressed more finely than Joan.

Joan was still wearing the costume of the Blessed Virgin, the simple clothes of a carpenter's wife. But even if she'd been wearing her festive best, Joan knew she would not have matched Lady Letitia's ladies, never mind the lady herself.

It didn't matter, since they immediately stripped her down to her skin and placed her tenderly in a huge perfumed, linen-lined bathtub. Despite feeble protests, soon every part of her body was being lovingly attended to by someone. She lay back and stared up at Lady Letitia, who was orchestrating this.

Edmund's sister lacked his spectacular beauty. Medium height, medium hair somewhere on the brown side of blond, medium figure. It was confidence and a fortune in silks and jewels that made her seem like a goddess.

"What's happening?" Joan asked.

Lady Letitia smiled, a full and joyous smile. "My brother will recover," she said, as if that answered the question.

"God be praised. But I meant, why am I being treated like—" she couldn't think what she was being treating like, except that it had never happened before "—an honored guest," she ended limply.

"But you are!" Letitia exclaimed, and sank to her knees to take the comb from a servant and work it gently through Joan's tangled hair. "You saved Edmund."

Joan hadn't even realized that her hair had come free from her plaits and must be a tangled mess. She suspected that despite Joan's status as heroic maiden, Lady Letitia would not be pleased to learn that her brother had created most of the destruction. She was tempted to laugh, or cry, or both.

If marriage between them wasn't impossible because of their families, she saw now that it was impossible in every other way. She'd felt like a poor relation at Woldingham. Here, she felt like an intrusive pig-girl.

She surrendered and let them wash her, dry her, lay her on a bed and massage her with perfumed oils. As she drifted off to sleep, she thought idly that it was not the treatment given an honored guest. It was more like the special care given a lamb destined for the Easter feast.

A sacrifice. Which is exactly what she was to be.

The next step was to hand her over to Uncle Henry in exchange for Gerald de Graves, and then the slaughter would begin.

Chapter Six

Joan was awoken by a gentle hand shaking her, and for a moment a strange softness and perfume confused her. Where was she? Then, reality rushed back, and she sat up straight, ready to face her fate.

She winced. She was sore and stiff in many places, some of which she would never admit to. Despite a hovering maidservant, she closed her eyes and tried to recapture a moment of the cave, a trace of her and Edmund, but it was like a dream, evading her conscious thoughts.

She opened her eyes and looked at the middle-aged woman. "Is it time?" Time to be handed over.

"Aye, Lady, it is. Come rise and let us dress you."

Joan saw two other servants, one older, one younger, and a spread of fine clothes. "Oh, that's not necessary." Perhaps if she was returned as the bedraggled Virgin, it would temper her uncle's fury. "What I came in will serve."

The woman pulled a face. "I'm sorry, Lady, but

that's all been tossed in the rag pile. Nothing special to begin with, and soiled with mud and blood."

Joan looked at the glowing fabrics again. She didn't even know what some of the garments were, but it was all silk, much of it wondrously embroidered. "Then perhaps something simpler?"

All three were staring at her. "For the feast?" the woman asked.

"Feast?" For an insane moment, Joan imagined herself the chief dish, dressed for slaughter.

The woman laid a hand on her hair, comfortingly. Perhaps her fear had shown. "'Tis Christmas Day, Lady Joan, and none here wishes you harm. Woldingham has agreed to return Lord Gerald safe tomorrow in exchange for you, so today we can celebrate. Soon all will be gathered in the hall."

Tomorrow.

What difference did a day make? And yet it did. She had a day before the ax fell, and why shouldn't she enjoy it? And if she was to feast with the de Graves, she welcomed the chance not to appear a pauper.

She rose from her bed and let them slip over her head a shift of linen so fine it felt like silk. The full length gown that followed *was* silk, a winter warmth of silk that puddled ungirdled at her feet like richest cream, for it was that color. By contrast, the tunic that they dropped on top was light as a feather and almost transparent, so finely woven it was, except where it was embroidered in jewel-colored flowers. Joan looked down and smoothed her hands over the shining pattern it made against the cream—like summer flowers against snow—and could have wept at the beauty of it.

For a moment she wanted to reject it as too fine, too fine for Joan of Hawes, but instead she gripped both layers of silk. Tomorrow would come. For today, she would dress in silk and feast in grandeur, and even let herself dream a little that this could be for her.

Next came fine woolen stockings and pretty cream leather shoes that fit. Then the plump maid, Mabelle, opened a chest and took out a glittering snake. The girdle of gold and pearls was clasped around her hips, yet still hung extravagantly down to her toes at the front. A fine veil was draped over her unbound hair and secured with a circlet as fine as the girdle. She wished she could see herself like this.

Had she, like ordinary Lady Letitia, been transformed into a grand lady for a while? Or, as she feared, did Joan of Hawes squat like a toad among flowers, unchanged and out of place?

She stiffened her spine. This was her chance to experience grandeur for a few brief hours. She would take it.

When she was ready, the maidservants escorted her out past a reredos into a staggeringly noisy and brilliant great hall. Banners hung from the high beamed ceiling, among coils of smoke from flambeaux, braziers and one great fire. The aromas of perfumes, spices and rich foods roiled in the air. Richly dressed people crammed tables all around, and servants lined the walls.

Waiting.

Waiting for her?

Embarrassed, she searched for her place, and Mabelle pushed her gently toward the grand high table to her right, raised on a dais.

Lady Letitia was there, and an older, even grander woman. A middle-aged man. Sir Almar.

Then she saw Edmund. Healthy?

No. Not Edmund, but the Golden Lion, sitting in the great central chair, dressed in crimson, with jeweled bracelets and a gold circlet on his hair—shimmering like a figure of gilt and jewels, scarcely human at all.

He was staring at her, too. Darkly.

He saw the toad.

Before she could panic and run, he pushed himself to his feet with his left hand—she could tell the movement hurt. Sir Almar, close by, and two attendants behind him, put out hands as if to help. When standing, Edmund bowed.

"Lady Joan. Welcome to my hall. Come, sit at my right hand."

To her breath-stealing panic, with rustles and scrapes everyone in the hall rose, even those at the high table. The knights bowed and the ladies curtsied, and the servants all went to one knee.

Joan stood there frozen.

Sir Almar came quickly down from the dais to her side and escorted her, dazed, up the steps and to the plain seat—but still a chair not a bench—at Lord Edmund's right hand.

She sat, and Edmund eased back into his seat. She noted that he accepted Sir Almar's discreet hand beneath his elbow to do it and that sweat glistened on his brow. He should be in bed. The hall sprang back into motion, but too many eyes lingered on her.

"I wish you hadn't done that," she whispered, head bowed, for she didn't know where to look.

His hand raised her chin and turned it to his pale face. She caught the flash of a number of large jeweled rings. "We do you honor, Lady Joan, that is all."

Once she met his eyes, he took his hand away, and, looking past him at the cool-faced older woman, she could only be glad. That must be his mother, the famous Lady Blanche de Graves, a grand lady in her own right, before marriage to his father. She was held to be at least partly responsible for the family's rise in fame and fortune.

The sort of woman he would marry next.

"I did not do so very much, my lord," Joan said.

"You saved my life, Lady."

"Thor would have brought you home safe, and you wouldn't have been in danger without me."

"You wouldn't have been in danger without me, Lady Joan, or *still* be in danger because of me."

"Ah," she said, breaking the disturbing connection

with his eyes to look out at the hall. "Honoring the sacrificial victim. I see, my lord."

Liveried pages presented food, and Edmund silently selected choice items for her silver plate. She drank from a jeweled cup and began to eat, for she was very hungry. She wasn't entirely sure it would stay down, however.

Minstrels were concealed somewhere, playing peaceful, beautiful music, which would doubtless have delighted her in other situations.

She felt him lean back in his huge, magnificent seat. "I have no choice now, Lady Joan, but to exchange you for my brother."

"I understand."

"It was your preferred course, if you remember." She could hear gritted teeth.

"But it's a shame I was forced to show my split allegiance so clearly."

"I didn't force you into anything. I ordered you to escape to Woldingham."

And it was clear he wished she'd done that. Perhaps it would have been better. They both would have been captured, but Lord Henry wouldn't have killed Edmund. To ransom the Golden Lion and his brother, Mountgrave would have had to give up the banner and all this would have been over.

But that wasn't true. If the de Graves lost the banner, they'd start a war to get it back. Their oaths demanded it.

"Lady Joan." She was startled into looking at his

guarded face. "Tell your uncle that you helped me in order to prevent my murder by his men, because you knew he would not wish it, and does not approve of bloodshed at Christmastide."

After a moment she admitted, "That's clever."

"I am, sometimes."

Eyes say things that lips cannot.

His mother broke the silent connection, leaning forward to speak around him. "You have my deepest gratitude, Lady Joan, for assisting my son." Her heavy-lidded eyes missed nothing, and her thin-lipped smile did not warm them at all.

"I would not wish anyone to die over a piece of cloth, my lady."

The woman's fine nostrils flared. "It is not merely a piece of cloth, girl."

"No," said Joan, meeting her eyes. "It has been forged into a shackle for the men of two families. Doubtless in time, Lord Edmund will require a binding oath of his son that he never bend, never negotiate on the matter."

Edmund's right arm must be heavily bandaged, but even so, he managed to grip her wrist. "Joan, be silent."

Joan saw his mother's features pinch, and it wasn't at her words. It was at Edmund's plain use of her name, and the tone in which he'd spoken. It had been a firm warning, but the tone had been almost intimate.

She saw him realize it. He removed his hand and pointed with his left hand, pointed to the right of the high table, where a length of dull cloth—faded reds and browns with some sort of stitchery on it—hung on a huge carved and gilded stand. "There it is."

The Bethlehem Banner. It hung like a figure of Christ on a golden crucifix.

War banners were rarely glorious after use, but this one was particularly faded and torn. Which, in a way, gave it additional power to move. She could believe that it had been carried into Jerusalem generations ago, had been stained with blood, then laid on the ground where Jesus had been born.

Or perhaps it was the suffering and blood through the subsequent years that gave it power.

Then she noticed how all the servants bowed to it as they passed.

She turned back to him. "Does it live there all the time?"

He was frowning at her tone. Perhaps everyone was, but she was intent on him. "Of course not. We have a special and secure chapel in the keep where it is kept, except at Christmas."

"It is locked away?"

"Six monks live close by to pray before it night and day, Lady Joan."

To pray for forgiveness, or to pray for yet greater glory for the de Graves, she wanted to ask. Seeing the grandeur in which he lived, sensing the reverence in which he was regarded, she understood better why the de Montelans believed the banner carried mystical power. Why they wanted it for themselves.

But it was all wrong. She felt as if that banner was trapped on that cross, as much a prisoner of cold-hearted men as she would be tomorrow.

He touched her again with his right hand, gently. "Joan, what is it? No need to curb your tongue, you know that."

A hint of a smile in his eyes invited her to another place and time, but that was past. Done. His mother's watchful eyes told her that. She owed him some honesty, however. "If we can speak together before I leave, my lord—speak alone—I will tell you my thoughts on this."

After a moment, he nodded. "So be it. For now though, as a kindness to me, enjoy the feast."

Since there was nothing else to do, Joan obeyed, taking particular comfort in Sir Almar's presence to her right. Though a quiet man, he spoke easily on a number of simple subjects, and encouraged her enjoyment of tumblers, magicians and riddlers. From time to time, Lord Edmund claimed her attention, too, with some polite comment or question, or to ply her with yet more delicacies, but that was all. She knew why he gave her this limited attention. He was the center of his world, and always watched, so he must not seem too fond with her. However, it would raise suspicions if they were to ignore each other entirely.

He had no choice. She knew that. Even if he truly wished to, he couldn't marry her, and without the exchange, his brother would languish in prison, or perhaps face torture and death. She knew without assurance that Edmund would try to bargain for her safety, to mitigate any penalty, but he had to give her over to her uncle, and once Christmastide was over, Uncle Henry would not be merciful.

And Nicolette, of course, was likely confined on bread and water even now.

She wondered if any kind of feast was taking place at Woldingham.

She wondered if Nicolette had been forced to confess the true and greater sin.

All appetite fled, and Joan began to feel sick.

A warm hand covered hers again, concealed by the rich table coverings, but he said nothing. She glanced at him, and his eyes met hers briefly, full of the same knowledge that lay bitter within her. They were both powerless within a pattern of events created by others but made more tangled by themselves.

Then the music picked up pace and entertainers ran laughing from the center space to leave room for dancing.

"I wish I could lead you into a dance, Lady Joan." It was a polite nothing, but she hoped she read a touch of honest sadness in his expression. She needed to believe that his feelings had some truth to them, some lasting quality. That it had not just been the cave and the night.

"I am in no mood to dance, my lord."

Lady Blanche leaned forward again. "There are many men here who would be honored to be your partner, Lady Joan."

Joan smiled at her. "I would rather not, my lady."

Lady Blanche smiled back, but her eyes flashed a clear message. *Harbor no foolish thoughts, girl.*

Joan watched the dance start, then said, "I assume your wounds are not too serious, Lord Edmund."

"Just painful and awkward, Lady Joan. They might have been worse without your skill with a stone."

She couldn't help a fleeting grin at him, though she controlled it quickly. "It was a game my brothers and I played, my lord."

She allowed him to draw her into talking about her home, her brothers and sisters, and the rough-and-tumble years of growing up with parents too harried by ten children—all of whom miraculously survived—to be keeping close watch on any of them.

"Of course, the boys left to be trained in other households, but they were replaced by other men's sons. Not many, my lord," she added deliberately, "for Hawes is not a grand holding."

Mountgrave bubbled over with pages and squires who had won the privilege of serving the Golden Lion.

"And none of these hopeful young men courted you, Lady Joan?"

"A few did. They were not to my taste, however. Too young."

"Ah yes, I remember now that you favor a sober, older man."

With that, carelessly or deliberately, he summoned

the memory of their night together, and as she had said that night, she whispered, "Don't."

His left hand lay on the rich cloth covering the table, and she saw it clench briefly. She also saw, made herself see, the three precious rings he wore, the worked gold bracelet around his wrist, and the heavy silk of his robe, embroidered red on red. He did not need to trumpet his wealth with gaudiness.

And then, she wondered suddenly how hard it was to be Edmund de Graves, the Golden Lion, at only twenty-five. She remembered him speaking of how wearying it was to be reverenced all the time.

Impulsively, irresistibly, she squeezed gently on the hand that still rested on her. He turned sharply to look at her, then carefully away. But beneath the cloths, his thumb gently, almost sadly, whispered against the back of her fingers.

After a moment, he eased his hand free and turned to his mother. "My lady, I fear I am too weary to preside over this feast any longer. May I beg you and Sir Almar to take my place?"

Lady Blanche put her hand to his face and kissed him. "Of course, dearest. You know I wished you to keep to your bed."

"I could not disappoint everyone." He turned to Joan. "Be free, my lady, to stay or retire. You share my sister's room for the night."

Joan colored. She'd not even thought of where she would sleep. "I don't like—"

"It is no imposition, is it, Letty?"

Lady Letitia, on the far side of Sir Almar, cheerfully agreed.

Lord Edmund raised her hand with his left, and gently kissed it. "I wish you good rest, my lady. Be assured that I will do my best to assure your safety as you did mine."

Both kiss and words were suitable for a hundred pairs of eyes and ears, and yet Joan bit her lip to force back tears. She watched as he was assisted to his feet by two strong servants and helped to limp away, obviously in serious pain. Under the floor-length gown, there was no way to know how badly he was wounded, but she didn't think he put much weight on his left leg at all. Even so, before the banner, he paused to bow.

For a little while, last night, that body had been hers.

Hers to play with. Hers to care for.

She caught Lady Blanche's thoughtful eyes on her.

"How seriously is he wounded, my lady?" Joan asked directly. No point in trying to pretend she didn't care.

"As Lord Edmund said, Lady Joan, painfully, but not seriously."

"I bandaged his calf, but there seemed to be blood from higher. There was no time to deal with that."

"A blade slid up beneath the mail," said Sir Almar, and Joan turned to him. "Not a trick anyone could pull off, one on one. He was lucky it didn't penetrate all the way or he could have spilled his guts instead of a barrelful of blood.''

Joan remembered the man on foot who'd charged with his sword. So close to death.

"But he will suffer no permanent harm?"

"If God is kind, Lady."

Infection. The ever-hovering danger. "He should not have left his bed. Surely he will keep to it now."

"He insists on delivering you to your uncle, Lady, and seeing his brother safe. But do not feel it is your fault. It must be done in person, on the neutral territory between the two lands. And no one wishes to delay matters."

"Neutral territory? I thought the lands met."

"They do, but at the start of this mess someone had sense to set apart four acres where the opposing parties can meet, honor-sworn not to spill blood. It's hardly ever used for that purpose, so the local folk use it as a common. They call it the Bethlehem Field."

She remembered a dark landscape and a flaring bonfire. "Do they light a fire there on Christmas Eve, Sir Almar?"

"They do, my lady. Peasants from both sides."

She looked at the banner and wished someone would throw it into the neutral fire.

"No, my lady," the man said as if he could read her thoughts.

She rose. "If you will excuse me, my lady," she said to Edmund's mother, "I would prefer to retire."

"Of course, Lady Joan. I will send some maids to care for you."

"There is no need."

"We would not want to fail in any courtesy."

Joan found herself accompanied by three younger maids, who she was sure resented being taken from the festivities, but who all insisted on remaining and settling to sleep on straw mattresses on the floor.

Alone in the bed she'd share with Lady Letitia, Joan smothered a grim laugh. Lady Blanche was clearly making certain that Joan engaged in no tryst with her son. It was flattering to be thought worthy of such measures, but a dismal confirmation that she was, after all, merely a toad.

Chapter Seven

Joan was awakened the next morning by early sun slanting through shuttered windows. It was warm under the heavy covers beside the sleeping Letitia, but the air nipped at her nose.

Though she didn't look forward to the day, she'd get up if she thought she had any clothes. She could hardly wear the feasting finery when she was taken to her fate.

Very soon a servant popped in to wake the three maids, and as they quietly began to dress and put away their mattresses, folding blankets into a large chest, she asked one to find her something to wear.

As she waited, Joan slipped out of bed and wrapped herself in one of the blankets. Then she opened the shutters a little and looked out over the castle complex and across the countryside that lay between here and Woldingham. Her breath puffed white, but she welcomed the sense of space, for even in this luxurious room, she felt imprisoned.

Perhaps an awareness of future imprisonment.

What would her uncle do?

She'd not just switched places with Nicolette for the Christmas play. She'd attacked, perhaps seriously injured, some of his men to defend a de Graves, and very actively helped Lord Edmund to escape. What was worse, if she'd not allowed herself to be brought here, there would be no hostage to exchange for Gerald de Graves, except the banner.

She'd try Edmund's clever suggestion, but her faith in it was weak.

She hugged herself against a chill deeper than the frosty morning. Poor, poor Nicolette, whose situation grew worse with every twist of this tangled event.

The door opened and she turned. It was one of the maids with an armful of cloth. Clearly no silk, this time, and not too bright of color.

"Thank you," Joan whispered, and waved the woman away. She began to dress herself in a sensible brown wool gown and a heavy tunic of russet color. Practical. Warm.

Letitia stirred and opened her eyes, obviously taking a moment to remember who Joan was. "Oh." Then, in a different tone, she said, "Oh, I'm sure we can find something better than that for you, Lady Joan." She began to scramble out of bed, but Joan waved her back.

"These are fine. I'll be going out, so something warm is welcome."

Letitia huddled back under the blankets and furs.

"If you're going out, you need more. I'll lend you my fur cloak. I insist."

Joan thought of arguing but didn't. It was a loan only. And she rather suspected Lady Blanche would prevent it.

She was tying the woven girdle when Letitia asked, "What happened between you and my brother?"

The question no one else had asked. "You know what happened."

Letitia shook her head. "He's in a strange mood over you."

Joan didn't want to create trouble here. "He considers me under his protection. He doesn't want to hand me back to my uncle."

Letitia pulled a face. "I'd hoped he might have fallen in love with you."

Joan gave a convincing laugh. "Hardly."

"Love has no logic. He looked at you once or twice last night, as if…well, as if."

Joan didn't want this conversation, but it seemed rude to leave. Instead, she posed her own question. "Are you not married, Lady Letitia?"

"I was betrothed, but he died of a festering wound."

Joan's heart missed a beat. It could happen to anyone, great or small. "I'm sorry," she said, but she longed to run to see if Lord Edmund was still healthy.

"So am I. He was a lovely man. I've not met the like."

Caught by her sadness, Joan sat on the bed. "How long ago?"

Letitia rolled onto her back. "Two years. Mother parades rich and handsome men in front of me like prize bulls, but Edmund won't let her push me."

"She wants you happy again."

"She also wants me well married. She takes pride in having well-married offspring. She's not going to like her younger son being entangled with Nicolette de Montelan."

"There's no choice now."

"Is Lady Nicolette strong?"

Joan knew what she was being asked. "Not in that way, but Ed—Lord Edmund said they'd live away from here, at one of his lesser properties."

"And never return. That will be hard for her. And Gerald."

"They made their own fates," said Joan grimly.

Letitia considered her. "Does that mean there's no chance you'll have a similar fate?"

Joan felt her face heat and stood. "Absolutely none."

"Oh." Letitia sat up, huddling coverings around her. "Are you saying that the Golden Lion doesn't attract you in the slightest? That makes you a very unnatural woman."

"That's what he said." Joan considered Lady Letitia's astonishment and laughed. "You're right. There are forces of nature that no one can withstand.

Of course, I'm in love with your brother. But I harbor foolish hopes.''

With that, she did make her escape.

The castle was strange to her, but she could hardly get lost. In the great hall she helped herself to some of the bread and cheese set out as a breakfast, and sourly regarded the Bethlehem Banner. Two armed guards stood beside it, and in front on his knees, a monk prayed. The passing servants still bowed.

She turned away, trying not to be bitter, but unable to forget that piece of cloth was the price of everything, and despite his fabulous wealth, it was the one price Edmund de Graves would not, could not, pay.

A young man appeared before her and bowed. A squire, she guessed, but close to knighthood, and with the gilded confidence of wealth and power. "My lady, Lord Edmund would speak with you, if you will."

Her foolish heart couldn't help a little flutter. "Where?"

"In his chamber, Lady."

She almost asked if it were proper, but the squire was not the person to ask, and anyway, Lord Edmund's chamber would not be a private place. She let him lead her back behind the reredos to the private quarters and to a richly carved door. With some wryness, she thought it looked like the door to a shrine except that an armed guard stood outside.

Who, exactly, did they think might attack their lord within his own castle?

The door swung open and she took one step

through before halting in amazement. She couldn't help it. She had never seen a room as magnificent as this.

What walls were not hung with brilliant tapestries were painted with flowers and animals. All the structural woodwork was carved and painted, as was every piece of furniture. Two windows lit the room, glazed in plain and colored glass and, between them, a roaring fire was set in the wall. Uncle Henry had a fireplace set into the wall of his chamber, but it easily belched smoke. This one had a hood that stuck out into the room—a hood of plaster, she thought, for stone could not be so finely detailed—sweeping up to the ceiling. It seemed to ensure that all the smoke went up the chimney and outside so that the room was pleasantly warm without smoke at all.

And on the floor at her feet, halting her, lay a thick woven cloth in a rich design of red, blue and cream.

There were many people in the room in addition to Edmund, who was on his dais bed, and they were all looking at her. They were all also standing on the precious cloth. Swallowing, she walked onto it, too, and curtsied. "You wished to speak to me, my lord."

His bed was like the resting place of a precious relic, carved and decorated like everything else here and hung with heavy cloth woven in rich colors. Thick furs lay folded near the end, for show, no doubt. No one would ever need furs in a room this warm.

"If it please you, Lady Joan, sit." He indicated a

chair by the side of his bed and the squire stepped forward to assist her to it.

As she brought her bedazzlement under control, she noted who was in the room. The squire, two manservants, a rosy-cheeked page, a monk at a desk writing on a long sheet of parchment and a black-robed figure who might be a doctor.

A chair, she thought, as she settled into it. And padded, too. Before coming here she had never sat on anything but a bench or stool. Was it as great an honor as it seemed, or just part of the astonishing luxury of Mountgrave?

Uncomfortably aware of an audience, she said, "I hope you are well, my lord."

"Healing wounds hurt, Lady Joan, but it appears I am healing, so I have no complaint."

"It might injure you to ride today."

"Dr. Hildebrand has sewn me up quite firmly and thinks I will not split again."

She could imagine the pain, past, present, and future, but supposed that even great wealth had not spared him from it in his life. And despite the pain awaiting her, she did want this over. This place was too rich, too grand, for her, and Edmund was too great a temptation. Even now, she wanted to lean toward him, to touch his hair, to soothe his hurts, to be touched, to be soothed....

She sat straight, hands in lap. "You had something you wished to say to me, my lord?"

"Last night, you said you had something you wished to say to me, Lady Joan."

Her heart sank. In the sillier parts of her mind she'd been thinking he had summoned her because he needed to, because, despite hopelessness, he wanted to see her one more time. Instead, he was just courteously granting her request for audience.

She glanced around. These were doubtless his trusted people, and he must carry on his private business in front of them all the time, but she said, "I request privacy, my lord."

A mere gesture of his hand, and everyone bowed out of the room. Joan watched the door close, then looked back at him. "It must get very wearying."

He laughed shortly. "And yet it is all I know."

He was reclining against full pillows and wearing a red robe under the covers. His thick golden hair waved down to his broad shoulders, and seeing him leisurely for the first time in daylight, Joan discovered that his eyes were not the clear blue she'd imagined, but a blue muted by gray and perhaps even by green. Softer, subtler, and somehow comforting.

"What are you thinking?" he asked.

"I think I heard an unspoken 'you wretched woman' after that, my lord." As his lips twitched, she said, "I was thinking that the Golden Lion should have piercing blue eyes. I like your eyes better."

She sat to his left, so when he extended a hand to her it was without pain. Knowing it was unwise, she put her hand into his, and at first contact, at the gentle curl of his fingers around hers, something inside cracked and melted.

That wasn't good. It melted into threatened tears.

"Don't," she said, and pulled her hand free. "Don't."

"Not even a touch?"

"If I'm any judge, your lady mother will be here as soon as she learns that we're alone. I would not like to distress her."

After a frowning moment, he leaned back. "As you wish, my wise and foolish virgin. What did you want to say to me? Something about the banner, I assume."

She saw him brace to refuse, to refuse to bend, to break his oath, and she almost held back her words. He would never understand.

"Tell me, Joan. At the very least, give me your honest tongue."

That made her color flare embarrassingly, but she met his eyes. "I know this will seem a madness to you, but when I looked at the banner hanging in the hall, it seemed to me like Christ hanging on the Cross."

He frowned. "The frame is supposed to suggest the Cross. It contains fragments of the true Cross."

She shook her head. "That's not what I mean. It seemed…it seemed trapped there. Hung there. Tortured." She stopped, hearing her words sound crazier by the moment.

"Joan, a banner is designed to be hung. It must be the strain of this—"

"And then you said that you lock it away," she continued, determined to spit it out and be done with it. "Like a prisoner in a dungeon."

"It's a *chapel.* It's more splendid than this room! It's a small monastery, with chambers beside for the monks who care for it and pray before it."

"And if you were locked away in here, my lord, would it be luxury or dungeon?"

He moved both hands, then winced and ran only one through his hair. "As you said yourself, Joan, it's a piece of cloth. What do you want me to do with it? Don't tell me. Burn it."

She sat resolutely silent.

"It has to be guarded. You must see that." After a moment he said, almost yelled, *"What do you want me to do?"*

The door opened and his mother glided in, trailing expensive sleeves, hems and veil. "Edmund? Is something the matter?"

Joan rose and curtsied, prepared to be thrown out.

"No, Mother, though I was speaking to Lady Joan privately." It was clearly a reproof, and the lady stiffened.

"I heard you shouting, my dear."

"Then I was shouting at Lady Joan privately." His lips had softened, however, and mother and son shared a loving acceptance of his ridiculous statement.

She walked to the right side of his bed and leaned to brush his forehead. Secretly checking for fever,

Joan was sure, as she'd wished to do. He caught his mother's hand in his left and kissed it. "I am well, Mother." Then he added, "I would ask you to do something for me, however."

"Anything, my dear."

"Go to the hall and stand before the banner. Look at it for me."

She straightened, frowning. "I do not need to look at the banner. I have seen it through Christmastide for thirty years."

"Yet that is what I wish you to do for me, Mother. Stand, or kneel if you choose, and look at it for me. For as long as it would take to say twenty Paternosters."

Clearly both puzzled and concerned, Lady Blanche looked at Joan with no kindness at all. "And Lady Joan?"

"Will stay with me."

"It is not proper, Edmund."

"I am in no condition to ravish her, and she is far too sensible to assist me to her ruin."

"Are you, indeed?" Lady Blanche asked Joan.

"I fear so, Lady Blanche."

After a startled moment, a touch of humor twitched at Lady Blanche's thin lips, and perhaps a prickle of womanly connection passed between them. But then she said, "I will do as you wish, Edmund, though it is folly," and swept out.

Joan and Edmund looked at each other, and for lack of alternative, she sat down again. She couldn't bear much more of his company, however. It was like starving at a feast.

"If times were right, would you be my wife?" he asked abruptly.

"We have not known each other long enough."

He didn't misunderstand. "Yet we have."

She gestured at his room. "I could not cope with this."

"You could cope with anything."

"You overestimate me, my lord."

"I don't think so. But if you wish, I would have it peeled back to wood and stone and whitewashed like a nun's cell."

She looked down at her clasped hands. "That would be a shame. Don't do this."

In silence she heard the fire crackle and the distant life of his bustling castle, and tried to estimate the length of time needed to say twenty Paternosters.

She looked up. "What do you expect your mother to say when she returns?"

"If I'd known, I would not have sent her."

"If you'll be able to ride shortly, you could have gone to the banner yourself."

"But I know what I want to see."

"I don't understand—"

They were interrupted by an autocratic child's voice beyond the door. "We wish to enter!"

The rumble was doubtless the guard. The response to whatever he said was, "But it's Christmastide!" and a wail that seemed to be a second voice.

Edmund pulled a face, but there was a smile in it. "If you please, Lady Joan, go and admit them."

Puzzled, she went to open the door to see the guard confronted by two blond children—a firm-chinned girl of about seven, and a much younger child in a trailing gown, thumb in mouth. They both instantly ran past the guard toward the bed, crying, "Father!"

Joan whirled. "Don't leap on him!"

Children. Why had she never thought that he must have children from his first marriage?

The girl turned with haughty anger, but then flushed. "We weren't going to," she said, but it was clearly a lie.

"You can sit on the bed if you're careful," Edmund said. "It's my right arm and my left leg that are wounded. And no bouncing on top of me for a while."

The girl lifted the younger child up onto her father's left side, and the toddler snuggled against him, thumb in mouth. Secure. The girl sat more sedately on his right-hand side, but Joan sensed she wanted to cuddle, too.

Motherless children, but at least they had one parent they loved and trusted, and who loved them.

"I will go," she said, but he shook his head.

"Wait until my mother returns. Come and meet my children. Anna, give Lady Joan your best curtsy, for she saved my life. Remi, you may stay where you are, but say thank-you to her."

The little boy extracted his thumb and said, "Thank you, my lady," then shoved it back in again.

Anna, who strongly reminded Joan of Lady Blanche, made a perfect curtsy. "We truly are most grateful to you, Lady Joan, and also that you will be the means to save Uncle Gerald from the wicked de Montelans."

Joan flicked one glance at Edmund, but then smiled at the girl. "I am happy to be able to prevent bloodshed, Lady Anna."

The girl returned to her seated study of her father, and, lacking an alternative, Joan went back to her chair. The boy's head turned, watching her curiously.

"The de Montelans are not wicked, Anna," Edmund said, though it sounded like a struggle.

Anna's straight spine straightened further. "Father, of course, they are!"

"But Lady Joan's mother is a de Montelan. And your Uncle Gerald is hoping to marry the Lady Nicolette de Montelan."

She frowned over that. "Then it is just the men of the de Montelan family who are wicked."

"Adults make a great mess of things sometimes, Anna. It is good to be faithful to your family's interests, but rarely is one group of people better or worse than another."

It was perhaps as well that Lady Blanche returned then, brow furrowed. She smiled at the sight of her grandchildren, however, and Anna went to hug her.

The wicked de Graves. A happy, loving family.

The wicked de Montelans. Even if Lord Henry was older and sterner, still it was a happy, loving family in its own way. She could even believe that he'd tried to bend to secure Nicolette's happiness.

How sad this all was.

"Well, Mother?" Edmund asked.

She sat in another chair, one closer to the fire than the bed, and Anna leaned against her. "What do you want me to say?"

"Whatever you wish. That is why I sent you with no guidance."

She sighed, staring into nowhere. "It is strange. I have never looked long and closely at the banner since I came here as a bride, and I do not recall what I thought then. But now..." She looked at her son. "At first I was impatient, thinking it a waste of time. Slowly, however, I began to really see it. It is a sorry piece of cloth by now, but that is not the point. It seems out of place on that huge, ornate holder. Perhaps we need to build it something smaller, more delicate...."

She looked at him, clearly searching for a hint whether she was saying the right things or not. Joan knew he was deliberately not giving any response. But what was the purpose of this? Even if his mother's reaction was the same as hers, what could he do other than give the banner a prettier frame and perhaps not lock it away from sight for most of the year.

"What's going on, Father?" Anna asked, standing straight, a slight edge of panic in her voice.

"It's all right," Edmund said. "Nothing terrible is happening. We are all just thinking about things long ignored. Mother, was there anything else?"

Lady Blanche frowned almost in exasperation. "It sounds foolish to say, Edmund, but the banner did not feel *happy*. I found myself wondering whether Christ Himself would like a holy relic that had touched the place of His birth being the cause of so much enmity. It wouldn't be the first time, however," she added. "The Crusades themselves have been fought over Christ's holy places."

"True, but this is our relic, and our responsibility."

"You cannot give it up," Lady Blanche stated.

"Father!" Anna exclaimed, but he raised his hand.

"Anna, this is not for you to debate. I must think on it."

"But *Father!*"

"No, Anna. You must take Remi now. I will spend more time with you later, after I have returned Lady Joan to her family."

Lady Blanche rose and shepherded the reluctant children away. She glanced once at Joan but did not herd her out, too.

Joan stood on her own. "I will leave you to think. I know there's nothing you can do, so I do regret putting this extra burden on you, my lord. I felt that I had to speak."

He nodded. "I understand." He held out his left

hand again, and she put hers into it, letting him pull her closer so he could kiss it. "Joan of Hawes, whatever happens today and in the future, know that I am honored to have met you. Never let the world cow you into silence."

Surrendering to folly, she leaned forward and lightly kissed his lips. "I'll do my best. God guide and keep you, Edmund."

Then she fled the room.

She found the castle strangely unaffected by the turmoil she was experiencing, though she gathered some traditional outdoor games had been postponed because of the planned meeting with the de Montelans at Bethlehem Field. In the bailey horses were being groomed and prepared to make a magnificent show. A number of men were already in armor surcoated in the livery of the Golden Lion. They were eating and drinking festive food in high spirits, though one or two glanced at her with casual compassion.

They knew her fate.

She supposed it was like this when men had prepared to take the sacrificial virgin out to the dragon. In this case, Saint George was not going to ride to the rescue.

She was surprised when Lady Blanche found her and insisted she return to the hall and eat, but the woman didn't say anything of importance, either about her son or the banner. She didn't protest, however, when Lady Letitia insisted that Joan wear her fur cloak.

As Joan left the hall she turned to look one last time at the banner, surprised to find that pity for it had driven out anger. Both emotions were foolish, she told herself as she went down the stairs into the bailey. It was an inanimate object.

It was men who had made it what it was, and men—and women—who suffered.

Chapter Eight

A fine dun palfrey had been prepared for her to ride, and Joan appreciated the quality of the horse, though she was surprised to be given one almost as big as Thor. The destrier waited beside, caparisoned magnificently and summoning a smile by the way he preened, knowing himself to be the center of attention.

Astride her tall mount, she watched Edmund emerge from the hall. When he let two men carry him down the stairs, she knew he was not recovered enough for the venture. He hobbled between the servants to Thor and she couldn't help but say, "You shouldn't be doing this."

"It has to be done, and I'll be better once I'm on the horse."

Getting him there, however, even with a mounting block was neither easy nor painless, and by the time he was in the saddle, he looked pallid.

"Edmund—"

"I do not need another woman to nag me about this!"

Joan literally bit her tongue to suppress words. At least this journey could be accomplished at a walk, and his saddle was a jousting saddle, high in the front and back and shaped to cradle his thighs. Even if he fainted, he'd probably stay on.

He wore no armor, but a magnificent crimson gown embroidered with gold thread. This, clearly, was not an occasion for subtlety. She realized she was the only person not glittering in the red and gold of the de Graves.

They moved out in procession, banner-carrying foot soldiers at the front, then herself and Edmund, side by side, with about two dozen armed squires and knights behind. She watched him anxiously. Perhaps he'd been right; his color slowly returned, and she sensed his pain lessened. He held Thor's reins in his left hand, however, and she suspected he'd rather his right was in a sling rather than resting on his thigh.

Needing to break the silence, she said, "Your children are delightful. Are there just the two?"

"My rare visits. Though Catherine was with child when she died."

"How sad."

He shrugged, and indeed, what was there to say about the hazards of life?

"Will your brother and Nicolette be able to marry?"

"It ought to be so, but first I must see Lord Henry

and try to judge his mood. He and I have only met once since my father died." He glanced sideways at her. "You do not look comfortable."

"I could have wished for something smaller to ride."

"I didn't think you'd be happy bobbing along at my knee."

"No," she said. "No, I wouldn't. Thank you."

"No matter what happens today, Joan, I want you to know that I'm going to have the banner treated differently. And I will continue to work for peace between the families. Surely in time we can break the shackles we have put on each other."

"I will pray for it."

"And I promise you, Joan, that my sons will not have to swear an oath on the matter."

"I wish such an oath did not burden you."

"Oaths have their uses. Will you swear to me to try to make the richest use of your life, your courage and your wit?"

She quirked her brows at him. "I think my courage will be well used, and soon, but my wit is best kept in check."

He tightened his lips and looked away. Perhaps she shouldn't have said it, but there was no point hiding from unpleasant truths.

They rode the rest of the way in silence, except for jingling harness and falling hoof. The day was cold but lovely, with clear blue sky and sunshine gilding frosted furrows and bare trees. Crows cawed as they flew from their dark nests high in the trees, but no birds sang until a robin fluttered to a hawthorn branch and trilled at them.

The Bethlehem Field was outlined by a thick hedge all around with only two breaks, facing each other. When they arrived, the de Montelans were already on the other side, banners flying, ready to enter.

Edmund raised his left hand and made a gesture. His squire rode up alongside. "Lady Joan and I go in alone."

The squire wheeled to pass the message back, and Joan went alone with him into the large, open space. They were sworn to peace here, so she hoped all would be all right, though clearly in the past the whole parties had entered.

She saw some consternation among her uncle's people, but eventually, Uncle Henry rode in, every bit as magnificently dressed as Edmund, only in the de Montelan's blue and gold. He was leading another horse by the reins. Gerald de Graves' hands were tied in front of him and to the pommel of his saddle.

It had never occurred to Joan to try to escape. Would that be held against her, too?

They met in the center, and her uncle's glare made Joan shiver inside the thick fur. Noble sacrifice was all very well, but in the end it was real and frightening.

As the two lords greeted each other, she looked at Gerald de Graves. He was lighter built than his brother, but nearly as handsome, even dungeon-dirty and bruised. He met her eyes sympathetically but sadly. He gained his freedom here, but not what he truly wanted—Nicolette.

Lord Henry was holding out the horse's reins to Edmund, but Edmund said, "If you will, Lord Henry, I would speak with you."

The reins were pulled back out of reach. "You break your word?"

"Never. I wish to speak of more important things. The banner, for one."

A smile touched Lord Henry's lips. A hungry one. "The de Graves have come to their senses?"

"You know we swear an oath never to give the banner to the de Montelans."

"And we swear an oath never to rest while it remains in the hands of the de Graves."

Joan had to suppress a sigh.

The silence lingered so long that she thought it was all over, but then Edmund said, "Lord Henry, do you wish this feud to continue, generation after generation, poisoning this area with enmity, costing lives and happiness?"

"I do not. But I cannot accept the banner being in your unworthy hands."

Joan sensed Edmund taking a special breath. "What if it were in neither of our hands?"

"Edmund, no!" Sir Gerald exclaimed.

Lord Henry's horse stepped back, clearly stirred by some unwary movement. *"Destroy it?"*

"No. What I propose, Lord Henry, is that the de

Graves and the de Montelans build a monastery here on Bethlehem Field, and house the banner in it. We would both swear to protect it, and to never try to move it from this place, and here it could be reverenced by any who wished to come.''

Lord Henry looked around, frowning, and Joan bit her lip. It was a brilliant solution, but would her uncle agree? He'd never struck her as a quick-witted or flexible man, but he wasn't stupid, and she suspected he truly was as weary of the enmity as Edmund was. And he knew Nicolette loved Gerald de Graves.

The still moment was broken by pounding hooves, and everyone turned to see a horse galloping toward the field. The pale gold flying hair could only belong to Nicolette. The horse soared over the hedge and raced foaming right up to them. Joan had never suspected that her cousin was such a magnificent rider.

''Father!'' she declared, ''I must go with Gerald.''

Joan saw a wince of exasperation on Edmund's face, but was herself tempted to wild laughter. Would nothing about this go according to plan?

''I left you locked up, daughter, where you belong!''

''I will not be kept from this, because it concerns me, Father. You know I love Gerald. If you will not permit our marriage, I must still go with him.'' She raised her chin, though she'd turned deathly pale. ''I am carrying his child.''

Lord Henry turned fiery red and swung on the bound man, fist rising.

"Stop!" Edmund's authority halted the older man. "I cannot interfere without starting a bloody battle here, Lord Henry, but I will not let you strike my brother. Save for the feud, he and Nicolette would be happily married, and if you consent to my plan, they can still be so. Proof of better days."

Lord Henry glared around, clearly teetering on the edge of bloodshed for bloodshed's sake. Nicolette extended her hand to him. "Father, I love you, but I love Gerald, too. And now, because of my sin, I *must* go to him. Pray heaven, I do not have to lose you."

Lord Henry's lips wobbled through his glower. "Sin indeed, daughter," he said. Though he doubtless intended to growl, it sounded simply unhappy. "But at least you didn't soil our tradition by playing the Virgin."

Joan stared at him. She had never expected such instant understanding and approval.

"And you, Joan," he said, turning to her. "You did well. But not," he added, voice recovering, "in helping de Graves to escape!"

Joan swallowed and produced Edmund's clever explanation. "I believed your men would kill him, Uncle, and I knew you would not want that."

Lord Henry looked nothing so much as baffled. "I see, I see."

Edmund spoke. "My death or serious injury would certainly have made peace more difficult, Lord Henry. If we do not settle this now, however, such a death might happen, sealing us all in turmoil for yet more generations.''

Lord Henry looked between Gerald and his daughter for a moment, and Joan could almost hear him muttering that this man was not worthy of her, but then he dragged Gerald's horse over to Nicolette and put the reins in her hands. "Here, daughter, have him." But he leaned to grasp the startled Gerald's tunic in his hand. "Harm her, neglect her, be unfaithful to her, lad, and there'll be violence that'll make this feud look like May Day."

"I love her, sir," Gerald said.

"Keep it so."

Lord Henry turned his horse. "What now, Lord Edmund?"

"You agree to my plan?"

Lord Henry nodded.

"Then the sooner the building starts, the sooner the banner can be moved. Perhaps by May Day."

Joan couldn't keep silent. "There could be a wooden chapel while the monastery builds. It could be up before the end of Christmastide."

Neither man looked pleased. She suspected Lord Henry glowered just because she had interrupted, but Edmund's frown could be because he'd rather delay the final step. But then he nodded. "It can be so. Lord Henry, will you lend men to help build?"

"To get the banner out of your hands? By Jerusalem, I will! In fact, I and my sons will help in this holy task."

To forestall Edmund stupidly making the same offer, Joan said, "Lord Edmund is wounded. But Sir Gerald will doubtless help. Perhaps he and Nicolette can be married—"

"Joan," said Edmund.

"Joan!" bellowed her uncle.

Her uncle continued, "Hold your tongue! I don't know what imp has invaded you, Niece, the way you speak out on men's matters!" He leaned forward and grabbed her reins by the bit, drawing her horse away from Thor. "Come. And you, too, Nicolette. Until you marry, you'll pretend to be a proper maid!"

Nicolette had untied Gerald, and they were both off their horses, kissing and exploring each other's tear-damp faces in a way that brought an aching lump to Joan's throat.

There was no true barrier now between her and Edmund, but clearly he'd realized that she was unsuited to be the bride of the Golden Lion. He was quite right, too. She'd be miserable in such a situation.

As she was led away, however, he spoke one last time. "Lord Henry."

Her uncle looked back and Edmund continued, "Of your kindness, do not punish Lady Joan for her adventures."

Her uncle's look at her was sharp and questioning, but he said, "If she keeps her tongue mild and respectful, she'll have no hurt from me."

Chapter Nine

The first reaction at Woldingham was consternation, but soon happiness bubbled up, along with a subtle warmth and relaxation that showed how deeply the frost of enmity had cut. Though resentful at first, her male cousins took their father's point of view, and threw themselves enthusiastically into the building of the wooden chapel, seeing it as a victory over the de Graves.

Mountgrave would no longer have the banner!

She wondered how everyone was taking it there. She was sure some would see it as surrender, as weakness of some sort, but Edmund's status as the Golden Lion would likely carry him over that. As for herself, she worked hard at banishing folly. Despite an unexpected friendship, there was nothing lasting between her and Lord Edmund de Graves.

Lust, a part of her whispered. She had to accept that, yes, there was lust. That wasn't enough, however. She wasn't trained to be a great lady, and he was doubtless wise not to tempt her with the notion.

The last thing she wanted was for anyone to guess at the foolish part of her mind, the part that would marry Edmund de Graves if asked and hope that a clever tongue could make it all work.

Meanwhile she tried hard to behave well, did her best to enjoy Christmas, and threw herself into her cousin's ecstatic preparations for her wedding. Gerald even visited, riding into Woldingham one day, unescorted, testing the truce.

Though to begin with, the air boiled with tension, Nicolette's warm greeting and sensible Aunt Ellen's welcome brought it down to simmering point. Soon, though rather hesitantly, the castle moved again, accepting the enemy in their midst.

Joan, however, had the task of chaperoning the two during the meeting. She sat in a corner, sewing and trying to ignore their soft murmurs and occasional laughter. At a silence she glanced over and saw them lost in a kiss she doubtless should not permit. But what harm in it?

Except to her.

She and Edmund had not kissed like that, a leisurely kiss that promised aeons. There hadn't been any aeons to promise. She was dreading Twelfth Day, when the wedding would take place, and the banner would be brought at last to neutral territory. Could she survive it without making a fool of herself? After that, she would go home, for what was there to keep her here?

Eventually light faded and Gerald had to leave, though clearly he'd rather have stayed forever. He took Joan's hand and kissed it. "You are a most excellent chaperon, my lady."

"From a suitor's point of view," she said tartly. Golden as his brother, he was a handsome man who could doubtless charm birds to his hand, but beside Lord Edmund he would pale.

He smiled. "Of course. But if Lady Ellen had wanted more decorum, she would have stayed herself. It's a clever woman who knows when the horse has left the stable."

Joan gave him a severe look. "I'll have you know, Sir Gerald, that I consider you a scoundrel for seducing Nicolette into what could have been disaster."

He glanced at his beloved. "Is it always the man at fault?"

Nicolette blushed, but Joan said, "It is always the woman who pays the price."

Gerald looked at her, head cocked. "Edmund said you were a very sensible virgin. I see what he meant."

And then he left.

Nicolette said, "Joan? What's the matter?"

Joan laughed it off, but she could have wept. A sensible virgin. It was likely to be her epitaph, and she'd like to die soon if that was the sum of Lord Edmund de Graves' assessment of her.

* * *

It snowed a little on the way to the wedding, but cleared to crisp gray by the time the de Montelan party approached the Bethlehem Field with its new wooden chapel to one side. The center of the field was left open for the monastery that would rise there soon.

The red and gold of the de Graves was approaching on the other side, but around, the ordinary folk hovered, keen to see this great day, and to see the Bethlehem Banner, but ready to flee at the slightest sign of trouble.

Joan didn't blame them. All around her, beneath handsome surcoats and cloaks, armor and weapons jingled. Most jaws were tense, most eyes watchful. No one truly believed that today could pass as planned, without violence. She hardly did herself.

This time both parties passed through the openings and into the field. The armed men formed opposing ranks, and the principal families rode to meet in the middle. Joan noticed Lady Ellen and Lady Blanche bow to each other with just as much caution as the men.

She scrupulously did not look at Edmund. She couldn't risk it.

Then the de Graves forces split, and through the middle passed the six monks, singing the Te Deum, the two front ones bearing the banner on a simple holder. Just in front of Joan, Lord Henry heaved himself off his horse and down on one knee. In the next moment, all his men followed, and then the men of de Graves.

Joan couldn't help but look at Edmund, but by then he was off and kneeling, and she couldn't tell what it had cost him.

The monks passed into the chapel, and the men rose. The ladies were helped down, and the two families followed. The air crackled with danger, and Joan saw that her male cousins all had their hands on their swords. Edmund and Gerald did not.

A good job had been done on the building. It was simple but straight and sturdy, and the main posts and beams had been carved with crosses. The walls were painted white, and ample long windows let in light. They let in cold, too, but that could not be helped. They also allowed those outside to glimpse events inside, which was doubtless wise.

On the end wall behind the altar, a frame had been prepared in which the banner could hang, with shutterlike doors that could be closed over it in harsh weather. The monks carefully placed it there and knelt before it.

Someone had clearly put together some kind of ceremony, for now Lord Henry and Edmund walked forward and knelt behind the monks. Edmund still favored his leg, but didn't seem to be badly troubled by it.

One monk turned and held out a crucifix to them. Edmund first and then Lord Henry, they vowed to guard the banner here, to never try to remove it, and to cease the feud, putting all lingering hurts aside. They bound their families and their heirs to this cause.

When they stood, a silence settled, as if no one could quite believe that it had happened. But then tentative smiles broke, someone laughed and, outside, people began to cheer. Aunt Ellen and Lady Blanche shared a genuine smile.

Lord Henry's priest came forward then, and guided Gerald and Nicolette through their betrothal and wedding vows, blessing their union, though his brow twitched when he said the part about going forth to multiply. Nicolette blushed a fiery red.

When the couple ran out into the fresh air, however, hand in hand, clearly nothing clouded their happiness.

Despite everything, neither family had quite been willing to attend a wedding feast in the other's castle, so food was laid here on trestles, and barrels of ale stood ready. There was plenty for everyone.

Joan nibbled a piece of pork and looked around at playing children and chatting adults content, despite her own unhappiness, with her work. There was lingering wariness, but the seeds of peace had been sown. She had created some of the seed, and it would be a worthy harvest.

As the ladies and gentlemen prepared to return home, leaving the remains of the feast to the peasants, she stepped into the chapel to contemplate the banner one last time. A monk was already in the first vigil there, and a number of simple people knelt in prayer.

She stayed back so as to not disturb them. The cloth was still as timeworn and stained, but she fancied it did look more content in this simple place, a cause of harmony not strife.

She turned at last to leave—and came face to face with Edmund.

"Oh."

Dimples showed. "Is that your most eloquent commentary on this all?"

Her throat ached with tears, but she must not show it.

"You startled me. It went very well, didn't it?"

"Exceedingly. This is all your work, you know."

She wanted to escape, but he blocked the door. "You came up with this solution."

"But you lit the way." He captured her hand. "I was going to wait, but I sense that you are about to flee."

"You're blocking the door."

"I am clever, sometimes. But I mean I fear you plan to leave from this area."

She tugged her hand, but could not free it. "It is time. I came to be companion to Nicolette." She looked back at the people in prayer. "My lord, this is not the place..."

"It is exactly the place." He captured her other hand. She noted that his arm must be healing well. "Joan, I had to wait until this proved successful."

"Wait?" she queried, looking up at him.

"I want you to know that about me."

She felt as if her mind was hopelessly tangled. "Know what?"

"That I cannot always do what I most want to. That I have to put head before heart."

"Heart?" She heard herself sounding like a complete fool.

"When we left the castle to exchange you for Gerald I wanted to speak then. To tell you that I wanted a chance to win you as my wife. But I couldn't. If I couldn't make peace, we couldn't wed."

Joan just stared at him, trying not to breathe too hard and blow this all awry.

"I've fought over twelve days not to send you a message. I snarled at Gerald because he could risk visiting Woldingham and I could not. But now it seems as if this has worked. Incredibly, perhaps we have peace." He went to one knee.

"Oh, don't!" She'd seen him wince. She glanced behind and saw the peasants had turned to stare. A woman grinned at her.

"Joan," he said, drawing her attention back to him. "You are a wise virgin. I value the first, but very much wish to change the second."

A laugh escaped her. Someone behind chuckled, and he grinned unrepentantly. "Be my bride. My wife. My truth sayer."

She sank to her knees in front of him. "But not stone thrower?"

"Reserve the stones for our enemies." He let go

of her hands and cradled her face, searching her eyes. "Do I have you?"

She covered his hands, part tenderness, part defense. "I don't know how to be Lady of Mountgrave."

"It needs your irreverent style, but my mother will teach you."

"Your mother doesn't like me!"

"My mother is waiting anxiously for me to tell her I haven't made a mess of this. She was only worried about yet more trouble with the de Montelans. Say yes, Joan. Please." He winced. "My leg feels tortured."

She leaped to her feet and helped him up, scolding. "How could you be so foolish! There was no need to kneel to me."

He captured her and kissed her. "Yes, there was. But if I'd not thought you'd run away, that was another reason to wait a week or two."

"What did you think I was going to do? Go straight to a convent and take vows?"

"I would put nothing past you. Or you might have seized the first lazy old man you saw and married him."

She snuggled against his chest, dazzled, dazed— and slightly scratched by his gold embroidery. She pushed away.

He touched her face with a grimace. "As you see, I will not always be a comfortable husband. You haven't said yes. I cannot change much for you, Joan.

I am the Golden Lion and the Lord of Mountgrave. Too many people depend on me.''

"I don't want you to change." She reached up to touch his face. "I'm sure there'll be days when I wonder why I fell into this gilded trap, but you make me so happy, Edmund. And you seem happy with me. With *me*.''

He turned his head and kissed her palm, then lowered to kiss her lips. "*You* are my most precious treasure, Joan of Hawes. You.''

"You're going to make me cry," she said, rubbing her face against his chest—and scratching it again. She pulled free. "Take it off.''

After a moment, he grinned, unfastened his belt and struggled out of the long, glittering gown to stand in a simple shirt and braies. "That, at least, I can do.'' He pulled her into a warm—and painless—embrace.

When they emerged from their kiss, cheers started, and Joan looked around to find every window crowded and a throng behind Edmund. She hid her burning face against his chest, and this time it didn't hurt.

Laughing, he swept up his rich garment and tossed it to his grinning squire, then led her out into the fresh air and smiling faces. His mother beamed, and brought his two children over to be the first to hear the news.

Before going to greet her new family, Joan turned at the last moment and curtsied to the silent banner. "Bless us all, Lord Jesus, de Montelan and de Graves, and all the simple people here. Bless us all forever.''

* * * * *

Award-winning author MARGARET MOORE actually began her writing career at the age of eight, when she and a friend concocted stories featuring a lovely damsel and a handsome, misunderstood thief nicknamed The Red Sheik.

Unknowingly pursuing her destiny, Margaret graduated with distinction from the University of Toronto with a Bachelor of Arts degree in English literature. She demonstrated a facility for language by winning the Winston Churchill silver medal for public speaking, as well as a place on an award-winning debating team. She now utilizes this gift of the gab by giving workshops for various writing groups, including Romance Writers of America and the Canadian Authors Association.

A past president of the Toronto Romance Writers, Margaret lives in Toronto, Ontario, with her patient husband, two wonderful teenagers and two interesting cats.

Margaret's next release will be *A Rogue's Embrace* from Avon Books. Set in Restoration England, it's the tale of a bitter cavalier whose goal is to get back his family's estate. King Charles decides to help him by arranging his marriage to the wealthy widow currently in possession of the land in question....

Margaret's Harlequin Warrior Series will continue into the new millennium with *A Warrior's Desire,* the story of Emryss DeLanyea's youngest and most ambitious son, Trystan.

The Vagabond Knight

Margaret Moore

To my parents, Clint and Donna Warren,
who give in so many ways.

Chapter One

Sir Rafe Bracton blew a damp lock of hair from his forehead with a frustrated huff. The snow fell faster and heavier now, and night would soon be upon them. The chill wind penetrated his thin cloak, and his bare hands were red and chapped from the cold.

"Saint David in a dungeon, Cassius," Rafe muttered, addressing his sole companion as he again pounded his fist on the heavy wooden gates in front of him, "the place doesn't *look* deserted."

The huge black warhorse snorted, his breath like smoke in the frigid air.

They had been traveling for hours, and although they had passed a few poor hovels and huts on the road, Rafe had been certain they would find better accommodation if they kept moving. When he had seen the stone wall divided by a massive gate looming just off the main road, he had been pleased to find his opinion justified.

Until nobody came in answer to his hail and his knock.

Perhaps the snow covered the desolation of an abandoned manor. Maybe the inhabitants had gone elsewhere to celebrate the twelve days of Christmas. Or it could be that all inside were dead of a fearsome disease....

A small panel in the gate slid open to reveal a wary, yet apparently healthy, pair of brown eyes peering out from beneath a snow-covered hood.

"Thank God," Rafe mumbled. He raised his voice to be heard above the wind. "I seek shelter from the storm!"

The eyes blinked stupidly.

"God's wounds, man, it's colder than a witch's teat," Rafe growled loudly, "and the storm is worsening. Be a good Christian and let me in!"

The man's eyes narrowed as Cassius snorted again, this time pawing his foot on the frozen ground as if as anxious as his master.

Then the gatekeeper glanced over his shoulder, appeared to listen a moment, nodded—and slammed the window shut.

A very colorful and remarkably obscene curse flew from Rafe's lips as he raised his fist to knock again. There was no other suitable shelter for miles around. He must and would gain entry here. He was a knight of the realm, by God, albeit poor and landless, and no one should—

The door slowly creaked open.

"That's better," Rafe mumbled as he grabbed Cassius's bridle and led him inside the small courtyard.

He looked at the short, rotund man who clutched the gate's latch. No wonder the gatekeeper was loath to show himself, if he was the only defense. He appeared scarcely capable of protecting himself from a bee, let alone a hostile intruder.

Rafe surveyed the rest of the courtyard. The buildings were in excellent repair, very neat, well kept and prosperous looking. There was a hall, with a kitchen beside it, judging by the smoke rising from the louvered chimney. Outside the kitchen was a well and a tidy stack of firewood. On the other side of the hall was what he supposed were storerooms and a large building he took to be a stable because of the hay visible through a small window on the upper level. There was another smaller building near the gatehouse. Its long, narrow windows suggested a chapel.

Rafe sighed with satisfaction at finding so comfortable a refuge. He turned to the gatekeeper, prepared to be magnanimous.

"Now, then, my man," he said jovially, his deep voice echoing off the nearby walls, "where am I? Is this a small castle or a large manor?"

The gatekeeper glanced nervously toward the hall. "Sir, you had best tell me who you are, and I shall inform—"

"Your master? Of course, of course. I am Sir Rafe Bracton, knight. I shall not intrude upon your master's hospitality for the Christmas festivities, if that is what you fear—unless he wants me to, for I have been told I am more entertaining than many a troubadour," he finished with a laugh.

"I do not think that will be likely," a woman's stern voice declared.

Startled by the tone as much as the words, Rafe stopped chuckling and looked in the direction of the hall.

A woman stood on the steps. She was tall and wore a black cloak, white wimple and black veil. That was all he could see through the falling snow.

"Good God, is this a convent?" Rafe demanded, turning to accuse the shivering gatekeeper. "Why didn't you say so?"

"'Tisn't, that's why," the man muttered defensively, "or I would have."

"This is my home, and I am sorry I cannot allow you to stay," the woman announced in a tone frosty as the air.

Emboldened by the knowledge that he hadn't inadvertently stumbled upon a convent, Rafe sauntered toward her. "What, no room at the inn and Christmas but two days away? Nay, lady, say not so!"

When he approached the woman who stood as motionless as if she were carved from a block of ice, he noted that she might be quite beautiful if she weren't so haughty and unfriendly. As for her age, she could be anywhere between nineteen and thirty, for her pale complexion had few wrinkles and he could see nothing of her hair.

He also noted that she wore no wedding band on the ungloved left finger of the hand clasped so tightly over the right.

A spinster, then, or a widow. She certainly didn't strike him as the timid sort, but the lack of a male head of the household might explain why she would not be pleased to have a stranger enter her yard.

He hastened to put her at ease. "Allow me to introduce myself. I am Sir Rafe Bracton, lately in the service of Baron Etienne DeGuerre," he announced, bowing with a flourish.

What might have been the slightest hint of amusement appeared in the lady's eyes. "I am Lady Katherine DuMonde, in no one's service." She ran another rather scornful gaze over him. "It would appear you have been some days on the road, sir knight. Or were you robbed by brigands and stripped of all but your poorest garments?"

Rafe's usually merry expression disappeared.

"If you were staying, I would require some proof that you are more than a vagabond. However, since you are not staying—"

"Is this your idea of hospitality to a noble knight, to make sport of my garments and then send me away to be benighted in a snowstorm?" Rafe demanded as he gestured toward the rapidly darkening sky overhead.

"It is not snowing hard and you have time enough to reach the inn to the south."

"Even an imbecile can see that the weather's worsening. Besides, I'm heading north."

"Only a greater imbecile allows an armed stranger into her home."

"I am a knight and sworn to chivalry. I'm safe as safe can be, my lady," he assured her. "No need to fear I'll ravish you in your bed, unless you want me to."

The gatekeeper's horrified gasp was distinctly audible, even with the wind, and the lady's face turned scarlet.

"There is the gate, sir," she replied imperiously, pointing, "and all I want is for you to go out of it!"

She meant it, Rafe realized instantly. She would send him out, storm or no storm, twilight or not.

Simpleton! he silently chided, almost smiting himself on the forehead. "Forgive my impertinence, my lady," he said, giving her his most winning and contrite smile. "I have spent much of my life among rude soldiers. Sometimes I forget how to address a woman of quality."

"Please leave," she replied, not a whit mollified. "There is an inn a few miles down the road. If you hurry, you should reach it before the snow gets much worse."

Rafe took another step toward her and regarded her beseechingly. "My lady, my horse and I have been on the road some days, as you so rightly guessed. Cassius is weary and in need of rest and shelter. If you cannot think of me, I ask you to consider my poor horse."

She glanced past him to regard Cassius thoughtfully.

"My horse is not young," he continued when she didn't respond, taking this for a hopeful sign. He made another little contrite grin. "Saint Hubert's hat, neither am I," he confessed. "I beg you to have mercy on us both. And the stable will do for us both, too, if it pleases you to give us refuge."

Whether it was because of Cassius or his offer to stay in the stable, Rafe wasn't sure, but at last the redoubtable lady before him regally inclined her head. "Very well. You may stay—in the stable, as you yourself suggest."

"Thank you, my lady. And Cassius, who has stood me in good stead these many years and in more melees than I care to count, thanks you, too."

The woman didn't even bat an eye. She simply turned on her heel and marched back inside the hall.

Rafe raised an eyebrow. "Not much of a welcome, but it will have to do, I think."

The wetness of the snow made the cobblestones slick and dangerous, so he walked carefully back toward Cassius and the gatekeeper, who was regarding him with wide-eyed awe. "What is it? Have I suddenly sprouted horns?"

"She's letting you stay," the man replied in a reverential whisper.

"I should hope so," Rafe replied with a shiver. He

tugged his worn cloak around his broad shoulders, then took hold of his horse's bridle. "It's bloody freezing! Is that the stable over there?" he asked, gesturing with his head at the likely building.

"But you're a *man!*"

"I'm a knight."

"Ah!" the gatekeeper sighed, nodding with sudden comprehension. "That's it, of course. You're a knight, so she has to let you stay."

"If I were not a knight, would she really have made me leave?" Rafe said as they made their way toward the stable.

"In a heartbeat. Unless you was really poor and shiverin' and starvin'. Then she'd likely let you stay in the kitchen."

"I gather your mistress does not overflow with the milk of human kindness."

The gatekeeper barked a laugh, then looked guiltily around the courtyard.

"That does not fill me with hope for a bite of supper at her ladyship's table," Rafe remarked as they came to the door of the stable.

"I'll tell you, sir, if I was you, I'd praise God for softening her heart enough to let you into the stable. Lady Katherine DuMonde has no use for men, except as servants, and doesn't trust any of us."

"What, men or servants?"

"Both," the little man said decisively before he turned away from Rafe to slip and slide his way back over the cobbled courtyard toward the gatehouse.

With a frown, Rafe shoved open the door and entered the large stable, which seemed very commodious for the manor. He was at once surrounded by warmth and the familiar smell of hay and horse. When his eyes adjusted to the dim light, he realized that this building was as neatly kept as the courtyard. In fact, it was the neatest, least malodorous stable he had ever been in.

A man in servant's garb—the groom?—and a lad, possibly the stable boy, stood inside, regarding him with grave expressions. Their garments were neat and tidy, too, and their faces remarkably clean.

The lady of the manor obviously prized cleanliness and order. He glanced down at his own rather shabby and unmended garments. Perhaps that was why he had not seemed to pass muster with her. "I am Sir Rafe Bracton, and Lady Katherine—"

The man and boy were already nodding.

"You know I am to stay here tonight?"

"Aye, sir," the man said, his voice a gruff rumble. "We heard it all." He gestured at a stall. "That's for your horse and you can take the one beside."

"You are the groom?"

"I am, sir, Giles," the man replied, tugging his forelock. "Been in her ladyship's service since she come here as a bride, nigh on fifteen year."

The lad gazed at Rafe with undisguised awe. "You're really a knight?" he whispered loudly. "Where's your armor?"

The groom cuffed him lightly on the back of the

head. "Egbert, mouth shut unless you're asked sommat! Besides, he can't be wearing it in the snow, can he? It'd rust." Giles gave Rafe an apologetic smile. "Forgive my son's impertinence, sir."

Rafe smiled kindly at the boy, who looked to be about twelve. A small sigh escaped him at the thought of the twenty years that had passed since he was twelve years old. "Indeed, I am a knight, and as your father wisely notes, snow is not good for armor. I keep it in that large leather bag when I am not wearing it," he explained, gesturing at the pouch strapped to Cassius's saddle.

Egbert grinned happily and rubbed the back of his sandy-haired head. "I want to be a knight someday."

"Egbert!" the man chided again as he began to remove the baggage.

"It's a fine thing to have dreams," Rafe replied as Egbert hurried to help his father.

Rafe picked up a wisp of straw from a manger and began to chew the end as he leaned back against one of the posts. "I seem to recall hearing of Lady Katherine's marriage," he lied.

In truth, he had never heard of the lady, but he was curious to know more about his reluctant benefactress. "She was quite young at the time, I think."

"Sixteen she was, and a beauty."

"She's not so ugly now."

He meant what he said. Despite her cold mien, her complexion was flawless, her hostile blue eyes large and bright, and her mouth...well, if she would stop pressing her lips together in a disapproving frown, he didn't doubt that she had lips worth kissing.

As the groom and his son began to rub Cassius down, Rafe remembered her lack of a wedding ring. "Unfortunate about her husband, of course."

"I heard he was a right glutton—" Egbert began eagerly, until a warning look from his father made him flush and fall silent.

So, she *was* a widow. "He was not the nicest of men, I recall."

His apparent acquaintance with the late lord achieved its anticipated result as Giles sniffed disdainfully. "That's one way to put it."

As tempted as he was to pry further, Rafe decided to take another tack. "He left her very well-off, I see."

The groom glanced at him over his shoulder. "He left her without a penny of ready money."

"She is an excellent manager of the estate, then."

"Estate?" That elicited a laugh from the groom. "There's no estate but what you can see outside. All the land she's got is encircled by yonder wall."

Rafe tossed aside the piece of straw. "But this place seems so prosperous."

"She's well paid for what she does, because she's the best at what she does," Giles replied.

"She's a whore?" Rafe asked, an idea that shocked him momentarily—but then again, she was not at all unattractive and he wouldn't be surprised if she proved to have a very shapely figure under that black cloak.

"God's holy heart, no!" the groom cried, turning around to stare at Rafe with outraged disbelief. "You should be stricken dumb for saying such a thing!"

"Well, my man, what else can a woman do? She does not look to be an alewife or a nursemaid."

"A nursemaid would be closer to it, if you would use the same term for the man who trained you in the skills of a knight," Giles said. "She teaches young ladies in the duties and arts that will be required of them when they marry."

"And for this she is paid?"

"Aye, and well paid, too," the groom said, returning to his task. "You ought to see the way the nobles line up in the spring. Half of 'em bring their daughters with 'em only to be turned away. She'll only take twenty."

Rafe realized he had an explanation for the commodious stable. "Then this *is* a kind of convent, and it's no wonder she didn't want a good-looking, virile man like me about the place."

Egbert, who was filling the trough for Cassius, tried to stifle a giggle at Rafe's wry, self-mocking words.

Even the groom chortled softly. "Well, you're handsomer than lots we've seen," he said. "Some of them got faces you couldn't make any uglier if you took an ax to 'em."

"I'm flattered."

Finished, Giles put down his brush. "But it

wouldn't matter if you looked like an angel, because our lady don't have nothin' to do with men unless she can't help it.''

''Now that's a pity.''

Father and son both looked at him as if he'd suddenly declared an undying passion for their mistress.

''Even you must admit she is a beautiful woman, in that cold, Norman way,'' Rafe said. ''And I daresay she'd warm up if the right man came along.''

Rather unexpectedly, the groom grinned as he led Cassius into the stall. ''That'd be you, I suppose, sir?''

''Perhaps.''

''I'd sooner snuggle up to a boar,'' Giles muttered.

''All good knights enjoy a challenge. I believe I shall wash, then join Lady Katherine in her hall for the evening meal.''

Clearing his throat, Giles came to stand beside his son. ''Excuse me for asking, sir, but was you invited?''

Sir Rafe Bracton drew himself up. ''I am a knight of the realm. I do not require a formal invitation, for courtesy demands that she offer me the hospitality of her table whether she wants to, or not.''

Suddenly reminded that they were speaking to a titled, trained warrior and not a common man, the groom and stable boy flushed with embarrassment and shifted uncomfortably.

Just as suddenly, Rafe gave them a conspiratorial

grin. "Now, if I may have privacy, I must prepare myself to face the dragon in her den."

The boy grinned and his father chuckled as they went to the door.

Rafe watched while they hurried outside into the rapidly falling snow, the door blowing shut behind them. He wondered if the groom appreciated how fortunate he was to have such a fine lad for a son, and a comfortable place in which to live and work. From what he could see of the manor, Lady Katherine DuMonde's servants would not be wanting for the creature comforts any more than the lady herself.

They would never have to worry where their next meal was coming from, or hope that they could find a cheap, relatively vermin-free place in which to bed down for the night. Nor would they have to wonder if the tournament they were about to partake in would be their last because of death or serious injury, leaving them at the mercy of providence or the charity of the Church.

"I've still got plenty of time left to win a place in a lord's service and the estate that will go with it," Rafe muttered as he went to the leather bag containing all his worldly goods. "As long as I don't get drunk and feel called upon to list the faults of the next lord I serve at the top of my lungs."

He turned his wry gaze on to Cassius, placidly munching in his stall. "Well, old comrade, shall we see for ourselves if my lady really is as impervious to your master's considerable charm and good looks as she seems?''

The horse snorted.

''To speak the truth, I fear you may be right.''

The door to the austere hall opened with such force it banged loudly against the wall. The noise made Katherine jump as if someone had come up behind her and struck her between the shoulders.

She half rose, then quickly sat again as Sir Rafe Bracton strode inside. He threw off his snowy cloak and proceeded to shake himself like a dog, giving her an opportunity to study her unwelcome guest.

Sir Rafe's unkempt black-and-gray hair badly needed a trim, for it brushed his broad shoulders. His chin was shaven but poorly, and his leather tunic unlaced, as was the somewhat dingy linen shirt beneath. His dark woolen breeches were obviously old and worn, and his boots no better.

She also couldn't help noticing that, for a man of middle years, he was rather remarkably muscular and his lithe movements seemed as youthful as his brightly shining hazel eyes and impudent grin. Unfortunately, these were not points in his favor.

Sir Rafe tossed his unlined cloak onto the nearest bench and arrogantly strolled down the hall past the central hearth as if he were a king expecting homage. He ignored the shocked stares of the servants as they sat at table, and the serving wenches as they stood openmouthed, their duties quite forgotten.

To be sure, the man was hard to ignore, with his handsome, mature face, muscular body and easy manner, but Katherine DuMonde was not so easily impressed. Men who thought she owed them deference or respect merely because of their rank were often surprised to discover that she was singularly unmoved by that alone.

Nor was she a woman to be swayed by good looks or a genial manner.

She was the mistress here, and she would not permit this man—or any man—to make her feel subservient, for any reason.

"Saint Simon in a smithy, I'm nearly soaked through!" Sir Rafe declared, his deep, rich voice filling the hall as he came to a halt in front of her table on the dais.

"Then you should have stayed in the stable," Katherine replied with icy calm.

As she spoke, his expression altered. He still smiled, but the friendliness in his eyes disappeared, to be replaced with a rather unexpected sternness. She suddenly realized that no matter how pleasant and unthreatening his general deportment, he was a man of rank and pride.

"Sir, won't you please join me at table?" she asked, her tone slightly more polite. As she spoke, she glanced at Hildegard, the maidservant closest to her, and then at the nearest chair. Hildegard hurried to set it beside Katherine's.

The fierceness in Sir Rafe's eyes ebbed and a merry

twinkle took its place. "I shall be delighted, my lady," he said, coming around the table in a few athletic strides.

He nodded his thanks at the obviously impressed Hildegard, and then winked at the maidservant—as if her hall were a tavern! The middle-aged, unmarried, very thin, gap-toothed Hildegard hurried away, her face red as a holly berry.

Katherine was profoundly glad the last of her charges had returned to their homes for the Christmas celebrations. She shuddered to think of the disruption and tomfoolery the boisterous presence of a man like this vagabond might inspire among her girls. It was enough of a struggle to maintain order and discipline as it was.

"Something smells good, my lady," Sir Rafe noted, inhaling deeply. "I tell you, a good cook is worth his weight in gold," he went on, as if she must be interested in his culinary observations. "The Baron DeGuerre had a fine cook, and his men thanked him for it every day."

"I do not know the Baron DeGuerre."

The blushing Hildegard returned with a trencher, and another, equally ridiculously smiling maidservant brought a goblet of wine.

Sir Rafe winked again at the women.

It might have appeased Katherine somewhat if she had known that Rafe winked more out of habit than any intention to cause trouble, and he was really far more interested in the spiced, mulled wine than the woman serving it.

"The baron's got quite a family, considering he married late in life," Sir Rafe observed. "Three sons and a daughter. Big, strapping fellows they're going to be, fierce as the devil, too, if they don't kill each other first."

"How fascinating," Katherine replied in a tone intended to tell him she was utterly bored by his gossip.

"Yes, and a pretty little thing Valeda is, too. Spoiled somewhat, although you'd never have thought the baron would be the kind to soften so, even for a daughter. Mind, she's a sweet-tempered girl, and the image of her lovely mother."

The rest of the meal arrived, and Katherine breathed a sigh of relief, for surely Sir Rafe would have to stop talking to eat. She didn't want to hear anything more he had to say in that robust voice of his.

Regrettably she soon discovered that his presence seemed to fill the room even when he was silent, and that a full mouth did not deter him from talking. "Where are your charges?" he demanded as he ripped the leg from a capon. "Do they not eat in the hall?"

"How do you know about them?" Katherine asked suspiciously.

"Giles told me."

"Oh." She would have to remind Giles of the necessity of holding one's tongue in the presence of strangers. "They have all gone to their families for Christmas."

"That will give you more room for your company," he said knowingly before he belched. He surveyed the hall. "And more time to decorate this room. A little holly and ivy must make a great deal of difference."

Katherine wrinkled her nose at his coarse manners and told herself she didn't care what he thought of her hall. "I do not have company at Christmas, except for the priest who comes to say mass in the chapel."

Sir Rafe's wine goblet halted on its way to his lips and he gave her an incredulous look. "Why not?" he demanded as if he had every right to know.

She stiffened, prepared to tell him that her personal affairs were none of his business, until she met his gaze.

It had been a long time since anyone had regarded her with anything but the utmost respect, as though she were not quite human but some sort of supernatural creature. To be sure, she had striven to make it so.

But Rafe Bracton's frank hazel eyes looked into hers as if he truly could not understand why she spent the festive season of Christmas without family or company of any kind, and her heart started to race and her face flush. She felt like a shy maiden having her first intimate conversation with a man not her relative. Suddenly every twinge of loneliness that had ever resulted from people's deference seemed to pile on her shoulders and weigh her down.

Why not tell him the truth? her heart urged. He would not be staying. What harm could there be in a small, personal revelation?

Chapter Two

"I have no family living," Katherine replied.

"None at all?" Sir Rafe demanded. "No distant relatives to avail themselves of your delightful hospitality at Yuletide?"

"No."

"Neither have I," Sir Rafe unexpectedly confessed. "It saves a lot of trouble, doesn't it?"

Apparently unresponsiveness was no deterrent to Sir Rafe's inquisitiveness, and Katherine regretted revealing even that little about her past when he continued to interrogate her. "Surely you have friends who—"

"I have no special company at Christmas. I do not celebrate Christmas with a lot of extravagant waste. We have a special meal, and that is sufficient."

Sir Rafe could frown, at least with puzzlement. "Wasn't that a Yule log I spied at the side of the road some ways back?" he asked.

"No. A tree fell across the road earlier this year and will be cut into firewood when it is needed."

"Well, I don't celebrate Christmas with a lot of extravagant waste, either," he continued, unabashed, "but that's because I haven't got anything to waste. Mind you, I don't begrudge sharing what I do have with the people I'm with at a festive time of year."

"Perhaps that is why you have nothing to waste."

His grin did not diminish and a new expression came to his eyes, an intimately speculative one that made her blush, despite her efforts not to react to anything he said. "But I greatly enjoy the sharing."

"That I don't doubt," she retorted, "since you do not seem a prudent man. Otherwise, you would not have gotten caught in the storm."

"I will not contradict you," he said with a low chuckle that seemed as suggestive as his gaze.

"I can only wonder if you remember anything of your celebrating afterward."

He barked a boisterous laugh. "To speak the truth, I have woken up in more haystacks, gutters and strange beds than I care to count," he admitted without a hint of remorse or shame.

She didn't want to think about him in any kind of bed at all. Really, this man was too disgustingly disruptive, with his long, barbarous hair, broad shoulders, deep voice and roaring laugh.

"You don't sound at all sorry," she observed haughtily.

"I'm not."

She took a sip of the mulled wine spiced with cinnamon and reflected that she had never encountered a man so at ease with his shameful behavior.

"I've never done any harm when I've been drunk, except to myself and my prospects," he continued, just as jovially unrepentant. "Unless you count the time I spilled a full goblet of wine on a lord's fine new boots. That pretty much ruined them, of course. Not that I'm sorry for it. He was a vain idiot and dead drunk, so it was too good a chance to pass up. I tell you, Delamarch should be glad that's the only thing of his I ruined."

"Would it be Sir Frederick Delamarch of whom you speak?" she asked after a moment.

"You know him? If you've met him, you must agree he's the vainest creature in England," Rafe observed. "I doubt any of your young ladies could top him for vanity, which might be acceptable in a pretty girl, but is truly disgusting in a knight. I never saw a man so in love with himself. It was a wonder he could find the time to seduce maidservants." Sir Rafe laughed. "By Saint George's lance, you should have seen his face when his boots squelched from the wine."

Her head lowered, Katherine wiped her lips with a napkin. It occurred to her that it was going to be a chilly night. Perhaps she should allow him to sleep in the hall with the servants. After all, there were several of them, so he would never dare...

Her body flushed with unaccustomed warmth as

her imagination conjured up visions of some things this bold, impertinent fellow might dare.

A clatter at the entrance to the kitchen made Katherine look at the red-faced Hildegard, who hastened to pick up the fallen platter.

"I suppose the young ladies make good company," Sir Rafe remarked.

"They do not come here because I desire companionship. They come here to learn."

"Oh, yes, to be sure."

Satisfied that she had made him understand she was not lonely or in need of any kind of companionship, and weary of his chatter, Katherine rose majestically.

"Good night, sir," she said.

"What, you are leaving me already?"

"I fear I must." She fastened a stern gaze upon him. "I would not take kindly to anything or anyone who disrupts my household in any way," she said with an accompanying glance at the still-flustered Hildegard.

"My lady, I assure you your maidservants are all perfectly safe. I have no lustful intentions," he replied as if mortally offended. However, his sparkling, merry eyes belied the seriousness of his tone.

And then his lips turned up in a slow, seductive smile that Katherine could well believe would bring many a foolish maiden to his bed.

Fortunately, she was not a foolish maiden, and so was impervious to his devilish charm.

She turned on her heel and swept out of the hall,

then up the stone steps to her bedchamber at the top
of the western tower.

If Katherine had deigned to look back, she would
have seen Rafe and the servants watching her depart,
a speculative look on his face and a wary one on
theirs.

The arrival of a flushed and flustered Hildegard
bringing apples interrupted Rafe's study of the lady's
retreating form. He instinctively smiled at the serving
wench, who was not young and not pretty and in no
way nearly as fascinating as her mistress. He grabbed
an apple and bit into it so deeply the juice ran down
his chin. Absently wiping it off, he leaned back in his
chair and again surveyed the somewhat barren hall.

He had been in larger halls before, and ones more
modern than this, with their large fireplaces in the
wall. Still, this one was not uncomfortable, considering that it was of a more ancient design, with a
central hearth. The dais upon which he currently sat
seemed to be a newer addition. The plain furnishings,
apparently made with only function in mind, appeared
to be not many years old. Tapestries covered the
walls, and since they were not yet sullied by years of
exposure to smoke and dust, he could see enough to
suspect that they were the handiwork of Lady Katherine's charges rather than the efforts of true artisans.

Despite the simplicity of the furniture and plainness
of the hall, the rushes beneath the table were fresh

and sweet smelling and the meal had been the best he had had since leaving the baron a month ago.

Or rather, since having it pointed out that it would be wise to leave the baron's service, before he said something else to insult his overlord.

Rafe flicked his finger against the side of his now-empty goblet and the ensuing sound assured him that it was indeed made of silver.

So, Lady Katherine, who had no family, was most certainly well-to-do. She had money, she had servants, and she knew several nobles whose daughters she taught. She was frugal, perhaps, but judging by the food and wine, not a miser. And, if Rafe were any judge, she was lonely, despite the company of her charges and her servants.

Indeed, he was sure of the latter, for he had seen mirrored in her steadfast blue eyes—

Mirrored? No, for he was never lonely. He had a knack for making friends, and women vied for his attentions.

Not as much as they had when he was younger, of course, but even here, even tonight, that gap-toothed serving wench would probably come to his bed if he asked her.

Tomorrow night, he could have another wench warm his bed, and another the next, if there were any more worth having here. He wouldn't have to bother getting to know or care about them. Of course, they would never get to know or care about him, either, but that was good. As he had said about his deceased relatives, it saved a lot of trouble.

He had plenty of friends, too. He was always a welcome companion—until he said or did something foolish when he was in his cups.

But that didn't happen so very often.

Just often enough that he had yet to have a lord offer him a permanent place in his service, and an estate to go with it.

Rafe rose, straightening his shoulders. He still had much to offer a woman, at least temporarily, and especially one like Lady Katherine DuMonde. If not tonight, there was always tomorrow.

Katherine entered her bedchamber and firmly closed the door. No one, not even a maidservant, was allowed to enter there. It was her private place, maintained by her own capable hands, and probably far less luxurious than anyone suspected.

After her husband's death, she had been nearly penniless. She had tried to think of some way to earn money as she sold off her belongings one by one. Finally, after recalling certain noble visitors who had been complaining about their wives' woeful ignorance when it came to the duties and responsibilities of a chatelaine, she had decided to offer her services as a teacher to the daughters of the nobility. She had written to those nobles she knew had daughters of suitable age. Four had responded with interest. Determined to make a good impression upon them, she had used the last of her money to have good food, a comfortable hall and fine quarters for the girls when they arrived. That meant she herself had to do without, but it was worth it when the nobles agreed to leave their daughters in her care and pay for her expert guidance.

In the beginning, the financial straits of her daily existence had been another reason to send the girls home during a festive season that required special food and gifts.

As the years had progressed, Katherine had taken on more girls and improved the public areas of her home with an eye to impressing the noble parents. Her own comforts could wait.

They were still waiting, she reflected as she looked about her spartan quarters with suddenly dissatisfied eyes. She had but a plain wooden table, a stool and a rope bed bearing a straw mattress and covered with plain sheets and two coarse woolen blankets.

Katherine struck flint and steel to light the tinder in the brazier she had prepared before leaving her room that morning. When it was burning, she lit a candle—a rare extravagance here—then went to her chest and rooted about until she found the looking glass she had put there long ago. She should have sold it, perhaps, as she had sold the rest of her wedding gifts after her husband's death.

But some remnant of worldly vanity had compelled her to keep it for the last, so now she was able to look at her face. It was not so much changed as she

had expected. There were wrinkles at the corners of
her eyes and marking her brow, yet she did not look
so very old. Setting the mirror down, she removed
her cap and wimple and shook her hair free. The
chestnut locks fell to her waist, thick and curling.
Again she picked up the mirror, dispassionately noting the few strands of gray among the ruddy brown.

Then she frowned and hurried to return the mirror
to its place.

She was no vain, silly girl on the threshold of wom-
anhood to be examining her reflection. She was a mature, respected widow. She would not let the jolly
prattling of a handsome man reduce her to acting like
an immature, foolish female again.

Not after all she had suffered.

The next morning, Katherine awoke with a start at
the sound of a feminine shriek coming from the courtyard. Scrambling from her bed, she wrapped herself
in one of the rough woolen blankets and, regardless
of her freezing feet, ran to the window.

The first thing she noticed was that it had stopped
snowing. The ground was covered by a thick, white
blanket and the damp stone walls surrounding the
courtyard sparkled like diamonds in the dawning
light.

Then her gaze caught a white object sailing through
the air. The snowy missile came from the direction
of the slightly open stable door and landed with a

thud, audible even to her, square in the middle of the stout gatekeeper's back as he approached the kitchen.

Dawson bellowed with rage and ducked behind the well near the kitchen as Sir Rafe Bracton leaned out of the stable to fashion another snowball. At nearly the same moment, amid much female laughter, a large ball of snow went flying through the air from the kitchen toward the stable. She watched as it exploded when it hit the stable wall right above the knight's head.

Howling a battle cry, Sir Rafe rose and let fly his snowball in one surprisingly graceful and athletic movement, nearly catching Hildegard in the shoulder. Unfortunately for Sir Rafe, Dawson had been awaiting a chance for retaliation. He jumped up and threw, and his snowball struck Sir Rafe squarely in the cheek.

"Saint Simon's shadow!" the knight cried with what sounded like real pain as he staggered, holding his cheek. He took his hand away, and Katherine gasped when she saw blood.

There must have been a broken bit of a stone from the well in the ball, she thought with dismay as she dressed hurriedly. Swiftly tucking her hair in her wimple and affixing her cap, she grabbed her box of medicines, lifted her skirts and ran down the stairs, through the hall and to the door, where she met Sir Rafe and the others coming inside.

"Sit by the hearth," Katherine commanded, "and

I shall examine your injury. The rest of you, be about your business.''

Dawson and the others began to leave, warily glancing back over their shoulders as they obeyed.

Although he continued to hold his cheek, Sir Rafe waved his free hand dismissively and grinned at her, his eyes twinkling as though his injury were nothing more than a joke—but there was a very real trickle of blood on his cheek. "It's nothing. Merely a cut."

"I shall be the judge of that."

Sir Rafe frowned. "It was not your fault."

"I know that," she snapped. "I didn't initiate your game."

She pointed to a bench near the central hearth. "Sit here by the fire so I can see better. Hildegard," she commanded the maidservant, who still lingered in the kitchen entrance, "fetch warm water and some clean linen rags from the storeroom, and be quick about it."

Sir Rafe sat on the bench and Katherine set her medicine box beside him. "Lower your hand please."

He grudgingly did as she requested. Trying to keep any hint of her disgruntled thoughts concerning the childish behavior of men who should act with more dignity from her face, Katherine concentrated on examining the inch-long gash and surrounding bruise. To see better, she put her hand under his stubbled chin and turned his face toward the fire.

"You look flushed, my lady. I fear I have upset you."

"You are my guest, so of course I am upset that you are injured, no matter how it came about."

"I am very sorry to upset you, but I can never resist a battle," he replied, grinning, his flesh moving beneath her fingers.

Bearing a basin of steaming water and with some white rags over her arm, Hildegard sidled up to them. "My lady?" she said with extreme deference.

"Set them there."

"Your servants make too fine a target, too," Sir Rafe explained. He grinned at the maidservant, who giggled.

Until Katherine glanced at her. "Thank you, Hildegard," she said, her words an incontrovertible dismissal, which Hildegard quickly obeyed.

"My servants may be fine targets, but apparently they vanquished you," she noted as she dipped a rag into the basin.

"I must confess I was taken aback to discover they could throw with such accuracy, but they also behaved most unchivalrously."

Katherine gave him a cynical look before she started to clean the wound. "I was not aware the rules of chivalry applied to silly games."

His hazel eyes suddenly flashed a cautionary look, and she quickly drew back. "I'm sorry—did I hurt you?"

"I do not appreciate being called silly."

With a frown, she went back to gently wiping the

wound. "What else would you call it when a man of your years throws snow?"

"My years?"

Katherine opened her medicine box and searched for the appropriate salve. "We are both past the first flush of youth, sir."

"We are not yet in the grave, either."

Katherine took the cloth coated with beeswax off the top of a small clay vessel. "Now keep still while I apply this."

"Saint Swithins in a swamp, that smells disgusting!"

Her lips twitched in what might have been a smile. "Yes, it does, but it will help your wound heal."

"Very well, I shall submit—but only because I enjoy having a beautiful woman caress my cheek."

Rafe kept the satisfied smile from his face as Lady Katherine flushed. He was enjoying himself immensely, and not in the least because he really did relish having a beautiful woman touch his face.

And no matter what the lady herself thought, she truly was beautiful, her proximity as she attended to him giving him ample opportunity to study her face.

To be sure, she was not wrong in saying they were both past the first flush of youth and, indeed, even the second, as his aching muscles reminded him every morning. Nevertheless, he was right, too. They were not yet in their graves, or past the age of feeling the thrilling excitement that could exist between a man and a woman, an excitement that was making his pulse beat with some rapidity right this very moment.

Try as she might to hide it, he was quite sure she was feeling something similar, too.

"There now," she said briskly, stepping back and reaching for one of the rags. "That should heal quickly."

"I hope it doesn't mar my handsomeness too much."

Lady Katherine's brow furrowed.

"While I don't consider myself ugly as an ogre, I was but jesting," he said, his own expression growing graver. "I must confess, my lady, I have never met a woman who takes things so seriously."

"I take serious things seriously."

"What of comical things?"

"I rarely encounter comical things," she muttered as she began to seal the jar of stinking ointment.

"Do you not? I encounter amusing things all the time."

She slid him a sidelong glance.

"I pity you if you cannot see the humor and whimsy around you."

"Perhaps if I were a nobleman with few responsibilities, I might."

"And if I had such a comfortable home as this, I would be smiling all day long."

Katherine regarded him stonily as she picked up her box of medicines. "I have a comfortable home because I have worked for it. I have not had the leisure to enjoy what amusement the world might provide.''

Rafe rose, meeting her steadfast gaze. "Forgive me, my lady, if I have offended you. It simply seems a pity that you do not smile more, for truly, I think you would look lovely if you did.''

Katherine cursed herself for a ninny even while she felt a girlish blush steal over her features at his blatant, outrageous flattery. "Since the weather has cleared, you will be on your way shortly, will you not?''

"Aye, if I must.''

"Yes, you must.''

"Sir! Sir!''

They both turned to stare at Giles, who burst into the hall as if a horde of barbarians were storming the gates.

"What is it?'' Katherine demanded as Sir Rafe drew his sword, a very determined look in his eye.

"It's your horse, sir,'' Giles replied anxiously. "It's sick, sir. Breathing all queer.''

Rafe blanched but didn't say a word. He simply ran from the hall as if the horde of barbarians were now at his heels.

Katherine again snatched up her box of medicines and hurried after him.

"Oh, Cassius!'' Rafe murmured as he stared at his poor stallion, the horse's breathing labored and rough as he lay on the floor of the stable.

Rafe slowly knelt in the straw and ran a gentle hand over the animal's heaving side. "When did he lie down?" he asked the anxious boy hovering nearby.

"A little after you left," Egbert offered in a hushed whisper.

Rafe silently cursed himself. He had realized something wasn't right with Cassius this morning, but had ignored the altered sound of his horse's breathing to throw balls of snow at servants, then flirt with a woman cold as that same snow, and all the while his faithful horse was sickening.

In truth, Cassius should have been put out to honorable pasture years ago. He was far too old to be carrying an armored knight, and far, far too old to be carrying that same knight into melees at tournaments.

If only he had earned an estate, Cassius would be spending his days in comfortable retirement befitting a noble warhorse, and not carrying a man around the length and breadth of England seeking one more chance to prove himself.

Rafe glanced up as Lady Katherine came to stand beside him. "It's a thickening in his lungs," he explained. "I should never have ridden so far yesterday."

"You sound very sure of his trouble."

"I have spent years around horses, my lady, as well as knights. Indeed, more than one man who has met me in a tournament has suggested that I stop being a knight and become a dealer in horses, since I seem to know more about them than fighting."

However those thinly veiled insults had rankled at the time, he would forget them all if his skill could make Cassius better.

He took note of her box of medicines. "Do you have calamint?"

She made a little frown. "You would give calamint to a horse?"

"Why not? It loosens the congestion."

"I know, but I have never heard of dosing a horse with it. How much would you put in the water? How often should he drink it? Too much might be worse than none at all."

"I will judge by his weight, as if Cassius were a very large man."

"Ah! That might work," she said, truly impressed, not just by his opinion regarding the calamint, but by the alteration in his manner. Any sign of the jokester had disappeared, replaced by an intelligent, caring man who clearly knew what he was doing.

"I will dose him at the times you probably give it to your girls, sunrise, noon and sunset, more if his breathing gets very bad."

She nodded.

"I can pay whatever the calamint costs."

She stiffened slightly, disturbed that he would think she would begrudge his horse the medicine. "I would not withhold it when you are so desperate. Besides, it is nearly Christmas, a time good Christians should be generous."

His gaze faltered. "Forgive me, my lady. As you

say, I am desperate. Is the calamint in there?'' he asked, reaching for her medicine box.

She yanked it away. "Only I open this." Seeing his shocked countenance, she softened a little. "There are things in here that could make someone very ill if they were used incorrectly," she explained in a calmer tone.

"Poisons, eh?"

"No. I don't keep anything like that in here," she replied, setting the box on a nearby manger and opening it to take out the calamint. "It is only that I am used to the curiosity of girls, who are prone to meddle. I will go to the kitchen and prepare a draft at once."

He gave her the ghost of a grin. "You had better leave that to me. I am used to dosing animals."

"Then I will watch over your horse until you return."

"You do not have to do that. Egbert is here."

"I don't mind."

His expression altered ever so slightly. "Then I thank you. I am glad to have someone with some experience of nursing with him, if I cannot be, and since I have no page, I will use Egbert's help with the medicine."

Katherine made no sign that his heartfelt words pleased her out of all measure, while Egbert looked as if he had just been handed the keys to the kingdom.

Before Rafe departed, he took a moment to stroke

the stallion's neck and croon softly in the animal's ear as if the huge beast were a child.

Or his best friend.

After Rafe and Egbert departed, Katherine approached the horse somewhat warily, mindful of its huge hooves.

"*Are* you his best friend?" she whispered, reaching out to pet it.

As the beast shifted its head to regard her with its large brown eyes, she sighed softly. "At least he has you."

It seemed to take a very long time before Rafe returned with the medicine, carrying it in a wineskin under his tunic to keep it warm. Egbert trotted at his side, obviously full of admiration for Rafe's unexpected and unusual knowledge.

"The servants didn't give you any trouble, I trust?" Katherine asked, voicing a concern that had arisen as she had waited.

"No. I took some time with the measure of calamint. I didn't want to make the potion too weak."

"How are you going to get your horse to drink it? The taste is not altogether pleasing. At least a person can understand that it is intended to make him feel better."

"That is why I put it in a wineskin."

He took out the stopper and went to kneel beside Cassius's head. Then he tilted it so that the horse could swallow the liquid as he slowly poured it into his mouth. Cassius's lips moved like a man tasting a beverage that wasn't entirely to his taste but not too terrible to finish.

"I have never seen a horse drink from a wineskin before."

She thought Rafe flushed, but it could have been from the effort of holding the wineskin aloft.

"I used to make wagers on this," the knight confessed. "But I wouldn't give him wine," he hastened to assure her. "Ale."

"You fed your valuable warhorse ale?"

"Not that much. Not enough to get him drunk. Besides, is that skill not invaluable now?" Although Rafe's smile was wry and self-deprecating, it was a smile of warmth and companionship, too.

She backed away. "I hope the calamint helps," she murmured as she departed.

Chapter Three

Later that night, as Cassius lay wheezing in the straw, the stable door creaked open. Rafe raised his head, expecting either Giles or Egbert. He made no effort to hide his surprise as the pool of golden light from a handheld lantern widened and revealed Lady Katherine. In addition to the lamp, she had a basket over her arm from which toothsome smells emanated.

She wore a plain dark gray cloak, and that damned wimple and cap, but her cheeks were rosy from the cold—and the expression of genuine concern on her face made her even more lovely.

Although he knew he should stand upon a lady's entrance, he feared he was too stiff to do so without making that stiffness obvious. He wouldn't embarrass himself by struggling to his feet from his cross-legged position, so he merely nodded a greeting and turned back to his horse, hoping his worry over Cassius would excuse him.

Apparently it did, for her expression didn't alter as

she set the basket beside him and, placing the lamp on the ground at her side, sat on a stool on the other side of the stall. "Is he worse?" she asked softly.

"No, not worse. A little better, I am happy to say."

"You will need more calamint at sunrise. I will fetch my medicine box—"

He held up his hand to make her stay. "It will be some time before we need it. Sit with me awhile, won't you? I have had too many lonely vigils and would welcome your company."

She lowered herself back to the stool. "Very well." She looked at Cassius and sighed. "He is a very fine stallion."

"You should have seen him when he was younger." He grinned ruefully. "Saint Ninian's nose, I wish you had seen me when I was younger."

She didn't meet his gaze. "I have had lonely vigils, too. The girls sometimes get sick. I have often thought how welcome a little bread or cheese or wine would be at such times, so I brought you refreshment."

"I confess I suspected that's what was in your basket." He reached for it and pulled back the linen covering. "This is indeed very welcome." He took the small loaf of course brown bread and bit into it with relish.

"I suppose you have attended to sick horses many times."

"A few," he agreed.

"I daresay it is more difficult for a man like you to do so."

"A man like me?"

"A man who so obviously enjoys company."

"Well, sometimes even a man like me needs a little peace and quiet." He smiled ruefully. "That surprises you?"

"I must say you do not strike me as a person who would enjoy solitude."

"I do not *enjoy* it," he amended. "I said sometimes I need it. For instance, if I've just lost a bet and I'm ready to snarl at the next person who looks at me askance—then I like to be alone. Or if I'm tired. Or when I'm ill."

"I confess I enjoy being alone after spending a day with the girls. You would be amazed how much they can say about the simplest things! That is one reason no one is allowed into my sanctuary."

"Sanctuary?"

"My bedchamber," she admitted. "No one goes in there except me. I have heard the girls whispering their speculations as to the luxuries I have hoarded there, but it is really quite barren...."

Her words trailed off as she realized he was looking at her with an expression that made her feel outrageously warm.

She should not have come. She had debated sending Hildegard with refreshment for him, then decided it would probably be safer if she did. Otherwise, Hildegard might do something foolish that would bring shame to her household.

And if she were not careful, so would she.

She must remember that no matter how attractive this man was, she was the formidable, dignified Lady Katherine DuMonde. Despite that, she couldn't resist asking him another question. "Have you ever been married?"

"No. I never thought about it with any seriousness," he said lightly. "I was too busy trying to win prizes."

"With much success?"

"Some," he replied as if he were too modest to detail all the many and wonderful prizes he had captured over the years. "Cassius was one."

In truth, Cassius was the one and only prize of any great value he had ever won. He had never been first at anything. He had always missed the best prizes and rewards, sometimes by a little, often by more.

"You have traveled a great deal, too?"

"I have been to France, and London, of course. As far north as the Roman wall, and west to the coast of Wales."

"I have never been more than twenty miles from this place. My family lived that far away to the south, and I have not left here since they brought me to be married."

"I think that's a very good thing."

Her brow furrowed.

"If you had gone to London, your beauty would have thrown the entire court into an uproar."

"I am too old for flattery, Sir Rafe."

He shrugged and bit into the soft cheese. "Demure as you will, but it is the truth."

She ignored his comment. "I would like to hear about some of your travels."

His responses would, after all, be educational, she told herself, provided he spared her his ridiculous flattery.

Deciding it might be better to take refuge behind humor, Rafe grinned. "Since nothing pleases me more than talking about myself, and since you don't want to be flattered, I am delighted to do so."

As he continued to eat the bread and cheese and drink the wine, he told her of the sights he had seen and the people he had encountered. Usually he enjoyed regaling an audience with his tales, but tonight, with Katherine's steadfast gaze upon him, he began to wish he had accomplished more that could make him worthy of her respect and her admiration. Now every tournament seemed boringly similar to the next.

As for the places he had been, if she wanted a description of various taverns and brothels, he was her man. Instead, he stuck to the well-known attributes of famous buildings he had never actually seen, except from outside.

"I fear I am boring you, my lady," he finally said, wiping his wine-damp lips with the back of his hand.

"Not at all. I have never seen a tournament and have often wondered what they must be like."

"Well, I seem to have bored poor Cassius," he remarked wryly, nodding at the slumbering stallion. "Of course, he was there."

She looked at the horse. "He is breathing much easier, is he not?"

"Yes, and for that, I thank you and your medicine."

She smiled, and he saw that he had been right to suspect that her smile would make her the most beautiful woman he had ever seen.

If he had met her when they both were younger, when he was just beginning his life as a knight, full of vigor and pride and hope, what wouldn't he have done to make a woman of her beauty and intelligence like him? Saint Michael's miracles, what wouldn't he have done to make her love him?

But he was not young.

"You were the apothecary," she said. "All I did was provide the calamint."

"Without which, I don't know what we would have done. It is the best Christmas gift I have ever received," he said softly and sincerely. He leaned back against the stable wall. "Now tell me about your life."

A small wrinkle of displeasure appeared between her brows. "There is nothing to tell."

He doubted that very much, for surely there must be some good reason she had not remarried. However, he could see that it would be a mistake to press her for information she was not willing to impart. "If you do not want to talk about yourself, tell me about your pupils."

"I don't gossip."

He sighed and cocked his head. "You let me go on about myself for a very long time. Now you must reciprocate, or I shall feel as vain and stupid as Frederick Delamarch."

She still looked unwilling.

"If you will not tell me about your charges, just tell me about the one you liked the best," he cajoled.

"I suppose that would not be amiss," she mused. A spark of pleasure appeared in Katherine's blue eyes, a glowing ember of vivacity that seemed to melt her frosty manner. "My best pupil was Elizabeth Perronet. She was one of the first, too. She was with me but a year, and then her family put her in a convent. While it is no shame to be pledged to God's service, I was sorry to lose her."

"Was she beautiful?"

Katherine frowned, looking as annoyed as if he had insulted the girl's memory. "No, not what most men would call beautiful, I suppose. Nor did she make much of an impression at first, not like her cousin, who came to me much later. Genevieve had more spirit and she let everyone know it. Elizabeth was different. She was an intelligent girl, yet humble and quiet, too—so humble and quiet it was easy to forget she was there, I confess.

"Then one day, when she had been here a fortnight, some of the older girls were teasing a younger one. I overheard them and was about to interfere when Elizabeth went up to the oldest, who was a head taller than she, and said, 'Stop it.'"

Katherine shook her head at the memory. "I will never forget it, the force in those words and the expression in her eyes. It was like a sudden burst of fire on a dark night. Once you saw that fire, you realized it was always there—banked, but there." Katherine sighed. "She was a pleasure to teach, too. She always listened, and I knew she would remember all the things I taught her."

"I gather the same could not be said of many of the other girls."

Katherine made a wry little smile. "Unfortunately, you are right. Indeed, sometimes I think most of them will forget everything I've taught them the instant they set foot outside my gates." She shook her head. "It is not easy interesting them in practical matters. All most of them want to think about is men and marriage."

Rafe chuckled. "I've met several knights who could only think about women and wine. The worst of all on that score was Raynard Flambeaux. He seemed to think a title meant women should willingly drop into his bed—not that he would have any idea what to do if they did, I'm sure."

Katherine tried to subdue any and all reaction to the image of a man and woman sharing nocturnal adventures. "You're speaking of Sir Raynard Flambeaux of Castle Beautress?"

"You've met him?"

She laughed softly. "I tried to teach his sister."

"If she's anything like her brother, I don't envy you that. He's as big and slow as an ox."

"She's petite, but oxlike in her own way, and as for the arrogance, I believe she matched him there," Katherine confessed with another laugh that turned into a sigh. "I thought she would never, ever learn how to add even the simplest sum."

"Who was your second-best student?"

Perhaps it was the intimacy of the stable and the golden lantern light, or perhaps it had been too long since she had had someone with which to share her thoughts, or perhaps it was simply that he seemed so keen to listen, but for whatever reason, Katherine answered Rafe's question, and more. She told him things she hadn't told another soul about the joys of teaching the girls, and the heartaches. She smiled as she recounted some of the pranks a few of the braver girls had tried to play on her, and smiled even more when she confessed how she had thwarted their efforts. She sighed over some of their fates, and marveled at the progress of others who had, at first, filled her with despair.

She fell silent when, with a snort and a whinny, Cassius began to get to his feet.

"Oh!" she cried, happy to see the horse so improved. "The calamint has worked."

Rafe also staggered to his feet. He almost fell over, but she hurried to help him.

"Saint Bernard's bones, I'm stiff as a plank," he muttered as he leaned on her, his arm around her slender shoulder.

"You're cold, that's all," she said. "I should have found you a blanket...."

Her words trailed off as she felt the warmth of his hard, masculine body surround her.

He looked into her eyes, his gaze piercing and yet questioning. "I cannot thank you enough for helping us."

"It was only common courtesy," she whispered, her throat suddenly dry, her heart pounding.

He slowly lowered his elbow, dragging his hand along the back of her neck, and turned to face her. The lantern light made the flesh along the angle of his cheeks glow, while his eyes were deep in shadow. His other hand came to rest lightly on her shoulder. Then he gently pulled her closer and kissed her.

It had been so long, so very, very long, and even then, his kiss was not like any other's. His firm mouth took possession of hers with both surety and gentle query.

He was no selfish, vain young man seeking only another conquest.

He was no old man wanting a young wife to give him children.

Before he kissed her, he had already given her

something far more precious than flattery and empty words, or his name. He had given her friendship.

So now she could not resist the invitation in his lips and the question in his eyes. With a low moan, she yielded to the burning need to feel Rafe's mouth upon her own, to taste him, touch him and inhale the masculine scent of him, to remind herself that she was a woman capable of fervent desire.

Their kiss deepened as his arms tightened about her. She eagerly parted her lips for him, and when his tongue entered her willing mouth, she entwined hers with his.

She was young and alive, truly alive, in a way she had not been for years.

In a way she never had.

With a low growl of desire, he tugged off her cap and wimple, and his hands moved through her un- bound hair.

This warrior could surely have almost any woman, and he wanted her—the stern, the cold Lady Kath- erine DuMonde. In his arms she was no longer stern or cold, but vibrant with the thrilling excitement of passionate yearning throbbing in her heart.

A heart that had not given or received love in over fifteen years.

Then something nudged her from behind.

Rafe stopped kissing her and looked over her shoulder, a warning look in his eyes. "Cassius," he chided. "You will be fed soon enough."

Katherine glanced out one of the small windows

nearby and was startled to realize that the dawn was breaking over the manor wall.

"I had no idea it was so late!" she cried softly, disengaging herself from Rafe's embrace. "I had best go."

His smile warmed her more than summer sunlight.

"You will come to the hall to break the fast?" she asked, shy in a way she had not been in over fifteen years, either, as she bent down to retrieve her cap and wimple.

His expression grave, save for his merry eyes, he bowed. "I shall be delighted, my lady."

Drawing the cloth of the veil over her head like a scarf, she answered with a smile as she picked up the empty basket and hurried from the stable.

How glorious this morning was, she thought as she made her way across the courtyard through the snow. The air was cold but crisp, the sun glinted off the windows of the hall, the sky was clear and free of clouds.

It was a perfect winter's day, and this year she would have the perfect Christmas. She would order the hall decorated with evergreen boughs and holly and ivy. She would tell the cook to make her finest dishes. She would have the best wine and wassail. She would have music and dancing.

Why, she was so happy she could almost dance now, she thought with a quiet laugh. Indeed, the last time she had felt anything approaching this great joy was the day Frederick had told her he loved her.

She halted in midstep, all thoughts of music and dancing and celebration destroyed as a wall crumbles in an earthquake.

Frederick Delamarch, the man she had loved. Who had told her he loved her and had made love to her, only to callously abandon her afterward. Who had bragged of his conquest to his fellows so that her reputation was in danger, and her only defense to marry the old man her parents found willing to take her.

Frederick, the charming. Frederick, the sly seducer.

What would he be like now?

Very much like Rafe, no doubt, came the dismaying answer.

Suddenly she felt like a fool, and an old fool. For years she had tried to teach her charges to beware of men who spoke of love and promised their eternal devotion. They were surely lying and more likely to be duplicitous, treacherous, selfish creatures interested only in assuaging their own lust. It was better to be alone than used, abandoned, heartbroken and pride shattered.

She, of all people, should remember that.

Glancing around guiltily as she quickened her pace, she hoped none of the servants could see her, or had seen her come out of the stable. What might they think if they had?

That she had spent the night in Rafe's arms, coupling in the straw like a lustful peasant.

* * *

Taking in deep, invigorating breaths of the cold morning air, Rafe energetically swung his arms as he marched across the courtyard. He had washed and made himself as presentable as possible before joining Katherine in the hall. Not only did he have her company and a good meal to look forward to, but Cassius was definitely better.

Even more important, Katherine had kissed him.

And what a kiss! He was not quite so vain as to think it was his personal attributes alone that were responsible for her passionate response. Indeed, he was all but certain that he had guessed aright before. It had been a long time since a man had stoked her fires and, surprising though it may be, he was the first to rekindle the blaze.

But there was more to his happiness than triumph at a potential conquest. He had truly enjoyed their conversation the night before, more so than he would have believed possible. He had experienced a companionship and intimacy with Katherine of a kind he had never known with a woman. In the past, he had spoken to women only to flirt with them, his sole objective being to woo them into his bed.

Walking toward the hall, he suddenly realized that, while he shared her passionate desire and wanted very much to make love with her, his feelings went beyond lust. He wanted to have more long conversations with her. He wanted to hear all about her childhood and her life. He wanted to learn more about her pupils. He wanted to know her secret wishes and regrets.

Most of all, he wanted to make her happy, if he could, because she deserved to be.

"Saint Thomas on a toadstool," he muttered as a new thought assailed him, making his steps slow.

Was this love?

Could this overwhelming need to be near her, even to simply see her face—was that love?

Yet if it was, what could he offer her? He had no home, no land, no wealth. He was nothing more than a vagabond knight who could tell amusing stories, a man past his prime, a man who had accomplished... nothing.

In the cold, harsh light of the winter's morning, he realized he had squandered his life. He had nothing to show for his thirty-two years except a horse, his ancient armor and a change of clothing. He had nothing to offer a woman of Katherine's admirable qualities and accomplishments, nothing at all.

He was a pathetic jester in love with a princess.

Rafe turned on his heel to return to the stable. He and Cassius would leave. At once. He would walk Cassius and carry his gear himself, if need be.

Suddenly he heard a pounding on the gate. He stopped and watched as Dawson came bustling out of the gatehouse and peered out the small window to see who it was.

Then he opened the gate, and a donkey bearing a man wrapped in a dark robe ambled slowly inside.

Katherine had said she had no guests save a priest

at Christmas and, as the man dismounted awkwardly, Rafe decided that's who he had to be.

Between his concern for Cassius and his attraction to Katherine, he had completely forgotten about Christmas.

She had given him back Cassius, and he had nothing to give her in return.

He continued toward the stable. Christmas or not, he would soon be on his way and it would be better if he did not linger.

Seated on the dais in her hall after hastily changing her attire, Katherine held her breath as the door to the hall opened, then let it slowly out as someone who was not Rafe entered. It was a stranger dressed in the garb of a priest.

Katherine tried to subdue her immature disappointment. It was better for her if Rafe stayed in the stable, even though a sudden dread that his beloved stallion might have worsened nagged at her. She would send Hildegard to ask how the horse fared.

A subtle clearing of the priest's throat made her start and focus her attention on the man coming toward her.

"Greetings on this day before the celebration of our Lord's blessed birth, my lady," the portly man intoned as he approached her and bowed politely. "Father Bartholomew sends his regrets, but he was too ill to come. I have been sent in his place."

"I am sorry to hear that Father Bartholomew is not well. I hope he is not seriously ill, Father…?"

"Coll, my lady. I am Father Coll. No, it is merely a chill. Unfortunately, although the abbey is but a mile away, the weather did not seem auspicious, and it was deemed too risky to his health to travel," the priest replied.

The day was fine, Katherine thought, glancing at the narrow window nearest her. The sunlight was weak, to be sure, but that was to be expected in winter. Then, as if in answer to her questioning look, a howling blast of wind suddenly sounded outside and the sunlight diminished as though the wind had blown the sun out of the sky.

"There is going to be another heavy snowfall, I fear," the priest said.

She turned back to look at him and made a little smile of welcome. "I am even more grateful you made the journey."

"I was also told you set a very good table," he replied with a low chortle.

Katherine wondered what man would next expect her to find life a source of amusement. "Will you join me for some refreshment?"

The priest started slightly. "Before mass?"

Katherine colored. "Of course, we must have mass first," she replied. "If you will give me a moment to fetch my cloak, we shall proceed to the chapel."

After the priest nodded his agreement, Katherine went to her austere chamber as quickly as she could while maintaining a dignified attitude. Once in her bedchamber, she rushed to the window. The formerly clear sky was now filled with dark, ominous clouds. The freezing wind bent the trees, tearing off loose twigs and small branches and sending them whirling about the sky.

No one should travel in this weather. No matter how inconvenient and unsettling, Rafe must stay. She would simply have to be wary of him, that was all. She could keep a cool demeanor toward him.

She had to.

After putting on her cloak, she returned to the waiting priest and led him out of the hall toward the small chapel near the gate. The frigid building was only about ten feet by twelve, with no seating and a plain altar covered in a white cloth. The communion vessels, wine and some bread were already prepared, Katherine was pleased to note. That was one of Hildegard's tasks, and she was glad to see that the servant had remembered it.

Indeed, it seemed Hildegard's memory was surpassing that of her distracted mistress this morning.

Several of the servants, including Hildegard, Dawson, Giles and Egbert, filed into the chapel and took their places behind Lady Katherine. She could hear their teeth chattering, their feet stamping and arms moving to keep themselves warm.

She wished the priest would begin.

"My lady?" Father Coll said softly, coming to stand in front of her.

"Yes?"

"Is this all who are attending today?"

She glanced around. "I believe so. We shall have all the servants tomorrow."

"Have you no guests for the twelve days of Christmas?"

"No."

"I saw a man in the courtyard, a nobleman...?"

"Perhaps he does not care to attend mass."

"Perhaps he does not know we are having it," the priest countered.

Katherine's eyes narrowed ever so slightly. No one had answered her so impudently in years, until Rafe had come. Had his visit somehow altered her external appearance so that this unknown priest would also be comfortable speaking to her in an impertinent fashion? "I think you may proceed."

Apparently unmoved by her glacial tone, the priest said, "I am willing to wait while someone fetches him."

Annoyed at the priest, at Rafe and at all arrogant men in general, Katherine made a small gesture that brought Egbert hastily to her side.

"Go to the stable and ask Sir Rafe to join us for mass," she ordered. "Tell him the priest requests it."

Egbert nodded, then hurried out.

Katherine clasped her hands and assumed a blank expression as she waited, determined to act as if nothing at all were amiss—even though, unlike the rest of the people gathered in that freezing stone building, she was more than a little warm.

Chapter Four

"You're to come to Mass," Egbert said after he ran into the stable. He skittered to a halt, nearly slipping on the straw, then stared at the knight. "You're not leaving? There's going to be another storm."

"I *am* leaving, so I will not be going to mass."

"But sir, can't you hear the wind? And your horse is still not well!" the boy protested.

Rafe stopped fussing with the leather pouch that held his pitiful belongings and strode past Egbert to look outside. He had heard the wind, of course, but had told himself it was just an occasional gust. Now, however, as he looked at the dark sky, he knew the boy was right. There was going to be a storm, and worse than the one that had brought him here.

Leaving now was impossible, unless he was willing to risk his horse's life because he felt uncomfortable around Lady Katherine.

Uncomfortable? That was a mild way to put the tumultuous conflict she aroused within him.

He forced himself to make a wry grin as he turned back to Egbert. "I see you are quite right. I will have to impose upon your mistress's hospitality for at least another day. Now, about mass?"

"He said you had to come."

"Who said?"

"The priest who arrived this morning. He isn't going to start until you do, and it's perishing cold in that chapel, so won't you please hurry?"

Rafe glanced at Cassius. "My horse—"

"I'll watch 'im."

"You are not the only one who would prefer not to attend mass, Egbert."

The boy blushed and stared at his toe, which he moved in slow circles in the dirt of the stable floor.

"However, since I am a knight, I suppose it is my duty to go, especially when a priest requests it."

The boy looked up eagerly.

"Now you take good care of Cassius. He has been in many a tourney and saved my hide more than once, so he should be treated with deference and respect."

Grinning, Egbert nodded.

"It's freezing in the chapel?"

"Aye, I should say it is!"

Rafe picked up his cloak, noting just how many rents and tears it had. Saint Paul's piety, the next time he had some spare coin, he would buy a new one, he vowed as he resolutely marched from the stables. Unfortunately, this one would have to do for now.

The wind grabbed at his cloak. With a scowl, Rafe

held as tight to it as he did to what remained of his self-respect.

The moment he entered the chapel, he knew the boy had not been exaggerating about the temperature. The building was bare as Lady Katherine's hall, and cold as any place he could remember. If he had any doubts, the blue lips, chattering teeth and impatient movements of the servants gathered there would have provided more than enough evidence. Even the priest seemed rather chilled.

In fact, the only person who seemed impervious to the frigid temperature was Katherine.

Although he knew it was a weakness, he couldn't resist the temptation to stand beside her, especially when the servants made way for him. It was folly, of course, because he was only going to torment himself.

Katherine didn't even glance his way.

Well, perhaps that was to be expected, he told himself, when they were in a holy place.

Or perhaps, he thought with growing dismay, she had come to her senses and realized he was not worthy of her affection or desire.

As the mass continued, he struggled to keep his expression calm and unrevealing, even though he dreaded having to speak to her afterward or, what might be worse, still being ignored by her.

When the priest finished, Katherine turned to Rafe and, her expression utterly inscrutable, said, "Because of the weather, Sir Rafe, you must stay another night."

Because of the weather. Not because of any feeling between them. Not even because it was Christmas Eve. "Thank you again for your hospitality, my lady. Cassius and I are most grateful."

As the servants hurried out of the chapel, the priest came to stand beside Katherine and she turned to address him. "Father Coll, this is Sir Rafe Bracton."

Father Coll smiled warmly. "Delighted to meet you, sir," he said. "Are you perchance related to the Bractons of Upper Uxton?"

"My uncle lived in Upper Uxton," Rafe replied with some surprise.

He was even more surprised to see the priest's smile broaden. "A most kind and generous benefactor to the poor."

"Oh yes, he was," Rafe agreed.

In reality, he knew almost nothing of his late uncle save his name and the town where he lived. However, it seemed the man had been worthy of some admiration, and right at the moment, Rafe was desperate for any and all self-esteem he could muster, even willing to cling to that of an unknown, deceased relative.

"Father, Sir Rafe, shall we go to the hall and eat?"

"Since I have been on the road since first light, I am happy to take advantage of your hospitality," Father Coll replied jovially. "And truth be told, I am most anxious to see if Father Bartholomew was exaggerating when he enumerated your cook's accomplishments."

Katherine made a little smile as she turned to lead the way. "You must tell me if he has."

At the door, they regarded the courtyard with some dismay. Not only was the wind blowing fiercely, but it had started to snow. Mixed with that snow were little pellets of ice which Rafe knew would sting like pebbles if they hit the face. "My lady, please allow me to offer you my protection," he said.

Without waiting for her to speak, Rafe put his arm about her and enfolded her in his cloak as Father Coll hurried out into the courtyard ahead of them. "Come, my lady."

Katherine thought of shrugging off Rafe's protective arm, but his unexpectedly shy, yet definitely intense expression, silenced her. Something was different about him this morning. His manner had been subdued in the chapel, but that might be explained by the necessity of proper behavior in a place of worship.

Perhaps the presence of the priest squelched his natural bonhomie. Or maybe he had stopped acting the merry mortal because he realized she was no longer under the spell of his boisterous charm.

Which was good, of course.

The weather was definitely nasty and she would be foolish to refuse the shelter he offered. Besides, she had mastery of herself now. He was nothing more than an attractive, mature man who had momentarily kindled emotions long buried. She could bury those tumultuous feelings and urges again. She would, once he let go of her.

They proceeded out into the courtyard. The wind caught their cloaks, whipping them about their legs. The snow and ice made it necessary to nearly close their eyes, so their progress was not as swift as it might have been.

Over and above this, however, Katherine was very aware of Rafe's masculine protection. She had relied upon herself for years and would have only herself to rely on when he was gone. Still, she could not help enjoying this momentary and rare sensation of being cherished and safeguarded.

Rafe removed his arm from around her the moment they entered the warm hall. "Saint Mary's mother, that's wicked weather!" he muttered as he took off his tattered cloak and shook it.

Katherine likewise removed her cloak and handed it to the waiting Hildegard. She looked around the room and realized Father Coll was already at his place at the table, as unruffled as if it were a beautiful spring day.

Attempting to emulate him, she went to her place and waited for Rafe to join them on the dais.

"Are we not fortunate to have such a fine hostess?" Father Coll asked as Rafe sat and the servants began to serve the bread and ale.

"Indeed, we are," Rafe agreed.

"I would hate to be caught on the road in such weather. I was afoot in the Alps during a storm once, and I would not care to have the experience repeated."

"That must have been terrible," Katherine agreed.

"Oh, it was. Fortunately, I had a marvelous guide, a fine fellow named Otto. Let me tell you about him."

For the rest of the meal, the priest entertained them with tales of his travels. Katherine was very impressed, and not a little envious. Once again, all the constraints of her life seemed to envelop her.

With Rafe sitting so close, she felt even more trapped.

The stories told by the priest seemed to loosen Rafe's tongue. He began to tell tales of his own adventures, to Father Coll's evident delight.

As Rafe spoke, she noted the difference between the way he had talked to her last night in the stable when they were alone. Then, she had felt she was participating in his memories, with all the joys and frustrations and moments of triumph. Today, the very same yarns were only mildly amusing.

What did that difference mean? Anything at all?

She did not want to have to wonder at Rafe's change of manner. She wanted respect, she wanted dignity, she wanted order and she wanted discipline.

At one time, she had wanted love, but that had proved to be a snare that had ruined her life, so she did not want that anymore.

"If you will excuse me," Katherine said, rising when Hildegard had cleared away the last of the food, "I have my household duties to attend to."

Father Coll smiled. "Of course, my lady, I'm sure

the preparations for Christmas celebrations are most time-consuming.''

"I do not celebrate the twelve days between Christmas and Epiphany,'' Katherine explained, wishing Father Bartholomew had saved her the trouble. "We have a special meal on Christmas Day, and that is all."

"What, no decorations? No Yule log? No music or dancing? No games? No gifts for the twelve days?''

Katherine frowned. "We prefer to observe this as a holy time, not an excuse for senseless merriment."

"Then surely you can stay,'' Father Coll declared, apparently not at all taken aback by her barely disguised reproach. "Sir Rafe was just about to tell me about Arabian horses."

"Sir Rafe is very knowledgeable about horses, and sure to be fascinating,'' Katherine replied. "However, I must see to your accommodations. Father, Sir Rafe, until later."

"Until later,'' Father Coll acknowledged genially.

Rafe didn't say anything at all.

That Christmas Eve, at least one person enjoyed Rafe's tale of the knight who lost his boots. Father Coll had laughed and the servants would have, had their mistress not sat stone-faced and grim throughout the entire meal, her eyes darting daggers at anyone other than the priest who had dared to be amused.

After she had gone and he sought solace in his wine, Rafe felt as if last night in the stable, when

Katherine had been so companionable and desirable, had been a fantasy that disappeared with the reality of daylight.

Saint Anne's aunt, it was a damned good thing he was leaving just as soon as the weather cleared. He had never met a more confusing woman in his life, and he would be happy if he never met one like her again. He must have been mad to think he was falling in love with her.

As for Father Coll, the man had to be the most unobservant fellow in England not to sense the lady's tension before, and it had not abated a bit when she returned a short while later.

"The storm looks to continue for another day at least," Father Coll noted, breaking the momentary silence.

"There will not be many tenants coming for the service, perhaps," Katherine said. "They will be sorry to miss it."

"Not if they are warm," Rafe muttered, thinking of the shivering servants that morning. "I don't suppose you would consider a brazier or two in there?"

"No. We go to the chapel to worship, not to be comfortable."

Well, if he needed any additional evidence that she was in no humor to be amused by him, he had just received it. "Perhaps if I had a better cloak, I would agree."

"There is nothing wrong with your cloak that some mending wouldn't fix."

"I daresay that means you were not planning on giving me one for a Christmas present."

She looked shocked, and he was rather fiendishly glad to have gotten any reaction at all from her.

Then she flushed, but not with embarrassment. "The calamint was not enough?" she demanded, anger in her eyes.

Now he flushed, and not with anger. Saint Vincent in a vise, like an ungrateful wretch, he had forgotten that. "Yes, it was."

"I do not believe in giving gifts at Christmas," she explained to the priest. "Sir Rafe's horse was ill, however, so with good Christian charity, I gave him calamint to make a potion to clear his lungs. It seems to have worked."

"I am very glad," Father Coll said. Then he sighed, a far more serious expression on his face than either of them had seen before. "The giving of gifts when none is expected in return is indeed Christian charity."

"Sometimes people cannot afford to give gifts, even if they would like to," Rafe noted with a hint of defiance.

"The most important gifts of all do not cost money," the priest replied, "and if anyone would doubt that—" Father Coll turned his suddenly shrewd gaze onto the knight "—he need only remember the gifts our Lord received on the first Christmas."

"But the Magi brought very fine presents," Rafe pointed out. "Gold and frankincense and myrrh."

Father Coll smiled and pushed his trencher away. "To be sure, they did bring those things, but for me, the important part of the story of our Lord's birth is not what they held in their hands, but the other gift they gave that was far more precious. These important, wealthy and learned men paid homage to a baby in a stable. They gave Him respect, which is something no amount of money can purchase.

"And we must also remember the shepherds, rough men who had come to see their promised messiah. Think of what it must have been like to find not a prince in a palace, but a baby wrapped in simple swaddling clothes, lying in a manger in a humble stable. Yet they still trusted their vision and had faith that this was their future king as they, too, paid him respectful homage. Respect, trust and faith are truly wonderful, precious gifts," Father Coll concluded softly, "for they are the basis of love."

Rafe toyed with the bottom of his goblet for a moment before giving Katherine a sidelong glance. "Would you agree, my lady?" he asked. "Would you say that faith, trust and respect are excellent gifts?"

"Respect, certainly," she answered.

"What of trust?"

She rose. "One can misplace one's trust and live to rue it. I thank you, Father, for your very interesting and unique thoughts. Now it is late, so I must bid you both good-night."

The two men watched her disappear up the stairs leading to her bedchamber.

The priest sighed softly. "I fear a man has wronged our hostess at some time in her life."

Rafe nodded. "Yes. She sounded very bitter."

Father Coll regarded him with a shrewd eye. "She is not the only one sounding bitter tonight."

"Am *I*? It must be the wine," Rafe answered with a laugh. "I'm getting maudlin in my cups."

"No, I don't think that's it."

"I assure you, it's nothing more."

"Would you say too much wine was Lady Katherine's trouble, too?"

"No. I think you have guessed aright. At some time, a man has betrayed her trust."

"And you feel sorry for her?"

"Not sorry. I regret that it happened, but her history means very little to me."

The priest cocked his head. "Do you think me a fool, Sir Rafe?"

Wishing he had been more circumspect, Rafe flushed, then lifted his chin with a show of bravado.

"Why should her past mean anything to me?"

"Because you love her."

"What?" Rafe cried, looking about to see if any of the servants had heard the priest's startling pronouncement.

"You love her. I can see it in your eyes."

"Then you should have a doctor examine them, for you are seeing the impossible."

"Why should that be impossible?"

"Because...because it is!"

"Because you are poor and she is not."

"This is too ludicrous to discuss. I'm going back to the stable," Rafe declared, pushing back his chair.

The priest laid a detaining hand on his arm. "Rafe," he said, his bright eyes intense in his round face, "you and I both know that no matter what has happened to her in the past, there beats a passionate, loving heart inside Katherine DuMonde. I think she wants to love and be loved. Offer her that love, Rafe."

"She would scorn it."

"Why?"

"Because I have nothing to offer her!" he muttered, the truth spilling out. "I have wasted my life. I have lived only for the present, with no thought to the future." He lowered his head and confessed. "How bleak that future looks now. I have no home, no wealth, no family, and few possessions. I have managed to hide this truth from myself for a long time, but I cannot any longer. I have nothing. I *am* nothing."

"Look about you, Rafe," Father Coll said softly with an encompassing gesture. "Do you think Katherine needs material goods? Do you think she wants money or power? Don't you think she needs something else, something more precious, something you can give her? She needs love, Rafe, and as you crave respect, she needs to be able to trust again. You can convince her that not all men who love will betray."

"I don't want her respect or her love," Rafe protested.

"So you would like to live out the rest of your days alone, and you would condemn her to do so, too?"

Rafe's chair scraped loudly over the stone floor as he shoved it farther back.

"I know you are afraid, Rafe, but take the risk and tell her how you feel. Offer her your love. Otherwise you may spend the rest of your life regretting that you did not."

Rafe didn't answer. He strode out of the hall, away from this most unusual, troublesome priest and into the storm.

Sometime later, Katherine crept down to the quiet hall. Unable to sleep, she had decided she should insure that the fire in the hearth had not gone out. Otherwise, the hall would be extremely cold in the morning. She also told herself she might need to put a brazier in the chapel, depending on the temperature of the hall. She did not want to make the chapel overly warm, of course. As she had said to Rafe, they were not there for comfort, but to worship.

She halted on the bottom step and wrapped her arms around herself, hesitating when she realized Father Coll was still there, sitting on a bench by the hearth. The light of the flames flickered and a piece of wood fell, sending up a small shower of sparks that illuminated his portly shape. Despite the shooting sparks, he must have heard her, for he looked at her over his shoulder and smiled. "Ah, my lady, what brings you to the hall at this hour?"

Katherine approached him. "I wanted to be sure the fire did not go out," she said, gesturing at the hearth. "It is indeed very late, Father. Should you not retire?"

"Oh, I often stay awake for the whole of Christmas Eve," he replied with a smile. "I confess this is my favorite night of the year. I enjoy the quiet of the winter's eve and contemplating how it must have been for those visiting the Holy Child." He patted the bench beside him. "Will you sit, my lady?"

Since she didn't want to return to the barren surroundings of her lonely bedchamber, she did.

"I think Christmas brings you little joy," the priest observed.

"No, it does not."

"Unhappy memories, perhaps?"

"Yes."

"We all have the burdens of our pasts to bear."

"Some apparently bear their burdens more lightly than others."

"Or hide them better."

She gave the priest a wary, sidelong glance. "You find your past burdensome?"

"I was not referring to myself."

"You speak of Sir Rafe, perhaps?"

"And yourself, too, I think. You hide your pain very well."

Katherine stiffened. "I do not know what you mean."

"No?"

"No."

"I gather you think Sir Rafe is little bothered by his history."

"He could not jest about it so if he were."

Father Coll gave her a quizzical look. "Some people hide their pain behind austere dignity, others beneath a jester's hat, but that does not mean they feel nothing. Some would say it takes a great deal of strength to mask one's pain with laughter. In truth, I think Sir Rafe is a very lonely man."

"He seems to have a great many friends."

"I would not say friends. Acquaintances, perhaps. I note that he is not spending Christmas with any of his so-called friends."

"He was caught in the storm."

"I have not heard him mention any invitations."

Katherine realized that Father Coll was quite right. "No, he hasn't."

"So while he is friendly, I think he does not have many friends, and he hides his loneliness. He must sometimes wish for a good friend, especially when he is troubled."

Katherine thought of him in the stable as he tended to Cassius. He had seemed very glad of her company.

Perhaps he was far lonelier than she suspected.

As lonely as she.

"I don't suppose there are many people he trusts,

either. The trust that enables us to reveal our vulner-abilities is a rare and great gift, my lady," Father Coll said quietly, "especially from a man like Sir Rafe, who would prefer to hold everyone at bay by making them laugh."

Katherine eyed the priest speculatively. "You believe he amuses people as a defense?"

"Very much so."

Katherine thought of the tales Rafe had told her about his own life and suddenly saw them in a new light. The mistakes he had made, the prizes he had lost, the insults he had borne—he had made her laugh that night in the stable, but now, they were far from funny.

"He wants to be respected, my lady, but if that cannot be—or he believes it impossible—he plays the clown. Better to be laughed at than ignored."

"I respect him," Katherine replied. "He is a knight and my guest, after all."

"But nothing more?"

"He treated his horse's illness with skill," she noted, looking away from the priest into the glowing fire.

"That sounds better. He needs more than respect, though. Like all of us, he wants to be loved."

"I believe he has little trouble in that regard," Katherine replied. "He charms without even trying. My maidservants have been in a dither since he arrived."

"That is not the kind of love he needs, my lady,

although perhaps he thinks he deserves no better. He needs the love that sees beyond the banter and tales to the man beneath, the companionable love that will make a woman stay with him during a long, anxious night.''

Katherine's mouth fell open in surprise, but Father Coll didn't seem to notice. "He needs a love that is based on respect and trust and faith. He needs *your* respect, your trust, your faith—your love, my lady.''

She stood up and faced the priest. "I cannot!" she said firmly, believing it even as her heart ached with loneliness and despair. "I cannot tell you why, but I cannot!''

With a sigh, Father Coll watched her hurry away. Then he returned to his Christmas Eve vigil.

Chapter Five

Rafe peered out the door of the stable. Behind him, Cassius breathed easy. Before him, through the gently falling snow, a light shone from the window in the western tower like the Christmas star.

He wondered if Katherine was thinking about the vagrant knight supposedly sleeping in her stable. If she was, she was probably considering him a pathetic example of a life gone awry and looking forward to his departure.

But what if Father Coll was right? What if he could give her something, after all? What if she might miraculously welcome his love?

Doubt assailed him. He could easily envision her scorning him. By all the saints, he would never be able to make an amusing story out of that. Her rejection would be too painful, because he had never in his life wanted anything as much as he wanted Katherine's love. No prize, no reward, no honor he had ever sought could compare to this one—and none had ever been more out of his reach.

Sighing, Rafe turned away and closed the door behind him. "Well, Cassius, it will be you and me again, as always," he murmured. "There's nothing wrong with that, is there? And if I have not the heart to try for prizes anymore, I shall become an apothecary to horses."

He lowered his head and slumped against the wall. "Oh, God," he moaned, despair overwhelming him. He was such a failure, such a useless fellow, undeserving of any woman's regard, and Katherine's most of all.

"It would indeed take a miracle for her to love me, Cassius," he murmured. "A Christmas miracle."

Then Father Coll's words began to sound in his head, about the truly important gifts of Christmas, and the basis of love.

He loved Katherine with all his heart, and he would still love her if she came to him with nothing. She alone was the prize—not her manor, not her wealth, not her title. Just Katherine.

He would not give up. He would not regret the risk not assumed, the chance not taken, the prize not sought. He was many things, but he was not a coward.

He raised his head and pushed himself from the wall. "I have to do it, Cassius," he said fiercely. "I have to risk it, or I shall truly be a shameful failure."

With renewed vigor, Rafe yanked open the stable door and stepped out into the cold air. With equally determined steps, he marched across the crunching snow in the courtyard and into the hall.

Mercifully, no one was there—or at least no one Rafe saw—so he swiftly brushed the snow from his shoulders and continued on his way, up the stairs and toward the lady's chamber.

Once outside her door, he took a deep breath, then knocked softly and walked in without waiting for an answer.

Clad in her shift, her hair loose and flowing, illuminated by a single flickering candle, Katherine peered at him as he stood in the shadows. "Who dares to enter here?" she demanded.

"Rafe," he said softly. Humbly. Like the unworthy petitioner that he was.

She sucked in her breath but didn't move. "What are you doing here?"

"I must talk to you, Katherine," Rafe whispered, stepping out of the darkness and into the pool of light.

She flushed, feeling naked before him. "You must go," she commanded, wrapping her arms around herself protectively.

He didn't leave. Instead, he closed the door behind him.

"You have to leave before you are discovered here!"

"No one comes into your bedchamber. You told me so yourself the other night."

The other night, when he had kissed her with such passion.

"Katherine," he repeated with quiet sincerity, "I must speak with you."

"In my bedchamber in the middle of the night?"

His gaze faltered as if he were a bashful youth. "I couldn't wait. Please do not send me away. I have come...I have come to give you a Christmas present, albeit a poor one." He raised his eyes, went down on his knee and said, "I would give you my love, Katherine, and my heart, if you will take them."

Her gaze softened to one of disbelief. "You love me?"

"Yes."

A tremor went through her, like that of a horse that senses something it should fear. "I have heard vows of love before, but they proved to be meaningless."

"I thought as much." He rose slowly. "Who was he, Katherine?" he asked softly. "Who hurt you?"

She shook her head, unwilling to speak of it even now, for her shame was too great.

"In addition to my love, I would make you a promise, Katherine. If you can find it in your heart to trust me and have faith in my devotion, I will never betray that faith and trust. I give you my solemn vow."

When she did not answer, he felt a despair that was like a physical blow. Then, as he always did, he sought refuge in a jest. "If you require proof, I have been faithful to poor old Cassius for a very long time, and I have never told him I love him."

When she still did not speak, hot tears sprang into

his eyes, adding to his humiliation. He quickly turned away and went to the door.

"Rafe, don't go."

Scarcely daring to believe his own ears, he turned back.

Katherine took a tentative step toward him.

"I am afraid of you, Rafe," she confessed quietly, studying his face.

"Afraid? Of me?"

"Of the feelings you inspire." She clasped her hands and regarded him steadily. "When I was but fifteen, Frederick Delamarch came to keep Christmas with my family. He was very handsome, and charming, and I was young and vain. I was ready to believe that he could fall in love with me, and when he said that he had, I trusted him without a single qualm. We made love."

Her gaze faltered for an instant, but she bravely raised her eyes to look at him again—and he loved her even more. "Frederick left the next day without so much as a word of farewell. I hurried to the gates and there I heard him laughing and bragging to his companions about what he had done. I had been betrayed, but before that, I had been a fool. I was so ashamed and terrified. What if I was with child? What if my parents found out?"

His heart ached to hear her anguished words, the pain undiminished by the years. "I did the only thing I could think of to make amends. I agreed to accept marriage to the man my parents had been urging me to wed for months. I explained my sudden change of heart as evidence of a young woman's fickle nature. They were only too pleased to have my agreement and did not press for more of an explanation. We did not know he had gambled away almost all his wealth, so I married Alfred DuMonde, and the rest you know."

"I swear by Saint George's sword," Rafe growled, "if I had known what Delamarch had done, I would have tried harder to kill him."

"Are you making a joke?"

"No," he replied sincerely. "I have met him in melees and tournaments and he would not have been so very hard to kill because he is a stout, slow-moving sot."

"He doesn't matter anymore," she said, feeling the truth of that deep inside. "I respect you, Rafe, because you are a compassionate man. And I want to trust you and be able to have faith in you, because...because I think I love you, too."

"You do?"

She nodded. "If what I feel for you is not love, I have no name for it."

"Oh, Katherine!" he whispered, hurrying toward her and taking her in his arms. "I want so much to believe it is possible."

"I thought it impossible that I should ever love again." She drew back and smiled. "Now I think I have never been in love before."

He chuckled softly, then kissed her cheeks, her nose, her chin. "Oh, my darling, thank you."

"For loving you?" she murmured as she returned his kisses, thrilled to be in his tender embrace.

"For giving me, little more than a beggar at your gates, the finest prize of all."

"I am the poor beggar, Rafe. Without your love, I am impoverished. I have been trying to convince myself otherwise, but that is the truth."

He caressed her back, then buried his hands in her thick hair. "Katherine, I shall never leave you. I mean that with all my heart."

She smiled tremulously. "I believe you. I trust you. I have faith in you. I love you."

His brow furrowed with puzzlement. "What happened, Katherine? How is it a miracle happened and you love me, a jester, a man who has so little to offer you?"

"You have made me happier than I ever thought I could be, Rafe," she answered softly. Then, to his infinite delight, a sparkle of mischief appeared in her blue eyes. "And perhaps I have been serious too long and am in great need of a jester."

He grinned his wonderful, familiar grin. "My lady, if it is amusement you desire, I am your man."

"You are." She smiled and eyed him speculatively. "I think I fell in love with you because of your impertinence."

His deep chuckle filled the room as his eyes twinkled with both happiness and something that made her heart race. "What? And after all Father Coll's talk of respect?"

She twined a lock of his hair about her finger. "I did not say I don't want your respect, Rafe."

"As much as I respect you, my lady, there are some rather insolent things I would like to do with you," he muttered as he trailed his lips along her neck.

"And I must confess there is more I desire than amusement," she whispered breathlessly.

"But there is one condition," he murmured as he began to loosen the tie at the neck of her shift.

"What condition?" she gasped, gripping his shoulders as his mouth moved lower.

"The condition is that you agree to make me the happiest man in England and this the best Christmas by consenting to be my wife."

"Yes, oh yes!" she sighed, giving herself over to the pleasure of his kisses and caress.

Now she was no silly girl infatuated and flattered by an admired man's attention. She was a woman who could perceive the honest sincerity of Rafe's heartfelt words and the truth of his feelings for her.

She was a woman who was free again to trust, reborn in Rafe's love.

Her eyes shining, she smiled happily. "I love you, Rafe," she said softly.

He lowered his head, suddenly humbled by her declaration.

She pulled away, then took his hand and led him to her bed.

"Katherine?"

Her gaze faltered, as if she had become a shy maiden again. "You do not want to stay?"

He raised his head, his eyes gleaming in the candlelight with unmistakable passion and desire. "I did not dare to hope for this."

"There is an advantage to finding love at our age," she said in a husky whisper, running her hands up his chest in a bold caress. "I am old enough to know what I want."

Then she hesitated. "Perhaps I am being too undignified...."

"Saint Martha's mouth!" he cried softly, a grin again lighting his features. "I am not complaining." He sat on the bed and pulled her down beside him. "I simply cannot believe my good fortune. But now, my lady, soon to be my wife," he murmured as he slowly took her in his embrace, "I believe you are beginning to convince me."

"What more need I do?"

"That I leave to your own imagination, my lady."

With a throaty, seductive laugh that soon turned into sighs of ardent desire, she found a way.

Yawning, Katherine slowly stretched her arms over her head. The sudden chill of the cool air against her naked skin reminded her of what had happened last night, and she opened her eyes. She was alone in her bed.

She quickly looked around the room, but Rafe was not there. Had she dreamed their passionate lovemaking?

But it was not a dream. They had loved with feverish abandon, whispering endearments to each other, delighting in the sensations each aroused. She knew she had not imagined the weight of his body upon hers, or the thrill of their joining. Nor had she made up the movement of his taut muscles or the feel of his mouth upon hers. She had not dreamed the tension that had filled her or the incredible pleasure of release.

She recalled the moments after their lovemaking, when she lay in his arms, sweat slicked and happy, and they had talked of their future. He would breed and treat horses, since he would no longer be a wandering knight traveling from tournament to tournament to earn a living, while she would continue to teach her girls, if that was what she wanted. Of course it was, although a new, wonderful possibility had also arisen in her mind.

It was not inconceivable that she could bear a child. Rafe's child. What a marvelous gift that would be for both of them! Indeed, that hope filled her with so much joy it was almost too delightful to contemplate.

So where was Rafe now?

It occurred to her that he might have gone to see Cassius. Yes, that was probably it.

And it could be that he didn't want to be discovered in her bed, which was something she really should have considered. What would the parents of her girls think if they heard about that? Why, she would never have another pupil.

Sitting up in the bed, she looked at the sky outside her window. It was still dark, but faint streaks of orange-pink light told her it was dawn and that the snow had stopped.

She reached for her shift, lying discarded at the end of her bed. Shivering in the cold, her teeth started to chatter when her feet touched the stone floor, and she dressed quickly. She began to put on her wimple and cap, then paused. Rafe had whispered many complimentary things about her hair last night. Today, for him, she would not cover it. The servants would talk, but she didn't care. She would rather please Rafe than worry about their opinion.

She was very glad Father Coll was here. Surely he would not object to giving them a marriage blessing. Fortunately, she had no male relative to petition for permission and was not of sufficient rank or wealth that the king would care.

Then she glanced down at the dress she had chosen without much thought. It was plain and black, like most of her garments.

But this was Christmas Day, and she was in love. She wanted to look beautiful for Rafe.

With a joyous smile, she went to her chest and pulled from its depths a dress she had not worn since before her marriage. In fact, she had never worn it, for once upon a time, she had decided the rich gown of holly-red brocade and samite would be her wedding dress when she married Frederick Delamarch. After he had left her, she had never been able to look at it without mourning his betrayal.

Now, however, all she cared about was that it was a lovely, well-fitting garment whose deep red tones seemed to reflect the happy glow on her cheeks.

She quickly dressed, picked up her cloak and laid it over her arm, then went below.

"Good morning and a merry Christmas to you all," she declared jovially to the servants already working there.

She did not stifle a laugh when she saw the startled looks on their faces, shocking them even more.

As the servants exchanged dubious glances and muttered a subdued Christmas greeting in response, Father Coll appeared. He did not seem at all surprised by her appearance. "A merry Christmas to you, my lady," he called out happily. "Shall we go to the chapel for mass?"

"In a moment, Father." She laid her cloak on a chair and gestured to one of the servants who stood near a brazier. "Light that and take it to the chapel, please."

The man's eyes widened, but he nodded eagerly and quickly did as he was told.

Katherine spotted Hildegard. "Tell the cook to prepare the best feast she can. We will all celebrate today.''

''My lady?''

''Come, it is Christmas. Do you not want a feast?'' she teased.

Hildegard looked as stunned as it was possible for a human being to be.

Katherine quickly began issuing other orders to be attended to immediately after the celebratory mass, orders intended to prepare the hall for a Christmas celebration the like of which it had not seen in years, if ever. The finest linen was to be taken from the storeroom and laid on the newly cleaned tables. The rushes were to be swept and changed, and herbs generously spread upon them. Other servants were commanded to go to the nearby wood and collect holly, evergreen branches, ivy and mistletoe with which to decorate the hall. There was also to be a blazing fire in the hearth.

It was clear from the confused looks on the servants' faces that they were finding it difficult to believe this was their mistress speaking, and Katherine smiled genially at their befuddlement. She felt young and happy, as if all the barren, lonely Christmases of the past fifteen years were but a bad dream now fading in the daylight.

She spotted Giles standing near the corridor to the kitchen. He clearly thought she had gone mad, and she had to laugh at his suspicious expression. ''No, Giles, I assure you I am in my right mind. I have never felt better. Please take word to all the poor you can find and tell them that a Christmas meal awaits them in Lady Katherine's hall tonight. I want everyone to be as happy and content as I am today, and as thankful for God's gifts,'' she finished with a joyful sigh. ''Now, we must go to mass, to give our thanks in worship.''

The door to the hall opened and with a smile, Katherine turned to see—Egbert. Not Rafe. The boy glanced about uncertainly when he realized it was indeed Lady Katherine looking at him quizzically.

''Will you ask Sir Rafe to join us in the chapel for Christ's mass?'' she asked.

Egbert's gaze faltered and he shifted awkwardly. ''I, um, that is, I would if I could, my lady.''

''Why can't you?''

''Because, my lady, because he's gone.''

''Gone?''

The boy nodded. ''Aye, my lady, before dawn, and took his horse with him.''

''He took Cassius?''

''Aye.''

Father Coll stepped forward. ''Did he say when he would be back?''

''No, Father,'' Egbert replied sadly. ''He didn't say nothing. He left when we were asleep.''

The priest turned his worried eyes onto Katherine.

''Good,'' Katherine said briskly. ''Then he will be all the more surprised by our preparations when he returns.''

The servants exchanged wary looks.

"You think he does intend to return, my lady?" Father Coll asked quietly.

Katherine straightened her shoulders, a defiant gleam in her eyes. "Of course I do. I trust him."

Father Coll sighed with obvious relief. "I am glad to hear it, my lady."

"But he didn't leave his baggage," Egbert protested. "I think he's gone for good—and he took a harness, too."

"I never thought he was a thief," Giles blurted out guiltily, "or I would have set a watch on him."

"He is not a thief, and he must have needed the harness," Katherine said. "He will explain when he returns."

All the servants regarded their mistress as if she were truly deranged. Only Father Coll seemed to find her response satisfactory. She put on her cloak and led her bewildered servants to the small chapel.

They followed her, whispering among themselves, wondering what had happened to their mistress overnight. Some speculated a divine visitation, others an illness, one or two that the creature issuing orders wasn't Lady Katherine at all, but some sort of changeling. Either way, they all agreed, something extraordinary was going on and they didn't think they liked it.

As the Mass progressed, Katherine tried to concentrate on Father Coll and the holy meaning of the ceremony. Unfortunately, every sound from outside made her tense with expectation. Every time the door to the chapel subsequently failed to open and Rafe didn't arrive, she felt an increasing disappointment.

But she would trust that he was not gone away for good. She would believe that no matter why he had gone, he would soon return.

She had to trust and have faith, or the despair, disappointment and hurt would be overwhelming.

Surely she could not have been so callously betrayed twice in her life! Surely, she fervently prayed, the knowledge that she was indeed a dupe and a fool could not be her Christmas gift this year.

The mass ended. The servants quickly dispersed to their tasks, while Katherine lingered long in prayer. Finally she felt Father Coll's gaze and got to her feet.

She managed to smile. "I think I will order a brazier here during the whole of the winter."

The priest nodded, but his bright, black-eyed scrutiny didn't waver. "Are you all right, my lady?"

"I thought I would dress differently for the festivities."

"That is not what I meant."

"I assure you, Father, I am quite well. I am, perhaps, a little anxious over Sir Rafe's continuing absence and curious to know what might have caused him to leave so abruptly. Still, I do not doubt he will return soon and explain."

"You do doubt."

Her gaze wavered under his steadfast regard. "I am

trying very hard not to,'' she admitted quietly. "As you said, trust and faith are the basis of love, and I...I..."

Years of hiding her true feelings made her suddenly reticent.

"You love him."

She clasped her hands together. "I know he will be back soon, and that there is a good reason for his absence."

The priest's smile warmed the chapel more than the brazier. "I do not think your trust misplaced, my lady. I can generally tell who is worthy and who is not."

Suddenly there was a huge thud outside the manor gates. "What is that?" Katherine gasped.

Without waiting for an answer, she dashed into the courtyard, Father Coll right behind her. "What has happened?" she shouted at Dawson, who was peering out the slot in the gate.

"What ho! I come bearing a gift!" a most welcome and familiar male voice shouted on the other side.

"It's Rafe!" Katherine shouted happily, running closer. "Let him in! Let him in!"

Ignoring the curious servants who also rushed into the courtyard, Katherine literally danced with impatience as Dawson hurried to obey. She squeezed through the opening the moment it was large enough and halted, staring incredulously.

Rafe stood between an ox, who bore a harness that was attached to an enormous log and Cassius, whose bridle he held. Behind the log was one of the peasants who lived nearby.

"Is that you, Katherine?" Rafe demanded, a saucy grin on his wonderful face as he ran an admiring gaze over her. "Have you found a potion of eternal youthfulness? If so, you had better share it with your decrepit old admirer."

"It is I, and you are not decrepit or old," she replied. "But what have you been doing? Where did that ox come from?" She noticed the way he kept his weight off one foot. "Are you injured?"

"I have brought you a Yule log, my lady, my love," Rafe said, patting it. "It is not much of a gift, I know, but it was the only one I could think of. I wasn't going to bring Cassius, but he made such a fuss, I feared he would waken everyone. I apologize for my tardiness. I had to find a farmer who would loan me his ox."

The man behind the log tugged his forelock.

"Unfortunately the log rolled and I was not fast enough on my feet. Or foot, I should say. I suppose I have missed mass, too."

"Oh Rafe!" she cried, hurrying to put her arm under his shoulder to help him and take Cassius's bridle.

"My language was much more colorful," he admitted ruefully.

"Is it very bad?" she asked anxiously, looking at his swollen foot.

"I've had worse wounds in a tournament," he replied, smiling at her, the love shining in his eyes. "And never so lovely a helper."

"You will not be able to dance."

"Dance? I should say not." He paused, then noticed the band of servants carrying greenery. They appeared at the side of the road in single file, like a train of supplicants bearing booty. "What is all this?"

"Decorations for the hall. I decided that this year, we would truly celebrate Christmas." She lowered her voice so that only he could hear. "I have a reason to celebrate this year."

Rafe's delighted smile confirmed that he was pleasantly surprised.

She spotted Giles and Dawson and gestured for them to come closer.

Giles carried Rafe's leather pouch. "We found it under some straw," he explained sheepishly. "And I've shown my son the difference between an ox harness and a horse's harness."

"An old habit. I always hide my belongings, such as they are," Rafe said. "Did you think it was lost?"

"It doesn't matter now," Katherine replied. "Please help Sir Rafe take the Yule log inside the yard," she said.

Gazing warily at the huge length of timber, evidently already trying to figure out how they would maneuver it through the gate and to the hall, they nodded wordlessly. She ordered the other servants to carry on, then turned to Rafe.

"Now lean on me, my love," she ordered. "We

should get you inside at once. You must be chilled to the bone."

"I am counting on you to warm me up," he said in her ear. Then he gazed at her askance. "Why, Katherine! I do believe you are blushing like the most modest maiden in Christendom."

"And you enjoy teasing me."

"When my foot is better, I think I shall shout my love for you from yonder wall—"

"Do that, Sir Rafe, and I shall knock you off."

"Is that a threat, my lady?"

"Yes. Now let us get inside."

"I am only too happy to obey. It's very slick underfoot, you might have noticed," Rafe remarked. "We had best take care, or we could both land in an ignominious heap, which would be very undignified."

"I fear I have lost any claim to dignity today," Katherine replied. "Strangely enough, I don't seem to care."

"A Merry Christmas, Sir Rafe," Father Coll declared as they slowly made their way into the courtyard. "Although Lady Katherine kept her faith in you, I was beginning to despair of your return."

Rafe's grip tightened on Katherine's shoulder. "She trusts me," he said, not a little proudly.

"And justly so," the portly priest observed as he joined them.

"I am sorry I have missed mass, Father."

"There should be time for a private celebration in

the chapel before the feast is ready," Father Coll replied.

"Excellent! I must say a prayer of thanks." Rafe looked back to Giles and Dawson who were trying to get the ox to move. "I shall leave the rest to you, men," he said jovially. "I fear I would not be much help with this foot anyway. As my lady says, no dancing for me this Christmas," he finished mournfully. "And I am a very fine dancer, too."

His voice dropped to a seductive whisper. "We shall have to think of other ways to amuse ourselves."

"Shh!" Katherine chided, nudging him. "Father Coll!"

Thankfully the priest seemed unaware of Rafe's seductive remark.

They entered the hall, and Rafe halted in stunned surprise. "Why, this is excellent!" he cried softly, surveying the brightly lit, cozily warm hall. Already the servants had it decorated with holly, ivy, evergreen boughs and mistletoe. The scent of hot bread, roasted meat and mulled wine filled his nostrils.

Rafe pulled her close. "Father," he said, addressing the priest without taking his eyes from his beloved, "will you give us a marriage blessing today?"

"Of course, my son!" Father Coll cried, his mouth drawing upward into a smile and his eyes twinkling merrily.

Rafe plucked a sprig of mistletoe from the basket held by a startled Hildegard and held it over Katherine's head as he bent to kiss her. "Merry Christmas, my gift, my prize, my love," he whispered.

"Merry Christmas," she murmured as she lifted her smiling face.

His belly shaking with a delighted chortle, Father Coll placed his finger meditatively beside his nose. "Merry Christmas and may God bless us all," he murmured with happy satisfaction.

* * * * *

DEBORAH SIMMONS is the author of more than a dozen Harlequin Historicals. A former journalist, she turned to fiction when the birth of her first child prompted her to pursue her longtime love of historical romance. She makes her home in the country with her husband, two children, two cats and a stray dog that stayed. Readers can write to her at P.O. Box 274, Ontario, OH 44862. For a reply, a self-addressed stamped envelope is appreciated.

If you enjoy "The Unexpected Guest," be sure to look for Deborah's upcoming Harlequin Historical, *The Gentleman Thief,* which will be available in mid-January 2000. Set in England during the Regency period, it's the delightful tale of a beautiful brain who stirs up trouble during a season at Bath when she investigates a jewel theft. Her "assistant," quite remarkably, is the handsome and much sought-after Marquis of Ashdowne....

The Unexpected Guest
Deborah Simmons

For Jenny and David,
the best gifts that I ever got.

Chapter One

His sons were not coming home for Christmas.

Fawke de Burgh, Earl of Campion, stood with his hands clasped behind his back, facing the evidence that swirled before him. Alone in the solar, he had opened the shutters to one of the tall, narrow windows, only to be buffeted by a blast of chill air and its accompanying snow. The weather was worse than in living memory, and he could only shake his head at its fury. Travel during the winter was never easy, but no one would be fool enough to tackle the frozen roads in the week past, marked by a blizzard such as he had never seen. And Campion would not endanger his family simply to indulge a father's whimsy.

Still he could not deny his disappointment, for he had become accustomed to a Yuletide surrounded by his offspring. It was the only time they were all together these days, and Campion had yet to meet one son's wife and see his newest grandchild.

Perhaps the holiday would have been more bearable if so many were not away, but out of his seven sons, only two were here at Campion Castle, the most meager gathering yet. And although he loved them all, the earl knew that Stephen and Reynold were those least likely to cheer him. A clever lad, Stephen had so far squandered his talents in too much wine, while Reynold, cursed with a bad leg, went through life with a grimness that belied all his accomplishments.

With a sigh, the earl shifted, welcoming the bitter wind that reflected his mood. He had never expected all of his sons to stay at Campion, but neither had he thought so many would settle elsewhere. Who would take over when he was gone? His heir was Dunstan, but the eldest de Burgh was busy with his own demesne, in addition to his heiress wife's holdings. Both Geoffrey and Simon had recently taken wives and were content to live in the homes that marriage brought to them. Robin was overseeing one of Dunstan's properties in the south, and Nicholas, eager for new adventures, had joined him there.

Campion was proud of their achievements and their independence, and yet he knew a certain melancholy at their absence. Not only would he miss them, but the holiday itself would not be the same. Such celebrations were the venue of women, as Campion, who had buried two wives, knew well. In the past few years, Dunstan's lady had made sure the hall was decked in greenery and all the traditions observed, but without her, who would see to it?

They had managed to drag the Yule log inside during a break in the weather and, of course, there would be feasting, but who would take the time to make a Christmas bush and insist upon all the games and gifts and songs? Campion pictured himself stepping into the breach, but he could not rouse much enthusiasm for the prospect, especially since Stephen and Reynold would little appreciate his efforts.

The sound of footsteps made him lift his hands to the shutters. It would not do for the Earl of Campion to be seen mooning out the window like a dispirited lad. Worse yet, he did not care to have a servant hurrying to shut the cold away from him as if he were enfeebled. Lately he had noted a certain subtle fussing over him that did not sit well. He might not be as young as he once was, but he was lord here, and he could still hold his own against his knights, if not his brawny boys.

Campion's fingers stilled at the sight of dark movement among the swirling white outside, and he leaned closer, but the snow obscured his vision of the land below. Although it was probably nothing, he would send a man out to check the grounds, he decided, just as the sound of his steward's voice rose behind him.

"My lord! My lord! Ah, there you are! Have you seen them? Someone is at the gate, a small party, struggling against the elements."

Not a trick of the eye then, but arrivals in these conditions and so late in the day? It was nearly nightfall. "Let them in," Campion said. Closing the shutters, he turned even as he wondered who would be abroad so recklessly. If it were one of his sons, the earl's enthusiasm for the company of family would be tempered by dismay at such a misjudgment. But who else would be about? Certainly no enemy, even one foolish enough to attack the famous stronghold of Campion, would dare the elements, while pilgrims and anyone else with any sense would be inside.

Perhaps a messenger from court, he mused, but such missives were ill news more often than not, and he left the solar with a distinct sense of unease. Still he knew his duty, and he would welcome any traveler who braved this weather to reach the haven that was his home. He moved down the winding stairs into the great hall, where he gestured for a servant to light additional torches and called for food and lodging for those who would soon enter.

The steward, having delivered his message to a waiting knight, returned. "My lord Reynold has gone to meet them," he noted, and Campion knew that his son would see that those at the gate made it to the hall no matter what the conditions outside. Despite the leg that pained him—or perhaps because of it— Reynold's will was stronger than any of the others.

"Shall I have the hot, spiced wine brought out?" the steward asked, and Campion nodded, tamping down his annoyance at such mundane questions. When Dunstan's wife had lived at the castle, she had served as chatelaine and handled all the details of food and household so well that Campion missed her woman's touch.

In more ways than one, the earl thought, frowning at the thought of the Christmas ahead. Someone would have to place the holly and ivy and bay about the hall in celebration of the season. And although the castle was cleaner than before Marion's tenure, Campion saw that the walls could use a good scrubbing. After Epiphany, he would set the servants to a thorough wash, he decided. Meanwhile, the Yule log burned in welcome in a hall that was spacious and well-appointed, and visitors, this night, would be grateful for any kind of shelter.

Outside he heard horses, while nearby the murmur of voices rose expectantly. Among them he recognized that of Wilda, one of the female servants, who eyed the entrance anxiously. Always superstitious, Wilda was staring at the doors with great significance, and Campion smiled. Not only did Wilda hold firm to the old belief that the first person to cross the threshold after midnight on New Year's Day was a harbinger of the year ahead, but she thought that those who appeared on Christmas Eve gave an indication of the holiday's happiness.

The arrival of a dark-haired man was thought to be lucky, and since Campion had been blessed with seven such sons, the comings and goings of his own family had provided plenty of omens of good fortune during winters past. Of course, he did not put faith in such nonsense, but his household was more peaceful when the credulous among it were appeased.

And so he watched for Reynold, who was well aware of the servants' expectations, but when the doors were thrust open, it was not his son who was first to step over the threshold. Several people burst inside, shivering and stomping with the cold, and in the lead was a slight figure in a voluminous cape that fell back with a movement to reveal a swish of skirts. No man at all, but a woman, Campion realized, as the servants gasped softly. While they all stood gaping, she flung back her hood, and a mass of black curls spilled out over the green mantle of snow-dusted wool.

"Humph. Well, at least she's got dark hair," Wilda muttered, and Campion swallowed his astonishment to step forward. Although he put no credence in forecasting the festivities based on his guest's coloring, nonetheless he was as surprised as anyone to find a woman about in such foul weather and on Christmas Eve.

"Father, may I present Lady Warwick, who is seeking shelter from the storm," Reynold said, stepping forward.

"Lady," the earl said with a nod. "I am Campion. Welcome to my home. Please sit down and rest from your journey." A small nod of a pale oval face made Campion push his own heavy chair toward the hearth. She went into it without complaint, and he stood beside, studying the other members of the party.

There was another woman, not dressed as finely, who might be an attendant, several men-at-arms and a handful of male servants. No other man was in evidence, and Campion wondered if some disaster marked his absence and the party's presence in his hall. As his own servants took wet cloaks and brought blankets for the group that huddled near the fire, Campion's gaze returned to the dark head by his side.

The mass of hair was rather amazing, for few except young unmarried ladies left theirs down. And even damp, the black curls were such as Campion had never seen before, so thick and rich that he was tempted to reach out and test one fat lock. Stifling the odd urge, he watched the heavy mane slide over one slender shoulder, his attention drawn downward only to arrest itself suddenly, for the lady was removing her boots.

Obviously they were wet and chilling her, but Campion was momentarily taken aback. Surely she would rather disrobe in private, and he leaned forward to offer her a chamber in which to do so. But his mouth seemed strangely unable to work as her slender hands tugged at the hose beneath her hem. Campion caught a glimpse of pale skin, the curve of a well-turned ankle and the instep of a small arched foot, before he recovered himself and straightened.

He slanted a quick glance at Wilda's back, glad that the superstitious woman had not seen Lady Warwick's toes, for a barefoot person was not welcome at the Yuletide fire, according to some ridiculous belief. Perhaps because the sight was so unnerving, Campion thought as he sought to regain his own composure.

It had been a long time since he had entertained a woman outside of his own family, so perhaps he was out of step with current manners, Campion told himself. Certainly the circumstances warranted swift action, for the whole party might well be frostbitten. It was his own reaction that bore censure, Campion thought ruefully. He had no excuse for his staring or for the slow, seeping warmth that had invaded him at the sight of a little bare flesh. By the rood, he was much too old for such nonsense!

"We have readied a chamber for you, my lady," he said, his voice a hoarse rasp that made him clear his throat. Reluctantly he peeked at his guest, but she had already tucked her feet beneath her and was taking a cup of spiced wine from a servant.

"Thank you, my lord. I admit that a warm bed would be most welcome." The statement was uttered in a serious tone that held no subtle inflections, so why did it conjure visions of linens heated by his own body? Campion looked away. Perhaps he had been too much in the company of his randy son Stephen of late. And just where was Stephen? Warming a bed, no doubt, and not his own, Campion thought, his lips thinning into a grim line. He had not taught his boys to live like monks, but neither did he approve of Stephen's careless dalliances.

"Thank you for taking us in, my lord," Lady Warwick said, and Campion's attention was drawn to her once more. A woolen blanket had been draped over her shoulders, and she held the wine in both hands to thaw her fingers, pink without the covering of her wet gloves, but she seemed to be feeling better, for she lifted her face and smiled, causing Campion to take in a startled breath at the sight.

She was lovely. The fire suffused her cheeks with life, and now he could see clearly the smoothness of her skin, the thickness of her black lashes...and her eyes. They were a most unusual shade of blue, almost the color of spring violets, and Campion stared again before he caught himself. No wonder his family had begun fussing over him, for only a fool or a dotard would be so dazed by a pretty face. A *young* pretty face.

He returned her glorious smile with a dignified nod. "You are most welcome, of course, but may I ask how came you to be traveling in this foul weather?" *There. Now he had command of himself as he should.*

She drew herself up, and Campion saw a strength that belied her years. Her violet eyes shone with a determination born of possession, of a maturity that made him reassess her age. She was no girl, he realized, but a woman. Still she was no older than most of his sons. Where was her husband?

"I was on my way to celebrate Christmas with my cousin when we were driven to ground by the storm," she explained. She met his gaze unflinchingly, as if daring him to pass judgment upon such a foolhardy scheme, but Campion said nothing. Often he found it wiser to remain silent while others spoke, and in this instance his judgment was correct, for she soon continued.

"Truth be told, it was not so treacherous when we started," Lady Warwick admitted. Although she was aware of her error, the firm set of her chin told him that she would take no rebuke from him, and Campion felt his lips stir. "We were forced to seek shelter last night at a public inn, and I daresay were plagued with bodily pests for our trouble. We had hoped to reach our destination before Christmas Eve, but, as you can see, we must throw ourselves on your mercy, my lord."

Lady Warwick took no pleasure in seeking assistance, that much was obvious, and Campion had to admire her spirit, although he still had reservations about her single-minded journey. "I am happy to offer a place to stay for you and your company, but what of your husband? Is he waiting with your cousin perhaps?" he asked.

At Campion's question, Lady Warwick's expression became positively mutinous. "I am a widow, my lord, and have commanded myself and my household for many years," she said in a haughty tone he suspected was intended to put him in his place. He bit back his smile, for if the most arrogant and fierce of men had failed to subdue him, this stubborn young woman was certainly no threat.

"I see," Campion said, keeping his thoughts to

himself. The men in her party moved over to the trestle table to partake of some food, but he motioned for a servant to set her portion upon a nearby stool.

"Thank you," she murmured a bit stiffly. At his silence, she seemed to relax and, setting down her cup, she reached for a portion of cheese. "Your hall is the most beautiful that I have ever seen."

"Ah, but sadly unprepared for the holiday," Campion noted. "I fear we lack a woman's touch, and my sons will not be bringing their wives in this foul weather. In truth, I was uncertain what sort of celebrations the season would hold, so your arrival has been most timely."

She looked a question at him as she nibbled daintily.

"Guests will surely enliven what might have been a rather quiet twelve days of festivities," Campion added. Despite her reluctance to seek help, she must see that there was no shame in accepting his hospitality. Travelers were welcomed any time of the year, but most assuredly at Christmas.

Violet eyes widened as she swallowed hard, and Campion leaned forward, concerned that she might choke, but she straightened and held up a hand as if to ward him off. "No. I...oh, but we cannot stay. I mean, we would not wish to impose upon you for such a time."

"But you surely cannot think to travel in this weather?" Campion asked in surprise. Already she had admitted the folly of her journey; to attempt it again would make her devoid of common sense.

"Oh, it will probably clear tomorrow."

Campion gave her a jaundiced look, and her gaze slid away from his, making him wonder if there was something to her trip other than what she had revealed. Even if the snow stopped, it already covered the roads, as she well knew. Her speech and bearing marked her as an intelligent woman. Why would she risk her life to pay a visit?

Campion was not a man to pry unless she made her business his own, but if Lady Warwick thought to leave on the morrow, she was mistaken. The stubborn woman was liable to end up frozen to death in a drift, should he accede to her wishes. And no matter how accustomed the lady was to making her own decisions, here at Campion, he ruled.

Still, he had not done so by acting unwisely, and so he kept his own counsel, hoping that after a good night's rest, Lady Warwick would be better able to see reason. In the meantime, he made her as comfortable as he could, offering her more food, more wine, another blanket....

"Greetings!" The sound of Stephen's voice made Campion glance across the hall. The handsomest of his sons appeared, looking no worse from his apparent frolic except for a slight tousling of his hair. At the sight of the guests, he flashed a smile that could melt the coldest of hearts, and Campion was caught between pride in the boy's charm and dismay at his poor use of it.

"What have we here, Father, visitors upon this Christmas Eve?" Stephen asked, moving closer.

"Lady Warwick, you have met my son Reynold. This is my son, Stephen," Campion said. "Lady Warwick will be staying with us until the weather abates," he explained. To his amusement, she lifted her chin as if to protest, but Stephen stepped toward her and bowed low, demanding her attention.

"My lady. It is indeed a pleasure to be graced with your presence." Stephen's rather smug look suggested he anticipated the usual feminine response to his attractions, but Lady Warwick only nodded in greeting, as if he held little interest for her.

Stephen's dismay at her less than enthusiastic response was almost palpable, and Campion had to curb his smile as he turned to study the lady more thoughtfully. She was an interesting woman—beautiful, intelligent, confident and too discerning to be swayed by Stephen's rather jaded appeal—certainly a rare guest in his household.

Stephen did not give up easily, however, and managed to seat himself on the stool, placing her tray of food on his lap, where she would have to reach for it. Campion frowned. His sons were too old to receive rebukes from their father, and yet, he just might have to speak to Stephen, who seemed to be growing more heedless by the day.

"Have you been traveling far, my lady?" the boy

asked, carving a piece of cheese and offering it to her on the point of his own knife. It was very nicely done but for the drawl in Stephen's tone that told Campion his son was up to something.

"No, not very far," Lady Warwick said as she gingerly removed the cheese with her dainty fingers. Her answer was oddly evasive, and Campion wondered if she sought to avoid the intimacy Stephen was forcing upon her or if the question itself disturbed her.

"Ah, but how is it then that I have never met you? Just how close do you make your home?" Although Campion frowned at Stephen's silky sarcasm, he, too, would know more of his guest.

"I live at Mallin Fell, at the manor there."

Campion hid his surprise. That was no simple day's journey even in the best of times, but several days' ride to the east.

"Ah," Stephen said as she nibbled at the portion of cheese. "I am not too familiar with that area and know of no Warwicks there. Who owns the holding?"

The lady bristled. "I do. Now if you will excuse me, my lords, I would see my rest." Eliminating the opportunity for any further questions, she rose to her feet, and Campion had a glimpse of slender ankle as she stood, obviously having forgotten her lack of footwear. But her attendant appeared at her elbow with fresh slippers and she slid them on swiftly.

"Wilda, see Lady Warwick to her chamber, please," Campion said, before Stephen could offer to escort her. The servant did his bidding, and he watched Lady Warwick move toward the stairs. Although not tall, she held herself so well that her very bearing drew respect. Indeed, she might have been a queen or an abbess or any other powerful woman— but for that rich mane of hair. It fell wantonly down her back to her waist and flowed when she walked...

Campion's inappropriate thoughts were interrupted by a snort and a thump as Stephen took the vacated chair with a disgruntled expression. "Haughty wench," he muttered. "She's probably some kind of man hater."

Reynold grunted from his place near the hearth, stretching his bad leg out before it now that the lady was gone. "Just because she didn't fall into your lap, like every other female?"

Stephen scowled. "If you're so clever, tell me this—how is it that a young, beautiful widow with a manor and lands, no less, remains unwed?" he asked, lifting a dark brow.

Reynold shrugged, obviously uninterested in such things. "She is not that young."

Campion glanced at his son in surprise, for surely Lady Warwick was not much older than Reynold himself. He again wondered at her age, for Reynold obviously saw the maturity that belied her youthful face.

"Perhaps she is barren," Stephen mused.

"Stephen!" For once, Campion reprimanded his son.

"Well?" Stephen said, sliding him a sullen glance. "What else would keep her from another marriage? Unless she's a shrew, of course, which might be a possibility, considering the set of that pretty little chin."

Campion rose to his feet. He had no intention of watching Stephen sulk because the lady had not swooned over him in the manner of most others of her gender.

"She's too old for you anyway," Reynold muttered as he rubbed his thigh. The piercing cold outside had probably done little to help it, but Campion knew better than to comment.

Stephen snorted. "She isn't any older than I am. And, anyway, there's nothing wrong with a more experienced woman. And being a widow, she ought to know exactly what she wants," he added lewdly.

"Apparently, it isn't you," Reynold commented.

Choking back a laugh, Campion coughed to cover the noise and headed toward the stairs. Any woman who ignored Stephen promised to enliven the hall, and the earl found himself looking forward to discovering more about the intriguing Lady Warwick. His steps to the great chamber were lighter than before, and he realized, with some surprise, that his heart was more buoyant, too.

Perhaps the Yuletide wouldn't be so dull after all.

Chapter Two

Joy Thorncombe, Lady Warwick, eyed the thin light filtering through the shutters with dismay. Not only had she slept far too long, but the gloom that seeped into the chamber did not bode well for travel. Lying there comfortable and warm in the huge, elaborately carved bed, she felt tempted to stay where she was, to revel in the luxury and relative security of Campion Castle. But she would not trust herself to the hospitality of a man, even one with such a sterling reputation as the earl, and so she rose swiftly, calling for her attendant.

"Roesia, get up! 'Tis late, and we must be on our way."

"Oh, my lady, must we? I've never slept half so well in my life," Roesia said, stretching slowly. "This place is wonderful!"

Joy could hardly argue. The room was beautiful, furnished with chests and a settle and even some kind of soft carpet to cover the tiles and with a wide hearth to stave away the chill. It was at once both cozy and elegant, and the thought of returning to a frigid ride along frozen roads held no allure, but the need to reach her destination pressed upon her as she reached for her clothing.

"Could you believe the size of the hall and these chambers? Fit for a king! And what about the food that they brought us, even though supper was over? That spiced wine was delicious, and did you try those little tarts with the dusting of sugar?" Roesia asked, sighing with the memory.

"No," Joy answered, oddly piqued at her attendant's enthusiasm for Campion. At Mallin, they did not have enough money to buy all the expensive spices that were used in such delicacies, but they ate well enough—simple fare that was probably better for the digestion, Joy thought righteously.

"And the hot bath, practically waiting for us here in our own chamber!" Roesia added.

"With servants aplenty to bring it," Joy noted, but she had to admit that the gesture had been a thoughtful one, and more than welcome when they were sodden and chilled from their efforts to find shelter. The memory brought her thoughts grimly back to the journey ahead, and she dressed swiftly.

Roesia moved more slowly. "I could grow accustomed to this sort of life," she muttered as she laced up her gown.

"As could anyone, I'm sure," Joy answered in a dry tone. The de Burghs were wealthy beyond her imagining. And yet, the castle inhabitants, even those who served, seemed genuinely kind and welcoming. Perhaps it was the Christmas season that moved them to such benevolence, Joy thought with a trace of asperity. But whatever the motive, she was not accustomed to charity, and so she remained resolved to leave as soon as her train could be readied.

It was with that purpose in mind that Joy made her way down the curved stairway to the great hall, but on the bottom step she halted in surprise at the sight that met her eyes. Last night in the dim light of torches and candles, the vaulted room had been shadowy and huge, but now... Joy drew in a deep breath, for she had never seen anything like it. It was vast and bright and clean, with painted walls and tall windows, with cupboards and settles and chairs and so many trestle tables that Joy blinked in astonishment.

And everywhere people rushed to and fro, from those dressed in the finest clothing to the lowliest garb. Men and women talked and smiled, their voices creating a constant din, while around them children dashed, laughing and squealing. Servants were busy with flagons, ale flowed and cups were raised in salute, while the scents of cooking food and spices drifted in from the kitchens.

"What madness is this?" Joy whispered.

Behind her Roesia laughed softly. "'Tis Christmas Day, my lady. Or have you forgotten?"

Joy *had* forgotten, and she felt an unaccountable sadness at the knowledge. But the celebrations she had known were nothing like this. Although she had always done her best to observe the traditions and provide for those at Mallin Fell, here all was on a grand scale, far beyond her meager efforts. There was simply more noise, more people, more food, more laughter and more happiness than Joy had ever imagined. She told herself it was an illusion, a trick wrought by wealth and power, but when she glimpsed her host approaching, the man looked disturbingly real.

Had he been this tall last night? Joy wondered, keeping her place upon the step so she need not crane her neck upward when he reached her side. Had he been this regal, this graceful, this...handsome? Joy swallowed hard as the Earl of Campion dipped his dark head toward her in greeting, his very being emanating authority and strength, yet when he spoke it was with a gentleness that she felt right down to her bones.

"My lady, may I wish you a good Christmas and bid you join our celebration," he said, smiling pleasantly.

"Thank you," Joy answered, her mind vainly groping for a more intelligent reply. The earl's gaze held her, and for a moment she had the absurd notion that he could see right inside her. The idea brought her wayward thoughts back to her purpose and she lifted her chin, determined to politely refuse his welcome and be on her way.

Usually Joy, set upon an objective, was formidable,

despite her dainty frame. Indeed, Roesia often said that when determined, her mistress was an irresistible force. However, neither one of them could have ever anticipated the Earl of Campion, who, for all his cultured manners, took on the appearance of an immovable object.

He simply would not budge, Joy realized as he led her to a chair at the great table, yet he did so in a quiet, elegant way that disguised his high-handedness so well that another woman might not have recognized it. Although Joy was not deceived, she was forced to admit that she liked his style. No matter what she said, Campion smiled and nodded, as if in agreement with her, and then insisted that she stay for the feast.

She told him that she must go, but he would not hear of it, and he turned aside her every protest with a graciousness that was neither bullying nor condescending. As they argued in a most civilized manner, Joy wondered if the earl ever lost his temper or if he even possessed one, for he seemed to be the most composed of men. He would make a formidable enemy, she suspected, and the knowledge made her reluctant to continue her protest.

Even as Joy reconsidered her position, it became apparent that the meal was about to begin, and she knew she would be churlish to delay it with her departure. When she saw the faces of Roesia and her men, only too eager for fine food and some holiday cheer, Joy found she could not refuse them. With a lift of her chin, she nodded to Campion, her manner poised despite her capitulation.

"Very well, but only for the feast. Then we must go," she said. Campion's answering smile was nothing more than a courtesy, and yet Joy felt a warmth that she could not explain, as if he were truly pleased by her presence. She told herself it was nonsense, but she could not deny that the earl had a way about him that was very appealing. His paternal air was deceiving, Joy realized, as she studied him more closely, for he was not old. Indeed, he was still young and vigorous, and there was something about him that she found attractive.

Smiling at such foolishness, Joy shook her head, but her gaze followed Campion as he rose to announce the beginning of the feast and to introduce his guests. Joy stood and murmured some pleasantries, though she could not help feeling a little awed as she looked down the long line of trestle tables filled with castle residents, knights, servants, villeins and freemen from the vast lands of the de Burghs. A great, deafening shout rang out as they raised their cups, and then the boar's head, the traditional Christmas delicacy, was carried in to much fanfare.

Roesia's words echoed in her head. *I could grow accustomed to this.* Although Joy had never paid much attention to food, she could not ignore the taste, the variety and the sheer size of the courses. Certainly there were more than the twelve special dishes called for by the holiday, as platters of beef, mutton, turkey and cheeses were accompanied by sauces, mustard, apples and nuts, and followed by frumenty, posset, mince pie and pudding.

While she ate, Joy studied the great hall and its inhabitants. The household was predominantly male, and when Campion spoke to her of his seven sons, she was not surprised. There was no chatelaine, and no ladies-in-waiting. The few women who sat at the lower tables appeared to be wives of the many knights, while farther down there were those who were villeins or married to freemen.

Joy sat on the earl's right but found herself sharing a trencher with his son Stephen. A more typical example of his gender, Stephen was spoiled and arrogant, and but for the looks they shared, she would hardly think him Campion's son. The other son in residence, Reynold, was also little like his father in demeanor. He was quiet and rather bitter looking. Foolish boy, Joy thought, as she saw all that he had before him. He should be thankful for his lot instead of ruing a slight limp, but wasn't that just like a man?

Lost in her thoughts, Joy was startled when Stephen leaned close, brushing against her breast as he cut her meat. "Thank you, but I can do that myself," she said, putting him in his place with a cool smile. Although he moved back an appropriate distance, the boy sulked for most of the meal, drank too much wine and then began taunting his brother. Joy felt like smacking him on the head and ordering him to behave, the spoiled churl.

Finally he took an interest in her attendant, and though Joy would not wish such a fellow on Roesia, she enjoyed the relative peace that came with the engagement of his interest elsewhere. Peace and prosperity. It was evident in every filled cup, in each voice raised in speech or song between the courses that filled the groaning tables. There was no desperation here, no worries over harvest or money or allegiances, Joy noted with a twinge of envy.

And yet none of the revelers misbehaved. The loud voices never erupted in anger or drunken debauchery, for Campion set the tone for the hall. He was the calm, solid center of it all, radiating a power and strength that few men could wield on the battlefield, let alone seated in a chair at the head of a feast table. Joy had always disdained men of rank as bullies, but here was a true lord, a man who ruled through wisdom not force.

Looking around her at the happy faces and then back at the man who reigned over all, Joy knew a brief yearning to be a part of this place and its people. She had always thought of the de Burghs as mighty knights, but now she began to wonder if she were not seeing the real family now. It encompassed all of the earl's subjects, drawn together here in a realm of his making, where honor and goodness reigned.

Perhaps she had partaken of too much spiced wine, Joy thought ruefully, or more likely, too much of the Christmas spirit. It pervaded the hall in a way that made her think such warmth was present year-round, when she knew that no home could be as wonderful as Campion Castle appeared to the eyes of an outsider. Visiting here was like a trip to some fantastic land of plenty, but as pleasant as it might be, her brief sojourn had to come to an end. And soon.

Despite the temptations of the Yule hearth and friendly people, the promise of singing and other celebrations that would drag the feasting on most of the day, Joy felt the press of time, urging her to be gone. And so she leaned close to Campion's chair, a finely carved oak piece that she immediately recognized as her seat of the night before. He had given her his chair, she realized, swallowing an odd lump in her throat at the gesture.

"My lord," she began, but he cut her off with a smile.

"Campion. Please call me Campion."

"Campion, I would thank you for this wonderful meal, but we must be on our way," Joy said firmly. Instead of dismissing her with a wave of his hand, as she expected, the earl bent toward her. He probably did so in order to be heard above the noise, but he was so near that Joy could see the strands of silver in his hair and the fine lines that fanned out from his eyes on his sun-darkened face.

And what beautiful eyes, Joy marveled. They were not as dark as she had first thought, but a light, clear brown that seemed to hold the wisdom of the ages in their depths. Joy felt herself drifting toward them, as if drawn by what she might find there—mysteries, truths, peace and something unknown. A blush rose in her cheeks as she jerked backward suddenly, aware of a strange, unsettling sensation.

Campion appeared not to notice. "Surely my home is not so lacking in Christmas welcome that you would refuse my hospitality?" he asked. Joy took a shallow breath and shifted warily as she tried to recapture her concentration. She had never learned the subtle game of convincing an arrogant man that her will was his idea. Indeed, she had been accused often enough of being unnaturally forceful, of not knowing her place, and worse.

"Nay, my lord, but I have dallied too much already at your fine table and must hurry to my destination," Joy explained. She forced a smile that she hoped was cajoling, but too many years as her own mistress probably made it more intimidating than anything else.

Campion studied her silently, and if he had been any other man, Joy might have known a twinge of fear. One could never be too careful with the volatile members of the opposite gender, to whom an unprotected woman was often fair game in terms of property, money or desire. But it was hard to impute Campion with such motives. Indeed, he was the first man Joy had ever met who seemed wholly comfortable with himself. He had lands, wealth and power aplenty, and the very thought of the calm, collected earl suddenly succumbing to fleshly urges was nearly laughable.

So why wasn't she laughing? Instead, Joy felt an
odd sort of warmth at the very notion. Campion's
head was tilted toward her slightly, his attention almost a tangible thing, such was the intensity of his
regard, and Joy suppressed the impulse to squirm un-
derneath the direct gaze of those enigmatic eyes.

"I understand your wish for a swift journey, but I
fear that you will make little progress in this
weather," the earl finally said. "I'm sure you do not
want to repeat your experience of last evening, yet
the conditions are little better today, for the villeins
and freemen who journeyed only as far as their own
farms this morning were full of stories of the fierce
elements."

It was no rebuke, but a gentle reminder, and Joy
frowned. A glance toward the tall, narrow windows
showed the light was still thin and pale, a sign that
the sky had not cleared, and she knew that yesterday's
drifts had been nearly impassable. The need to be off,
and soon, warred against the temptation to linger here
in the stronghold Campion had carved for himself, an
island in a stormy sea of troubles, where the world
didn't seem to intrude.

But Joy had never been one to hide from her duties
or lean upon a man, even one as elegant and powerful
as Campion. She lifted her chin, resolved to depart,
yet even as she would speak, the earl leaned toward
her once more, as if imparting wisdom for her ears
alone.

"Forgive me for speaking plainly, Lady, but in this

weather, you are more likely to die upon the road than reach your destination,'' he said. Joy opened her mouth to protest, but at his somber look, so fraught with reason, she thought better of her speech. He was right, of course. She had let her fierce determination cloud her judgment.

Joy looked around the hall, at Roesia flirting with Campion's boy, at her men talking so easily with the knights of the castle, drinking their ale in warmth and comfort, and she felt a villain. Should she order them out, they would loyally do her bidding even to their death, and, as the earl reminded her, that was a distinct possibility. All too well, she remembered the blinding snow and the fear that they might not reach shelter before the horses reached the limits of their endurance.

Only a fool would dare such forces again, Joy thought, ruefully. Although no fool, sometimes she was so accustomed to taking charge, so intent upon a goal, that she could not see anything else. It was both her strength and her weakness.

"Lady." Campion's low voice startled her, for Joy had nearly forgotten his presence. When she turned toward him, she wondered how that had ever happened, for her senses hummed with awareness at his nearness.

"I cannot let you leave in such conditions," he said. His expression was gentle yet implacable, and Joy bristled. Did he truly think to stop her? "Tell me why you must hurry, and I will do my best to help you in any way I can," he added softly.

Joy glanced away from his probing gaze. "I wish only to be in familiar surroundings during the Yuletide. And although your offer is very gracious, let me assure you that I have taken care of myself for many years," she said.

"Obviously," Campion answered, his lips curving slightly, and Joy found her outrage seeping away. It was hard to remain angry with a man who had a sense of humor, especially when he was in the right. Joy had always thought males the far more stupid of the two genders, no matter what the Church's doctrine on the subject, for it was usually men who fought each other, who were ruled by their lusts for power and such.

Yet she could not imagine the Earl of Campion being ruled by anything. Here was a man to admire and even emulate, Joy decided, coveting some of his calm composure. For years, she had done her best to maintain her holding, making informed decisions with a clear head, but she knew there was a part of her nature that was given over to impatience and argument, which she did her best to subdue.

She saw no such imperfections in Campion. Indeed, it was difficult to find any fault with the earl. Although Joy had never been inclined to take much note of a man's appearance, she could not deny that she found him handsome. His face was narrow but strong, his dark hair sleek, and the streaks of silver in it only added to his innate dignity. It was obvious he was a knight, for his lean muscles were evident beneath the fine fabric of his tunic. Joy's gaze lingered momentarily along his broad chest before skidding away.

"Very well. I will accept your generous hospitality for another night," she murmured, trying to rein in her unusual thoughts.

"Not another night. You must stay for the entire Yuletide," Campion said. When Joy glanced at him in alarm, she found his manner serene, not threatening. "I have already told you of my sons and their families and how the weather has prevented them from joining us this Christmas. And since these same conditions have conspired to bring you to Campion, I charge you with staying in their place and bringing joy to our holiday," he said.

Joy stared at him in surprise. "How did you know?" she asked, wondering if the earl was omnipotent, if his eyes could truly see another's soul and the secrets hidden there. Or had he some knowledge of her, some word of which she was unaware?

"Know what?" he asked, his expression puzzled.

"My name. My name is Joy."

"How lovely, but I knew it not," he said, in a charming yet genuine manner that chased away her momentary fears. "I meant only that we wish for visitors at this time of year, to add to our happiness." His smile was oddly wistful, and Joy was rocked by a sudden, sharp realization.

He was lonely.

She looked about her at the vast hall filled with people, at Campion's sons and knights and servants and villeins, and she wondered how the man could want for anything. Yet he did. She knew it as surely as she now knew her name, and the knowledge made this man not so omnipotent, but oddly human. And it was that glimpse of vulnerability that swayed her far more than warnings of foul weather ever could.

Joy glanced back at Campion, at the polite smile that curved his lips, and she wanted to ask him outright if he missed his family. But would the earl, so dignified and poised as he faced her, admit to such a frailty? Joy wondered. She doubted it, and somehow she found his elegant veneer frustrating, as if that tiny peek had whetted her appetite for the true Campion. She let herself meet his gaze and wished that she could see behind those enigmatic eyes to the man who dwelled within.

"Only if you let me do something in return for your generosity," Joy said finally. "You have complained of the lack of greenery and such Christmas trappings. You must let Roesia and I hang some bundles upon the walls and help to organize the feasting, as your son's wife would do, were she here."

"If you wish, but I will hold you to no such bargain," Campion said. "You shall do only as much as you will and take Marion's place only when you wish," Campion said.

Although he sent her a courteous smile, Joy felt

oddly discomposed, as if all between them was not settled to her satisfaction. Perhaps it was caused by the earl's slow, confident smile that told her he had harbored no doubts about his powers of persuasion. Or perhaps it was dismay at her own unusually impulsive agreement, a decision based more upon emotion than logic.

However, Joy suspected it had more to do with his final words, for she wanted to be considered his equal, not as his relative. And, although she could not have said why, she especially did not want to be mistaken for his daughter.

Chapter Three

The day after Christmas dawned bright and clear, much to Campion's disappointment. After the gloom of recent weeks, he should have been glad to greet the sunshine, but his thoughts immediately turned to his guest and their bargain. Would she remain to honor it? His instincts told him she was a woman of her word, but he sensed, too, that she was not telling him everything.

What did it matter if she stayed or went? Campion chided himself, and yet he could not deny a particular fascination with the beautiful Lady Warwick. She was intelligent and competent, no simpering maiden, but a forthright woman with opinions on every subject. He smiled as he recalled the lively debate she had brought to his tired hall during the long day of feasting.

The old place was looking a bit livelier, too, for she had already hung some greenery, tied with brightly colored cloth over the doors, and had prom-

ised more. He chuckled at the memory of how she
had bedeviled his sons until they had braved the snow
to gather branches for her. Stephen had grumbled and
called her the Christmas Commander, but Campion
had admired the way she took charge without being
loud or brash. He could well use her firm, but gentle
aid year-round.

The thought gave him pause. Ever since Marion
left he had missed a woman's fine hand, the presence
of a chatelaine who would make her own decisions
without deferring to him. Idly Campion wished that
he could convince the capable Lady Warwick to tarry
after Epiphany, but she had a journey ahead that she
had already interrupted and her own manor to attend.
Why would she forsake it for Campion? And she
could hardly remain at the castle indefinitely unless
she joined the family, he mused, but the idea of her
marrying Stephen or Reynold somehow made him uneasy.

His mood suddenly soured, Campion listened to a
servant's report upon the dairy and the extra butch-
ering required for the holiday, but his thoughts were
elsewhere and he finally dismissed the fellow with an
absent wave before hurrying toward the hall. He realized, even as he made his way down the stairs, that
the anticipation seizing him surely exceeded what was
warranted by the presence of guests.

His relief, too, was excessive, but it rushed through
him, nonetheless, when he saw her. She was seated
in the massive chair next to his own, just as if she

belonged there, and Campion knew a distinct sense of satisfaction at the sight. Even Reynold, looking more grim than usual as he left the hall, could do little to disturb his odd feeling of contentment.

"Hail, Father!" Stephen said with a courtly bow, and Campion wondered, not for the first time, how his wayward son could carouse all night and then rise in the morning, looking no worse for it. "We're going skating," Stephen said, lifting aloft a set of sharpened animal bones.

Campion saw that several knights and a couple of their ladies were already donning their cloaks, and he knew that the weather would be perfect, crisp and clear after the recent temperatures, which ought to have turned the pond that lay outside the castle walls into a heavy sheet of ice.

"But I cannot convince our lovely guest to try the sport," Stephen said. Turning toward Lady Warwick, he bowed again. "I fear she is reluctant to trust herself into my care, but I will not let you fall, my lady. Come," he cajoled in his most persuasive tone. Although Joy shook her head firmly, Stephen pressed her, leaning close until Campion stepped forward.

"Perhaps I shall join you," he said. Stephen swiveled toward him to stare in surprise, and Campion could see the question in his son's gaze. It did not reach his lips, however, for Lady Warwick's attendant took the opportunity to seize Stephen's arm.

"I would be most grateful, if you would teach me, my lord," she said, flashing him a smile, and Stephen's momentary dismay was lost in an answering grin.

"Of course, mistress, I would be happy to teach you everything I know," he purred, and Campion shook his head as he watched them go. Although people were already crowding the hall, the earl found himself alone with Lady Warwick at the head of the high table, and he fought back the urge to apologize for his son. Stephen was old enough to handle himself, even if his behavior had veered wildly of late.

"Do not tell me that you really intend to strap these outrageous things to your boots!"

Campion turned his head to see Lady Warwick with an amusing expression of distaste upon her lovely features as she fingered the narrow bones. His attention caught, he smiled down at her.

"Yes," he said, and the word hung in the air in a manner that forced him to clear his throat. "I learned to skate when I was just a boy."

"But, why?" she asked, her dark brows tilting together as if truly bewildered, and Campion laughed.

"For the simple pleasure of it," he said, his mind drifting against his will to other pleasures that he had been too long without.

Lady Warwick looked dubious still, and he reached out to take her hand. "Come, I will show you," he said, leaning over her. It was a simple gesture, an innocent one, but the feel of her small fingers in his own was oddly enticing, and when his gaze met hers, he felt a moment's disorientation, just as though those violet eyes were calling him home.

It was over too swiftly for Campion to draw any conclusions, for she tugged her hand from his with an awkward air of confusion. "I don't think so. I am not one for games or frivolous activities," she explained with an air of dismissal.

Campion wondered just what she considered frivolous. She looked so serious, her dark head bent, her hands in her lap, that he frowned. Had she lost her sense of fun with her husband's death, or had she never been given the chance to cultivate it? Either way, he was determined to gift her with an hour of play.

"It is not dangerous. You need not fear injury," he said softly.

As expected, her chin lifted. "I am not afraid of hurting myself."

"Then come," Campion said, straightening. His words were a challenge, and as he suspected, Lady Warwick could not resist. A twitch of her lips told him that she was well aware of his tactics, but then a slow smile spread across her face that nearly knocked the wind from him. Joy was not merely lovely, she was breathtaking, and Campion simply stood staring at her for one stunned moment.

"Very well," she said, rising to her feet, and Campion found himself wondering about her late husband. Had the man appreciated his bounty, or had he been too often away to entertain his young wife? Had he been a man of intelligence who thrived on his wife's wit or an oaf who condemned her as stubborn and willful? Campion had always been interested in people, and he told himself that therein lay his curiosity even as he suspected he was becoming far too fascinated by Lady Warwick.

After they had donned their gloves and cloaks, Campion led his guest through the great doors of the hall into the bailey. The air was cold, and he drew a deep draft, enjoying its crisp flavor. Beside him, Lady Warwick eyed the brewery and various buildings with approval, and Campion felt an intense pride in his demesne that he had not known in a long time. Indeed, he felt better than he had in years as they followed the path of trampled snow, and when they reached the pond, he stopped to admire the scene, made singular by the winter's unusual amount of snow.

Around them, the world was covered in white, fluffy mounds that curved over a hillock and topped the gnarled oaks whose branches dipped beneath the heavy burden. And stretched ahead lay the water, shimmering in the sunshine yet solid as stone, for upon it several of those from the castle skated, along with some of the freemen from the village.

His land, his people, Campion thought, with a certain happiness. And beside him, his unexpected guest. He turned to see that Lady Warwick had thrown back her hood, revealing the thick black curls that fairly gleamed in the light. Her cheeks were pink with cold, her lips curved into a gentle smile that echoed his own wonder, and Campion savored the joy of the moment, of pleasure shared and anticipated. He urged her over to a large rock, where they donned their skates, but the rest of the group was too boisterous, so he led her to a more secluded area of the pond, where dark branches hung close to the frozen water.

Considering that he could not remember the last time the pond had frozen, let alone when he had skated its surface, Campion was surprised at the ease with which the skill returned. Sweeping ahead in a long curve, he returned to halt before his student and held out his hands. Although she gripped them, her initial steps were unsteady, so Campion slid an arm around her as he drew her onto the surface, keeping a solid stance while she struggled to find her balance.

He moved forward, taking her with him, and Lady Warwick swayed precariously, flinging an arm around his waist to grip him tightly. Campion took his time, adjusting himself to her tentative efforts as he began a gentle arch across the ice. They proceeded slowly, while he murmured advice and encouragement until, at last, his companion seemed to be able to stand without difficulty.

"Why would anyone want to do this?" she asked, but she followed the question with a laugh, and Campion could see she was enjoying herself. Skating might be a foolish pleasure, but life was too short not to make the most of each and every one of them, and Campion was glad to serve as her teacher. As she gained confidence, he took them farther across the ice, gliding smoothly for a long moment before he glanced down at her face.

That was his mistake, for the look of wonder there nearly took his breath away. Her violet eyes glittered above pink cheeks and pale skin, her delicate mouth was drawn wide in a white smile, and Campion faltered. Lady Warwick shrieked and they swung around, grasping wildly at each other, before regaining their balance, both of them laughing at the near calamity.

They were facing each other now, hanging on to each other's arms, and a sudden sway of Lady Warwick's body made Campion bend his head near. Suddenly he was aware of the scent of her, womanly and inviting. His lips brushed against a thick lock of her hair, and the sleek softness affected him in more places than he cared to admit.

With a low grunt of dismay, Campion gingerly set her away from him. They had been too close, and he put some space between them, sliding his hands down to hold her own. She was becoming more adept now, and he glided backward as she followed him forward. In this manner, they circled their small area of the pond, hidden by the curve of the water and the drape of the snowy trees, until Lady Warwick was laughing with delight.

"See how well you skate!" Campion said. "You like it."

"Yes, I like it," she said in a low, breathless voice

that made him clear his throat. He let go of her hands, and she shrieked in protest but continued on her own.

"Look!" she cried, obviously delighted with her new skill, and Campion watched in admiration as she gained speed, moving into a long curve. He thought of the women he had known since he had buried his wives, fancy ladies of the court who were interested in money and power but not in a rowdy family of growing boys, women only too eager to pursue a wealthy widower but far too elegant to dash about on a frozen pond.

Lady Warwick was different, Campion mused. If she enjoyed this, then wait until the flowers were in bloom and...he drew up short. Joy wouldn't be here come the spring, he realized, and he felt the slow seep of disappointment into his bones. His smile faltered, and he glanced away at the white hillside where Campion rose, its golden towers no longer as shiny as they once were, the haven it provided somehow lacking.

"Oh! But how do I stop?" Lady Warwick's cry brought Campion's attention back to her, but it was too late. Her eyes wide, she was heading straight for him, arms flailing, and even though he reached out to slow her, she was an irresistible force that knocked him off his feet. He fell backward, and they both landed in a heap on the ice, laughing as they struggled to sit upright.

"Are you hurt?" Campion asked, relieved when she shook her head in response. Despite their spill, he had never felt better, for this little jaunt had him pulsing with life, but it was not only the skating that affected him.

Joy was on his lap, beautiful and young and full of energy that seemed to feed his own, and suddenly he was assaulted by images and urges better suited to his randy son Stephen. He felt in the grip of something inexplicable, as if possessed, and to his horror, the pressure of her small derriere on his lap made him hard, painfully so.

Campion's hands shook as he lifted them to her face, and he wanted nothing more than to bury his fingers in her heavy hair, to draw her close, to kiss her lips and more...to slake this frantic thirst with her body. He dared a glance at her eyes, expected to see a reflection of his own shock, but instead she simply stared back at him, violet depths wide and precious as gems. The world stilled, the air around them so hushed that Campion could hear her breath and feel its warmth against his skin, as temptation warred with honor within him.

A shout from across the pond made them both start and, grateful for the distraction, Campion rose, sliding her from his lap and helping her to her feet. His hands fell away, and he didn't know whether to laugh at his own folly or apologize. He could not recall a situation so awkward, but then he could not recall ever being in the grip of so fierce a desire.

Desire.

Joy blinked, drawing her trembling fingers back to her sides as she tried to regain her lost composure.

For a moment she had been struck motionless by a blossoming heat that could surely melt the ice beneath her. And it had been so sudden, so unexpected that she had not even recognized the sensation for what it was.

Desire.

She had always scoffed at ladies who sought liaisons with men, for they did little to refute the Church's claim that women were ruled by their lusts. As a clearheaded female capable of managing her own affairs, Joy had held herself above such nonsense. Certainly she admired a handsome form as well as the next woman, but she had never been prompted to act upon such admiration. *Until now.*

Joy shivered at the thought of her position upon the earl's lap, her initial laughter fading in the face of his warmth. She had felt the strength of his power, of a protection such as she had never known, and then the slow curl of awareness, of his nearness. Her heart skittered, and she rubbed her arms as if to ward off the unusual reaction.

"Are you cold? Let us return to the castle," Campion said, looking maddeningly unaffected by their near embrace. Perhaps she had imagined the excitement in his enigmatic gaze, for now he evidenced nothing more than a polite interest in her welfare.

Joy nodded, eager to take a respite from the earl's heady company, and she moved shakily toward shore as she sought an explanation for her peculiar response to him. Campion was just a man, she told herself. He walked and talked like any other...except that his voice was so deep and husky that it managed to both soothe and rouse her, and he moved with an appealing grace possessed by no other, whether gliding over the frozen pond like something out of a dream or striding across his hall.

Joy swallowed hard, wondering why this man, among all of his gender, should affect her so. Of course, he was handsome. All the de Burghs were accounted dashing and good-looking, though Joy had not been particularly impressed by the attributes of Stephen and Reynold. They could not hold a candle to their father.

But it was more than his pleasing countenance that attracted her. His power, perhaps? Joy considered that as she sat down to remove her skates. The straps were tangled, and she struggled with the wet leather until a pair of hands pushed her own aside. Campion knelt before her, and Joy's eyes widened as she stared at his dark head. His fingers, without their gloves, were as elegant yet forceful as the rest of him, and Joy felt a renewed warmth at his touch. When his palm slid up to cup her ankle in an intimate hold, her whole body blazed in reaction.

Perhaps it was the way he carried himself, Joy thought, as he made short work of removing her skates. Power sat upon his shoulders so easily, as if nothing could shake his quiet strength, and yet he was not arrogant. It was a confidence born of honor...and of knowledge, she decided, as he helped her to her feet.

Joy had often condemned members of the male gender as fools, but Campion was truly intelligent, with a mind open to differing opinions. Not only did he have a great store of book learning, along with his vast life experiences, but he possessed some kind of innate wisdom that shone in his eyes, which Joy found extremely provocative.

All that was very fine and cerebral, but how to explain the jolt of awareness she felt at his nearness, the rush of heat to parts of her that had never known any warmth? Joy felt the loss of his touch like a tangible thing as he moved beside her to walk the snowy path. She shivered again, for though she wished to shrug away those sensations or deny them, Joy had always been truthful with herself. And the truth was that for the first time in her life she wanted a man.

So startled was she by the admission that she halted in her tracks, staring blindly at the broad back of the male in question. The very notion of her being seized by overwrought desires ought to have been horrifying, shocking at the very least, but instead of gasping, Joy choked back a laugh. For what could possibly come of her wanton yearning?

Of all the men in the land she had surely chosen the only one who possessed far too much honor to succumb to passions of the flesh.

All through the feast, Joy watched him, trying to discover why Campion, of all people, should suddenly provoke her heretofore nonexistent ardor. But by the meal's end, she was no closer to answers than she had been when sitting in his lap upon the ice.

The want was just *there,* thrumming in her blood whenever she looked at him, and when she did not, it grew more insistent, like an unsatisfied craving. Never before had a man aroused such interest in her, and being of a curious nature, Joy was driven to closer scrutiny.

And the more she studied him, the more interested she became. Everything about him became noteworthy: the way the strands of silver streaked his dark hair, the way his dark green tunic fell across his broad chest, the width of shoulders that were imposing and yet not intimidating. Campion was not a man to wield his power recklessly, and that knowledge was almost as exciting to Joy as his physical form.

Her gaze dipped to his graceful wrists and long, slender fingers, and she flushed with heat as she remembered the feel of them over her own. Strong. Protective. Exciting. How could the sight of a man's hands, regal in repose, thrill her so? she wondered. It was absurd, and yet, undeniable. This incredible new feeling had seized her just as surely as the Christmas spirit had hold of all else in Campion's hall.

Indeed, Joy might have thought her desire some kind of strange consequence of the season or her luxurious surroundings, but she felt no such thrill when she looked upon Reynold or Stephen or any other man present. It was only Campion who affected her so. Of course, she rarely met men of the earl's rank, but those she had known had annoyed her more often than not. Not so Campion.

Joy felt giddy as a young girl, as the young girl she had never been, while she sneaked peeks at his elegant countenance. In the space of two days' time, it had become familiar to her, achingly so, like a favorite book one could not bear to put away. Even as she looked on, a child approached the earl's massive chair to speak with him, and Joy held her breath, but unlike most of his sex, Campion did not rebuff the girl. He leaned forward to answer her with a gentle smile that filled Joy with heat and song, as if the celebration around her echoed in her very being.

Not for the first time, she realized that when Campion gave someone his attention, he gave it full measure. He did not fiddle with his cup or glance away or evidence impatience of any sort. The earl did nothing idly, but focused himself wholly upon his audience, large or small, man or woman. And when that powerful regard was turned toward her, Joy felt she was the center of his world, the single most important person alive.

It was silly, of course, and at first, Joy had found the sensation rather disturbing, but now she coveted that concentration, wanting it for herself with a selfish yearning. *Wanting* Campion. Ever it came back to that, Joy realized, as her gaze drifted over his powerful form once more, dropping to the hands that rested upon his knees.

Joy wondered what they would feel like upon her, not in the companionable manner of her skating lesson, but as a man touches a woman. She no longer held any illusions about romance, but she had to admit to a curiosity about such things, recently fired by Campion. Her limited experience left her at a loss, and so she imagined touching him, instead, sifting her fingers through his hair, exploring beneath his tunic to the hard body below.

Joy shifted, restless in her seat as she took the fantasy further, envisioning herself in the earl's bed, sharing untold mysteries in the darkness of the night. How would it feel to have those strong arms around her without the fear that he would steal anything of hers, including her independence? Here was an honorable man, a man of the world who might teach her a thing or two.

As Joy sat there, lost in pleasant illusions, an idea evolved slowly, insinuating itself into her mind until she gasped with the audacity of it. And then she wanted to laugh in delight, excitement and relief surging through her, along with a low curl of warmth. Could she?

Why not?

Turning her head slightly, Joy studied the Earl of Campion with a new intensity. By all accounts, he was a man of honor who held himself apart from the common dalliances of others of his gender. She had heard no gossip about him, no rumors of lemans or mistresses, and the knowledge was both pleasing and daunting, for what made her think she could change his mind?

Her own formidable will, Joy decided with a smile. Roesia often complained about it, but Joy was driven, and when she wanted something, she usually achieved her goal. She had poured herself into Mallin Fell, turning the small demesne into a stable, if not highly prosperous, holding. And she had managed to keep it, against all odds.

And through the years, she had asked little enough for herself. Certainly she had never complained, considering herself well-off compared to most of the female population. Joy was accustomed to work and always thought of her people first, but now she found herself wanting something for herself, and the more she thought about it, the more determined she was to have it, despite the slight twitching of her conscience.

There had been few pleasures in her life; how wrong could it be to want to wring something from this holiday? To know a man's touch for the first time in her life? To finally discover the great mystery? Joy had been glad enough on her wedding night when her boy husband had turned away from her, no more eager than she to consummate their marriage. And she had known no regrets when he had died before growing more into his manhood, leaving her untouched.

A virgin widow.

But now her status seemed ludicrous, and the more

Joy considered it, the more she became determined to remedy the situation. She was a curious woman, after all, a seeker of knowledge, so why shouldn't she want to learn from the wisest man she had ever met? With seven sons, the earl ought to know what he was about in the bedchamber, Joy realized, flushing at the thought.

She lifted her chin as she became resolved. Just this once she would take from a man. They owned the world, had harried her most of her life and owed her more than she could ever claim. It was time she got something worthwhile from their gender and past time she discovered what she had denied herself, Joy thought, with new determination. This Yuletide she would give herself a gift.

Campion.

Chapter Four

After the feasting, Joy escaped to the solar, ostensibly to bundle Christmas greenery. In reality, she needed to think. Now that she had made her decision, she had only to execute it, but the methods involved in luring a man into her bed were something she had never taken an interest in before. Certainly, with someone like Stephen, she would not need to have a plan, just breath in her body, she thought with a grimace. But Campion was no randy rogue. He was a mature man seemingly unaffected by her presence.

Joy frowned, considering all that she had seen of courting behaviors, but those were usually among the lower orders, and she could not imagine plopping herself on the earl's lap with a giggle. Indeed, the idea was so horrifying that she dropped the sprig of holly she had been tying and bent to pick it up. Roesia and Stephen had brought in plenty of bay and holly when they returned from skating, and she and Joy were now gathering it into bunches of twelve to decorate the hall.

Idly Joy wondered if Roesia's trip to the pond had been as interesting as her own, and the thought made her pause. Laying the sprig in her lap, Joy slanted a speculative glance toward her attendant. Although younger than herself, Roesia had more experience dealing with men, claiming an appreciation of them that Joy had always disdained, yet now that knowledge might come to good use.

"Roesia, how do you go about making a man... notice you?" Joy asked. The question, although put forward casually enough, caused her attendant to spill her evergreens, scattering small boughs upon the tiled floor.

Eyeing her with a puzzled expression, Roesia knelt to retrieve her work. "Excuse me, my lady, but I thought you asked something about gaining a man's attention!" She laughed, seemingly amused at her own folly, but the sound died away when she looked at Joy's face.

"You are serious? I was not mistaken?" she asked.

Joy lifted her chin. "I have always sought to increase my store of knowledge by learning from others, but if you are unwilling to share your—"

"Oh, my lady!" Roesia interrupted. "Oh, this is wonderful! But I thought you were resolved against marriage!"

Joy frowned. "I am resolved against it."

"But, you said—"

"I said I was interested in the arts of seduction, not imprisonment," Joy said with a sound of disgust.

Roesia blinked at her in bewilderment. "Surely, you aren't talking about becoming a man's...mistress!" she objected. "You, with all your high ideals about women and all!"

"No, I most certainly will not become a mistress. I won't be around long enough to qualify as that," Joy answered, shifting in her seat uncomfortably at the reminder of her more vocal views. "I am thinking of a simple dalliance, the kind that happens all the time at court and even among my neighbors."

Roesia gaped at her openmouthed, and Joy bristled. "You are always prattling on about the pleasures to be found in a man's arms. Now would you deny your words?"

Roesia shook her head. "No, my lady, but I enjoy a good kiss or two now and then and maybe even a tumble with the right fellow, while you've never even looked at a man!"

"Well, now I am," Joy replied with a righteous expression.

"And that's all to the good, my lady! But a woman like you wasn't made for a quick toss. Why, I thought you couldn't stand Stephen...." Her words trailed off as she studied Joy. "Oh, my lord, it's Campion! 'Tis the earl himself who has caught your eye!" Roesia said, lifting a hand to her throat as if she found the discovery shocking.

"And what, pray tell, is wrong with Campion?"

Joy said in a dangerously low tone that warned her attendant to watch her speech.

"Nothing, my lady. Truly, nothing. Lord, what a man!" Roesia said with a sigh of appreciation. She seemed lost in thoughts of the earl for so long that Joy scowled at her, and Roesia gave her an apologetic smile before sobering. "But he's totally different! You can't take a man like that to your bed and wake up unchanged."

"Whatever do you mean?" Joy asked, genuinely puzzled. Of course, she wanted the experience to change her. She wanted, at last, to be a woman, in every sense of the word.

Roesia flushed. "You're talking about simple lust, my lady, but it's not always easy to separate your heart from the rest of you." At Joy's questioning look, she threw up her hands in exasperation. "What of love, my lady? Not all your fine ideas or stubborn will can protect you against it."

"Love!" Joy scoffed. She had always thought that so-called romance was a bunch of foolishness conjured by wandering minstrels in order to trade upon the good graces of the lady of the castle. "I fear it not!" she said with a laugh.

Roesia simply shook her head. "And what of Campion? He's not like Stephen, eager to get under any woman's skirt! I know more of men than you, my lady, and I tell you that he's not the sort to take a woman to his bed unless he loves her. Do you think he'll just perform like a stallion and then let you go?"

Joy stiffened at the implied threat to her coveted independence. "He will have no choice," she said, "for I am my own woman. He can make no claim upon me."

Roesia sighed as if put upon by a poor student. "My lady, you don't know a thing about males, if you think that. For all that he looks gentle eyed and calm, the earl has a fierceness in him. Else how could he have ruled these lands and built this dynasty of his? And I would think you ought not give yourself to him unless you mean it. Forever."

Just as Joy opened her mouth to argue, Roesia gave her a hopeful smile. "If you've got your sights set on the earl, why not wed him? That would solve all our problems! And I can't say I'd mind living here," she added with an admiring glance toward the castle's luxurious furnishings.

"I will not marry again," Joy said. She had hated being torn from her home to wed a stranger, had resented her lanky boy of a husband, and, after his death, had come to prize her independence. Men controlled everything about a wife—her money, her property, her very life. Even friendships between women were discouraged, for a wife must keep her mind upon her duties.

Since the Church decreed that God had made womankind subject to male control, a woman who acted for herself was believed to be possessed by the Devil. And the courts were no more favorable than the Church. If a wife killed her husband, she was executed for treason because her husband was her master, while a man could buy a pardon should he be moved to such violence against his spouse. While men ruled, they conspired to keep women as less than chattel, and no doubt would do so until the end of time, Joy thought bitterly.

"Well, Campion is no boy forced upon you by relatives. He's a man, with power aplenty to control his fate, and marrying him would be wholly different. No more worries over the harvest or holding your demesne or *anything.*" Roesia sighed at the notion, and Joy felt a bitter guilt at the lean years. She had done her best to run the small household and bit of lands surrounding it without help from anyone, but she had precious few funds and there was always something to eat away at them.

Oblivious to her thoughts, Roesia smiled wickedly. "And since you've a taste for the earl, you could ease it every night, or day for that matter!"

Joy frowned at her attendant's exuberance. "As appealing as that notion is," she answered dryly, "I am hardly ready to give up my life for it."

"But the earl's not like most men! He thinks differently, having read so many books and all. And you don't see him treating anyone badly."

It was true. Campion seemed so wise, so...understanding, but as her husband, he would still own her, and Joy refused to submit to anyone's possession. She had struggled to make a life for herself at her small manor, a life in which she had all that she needed.

As if reading her thoughts, Roesia glanced about the well-appointed solar, a far cry from the close quarters to which they were accustomed. "And this castle is the most beautiful place I've ever seen, with so many lovely things. Why, living here would be like living a dream," her attendant said.

"For you, perhaps. But for me it would be bondage, of a sort, and I am not bargaining away my freedom for a few pieces of furniture and delicacies upon my table."

Roesia sighed as she reached for a ribbon to tie around her bundle of greenery. "You're a hard woman, my lady. I just hope that you won't one day rue those precious views of yours, for they won't keep you warm on a cold night."

Her words turned Joy's thoughts toward Campion, and she imagined his strong body heating hers, holding the chill and all else at bay. It was a tantalizing notion, but one which she dismissed with a frown. An extra fur would work as well, she told herself firmly. And it would be a lot less trouble in the bargain.

Irritated with her attendant, Joy had finally returned to the hall, where she had spent the evening desultorily weaving the rest of the greenery around a wooden frame into a kissing bush. Roesia had been no help at all. In fact, the woman who had perpetually urged her to find a man now refused to aid Joy in interesting one. Capricious creature!

Although Campion had presided over the light supper served earlier, he had disappeared since, and Joy knew a sense of disappointment, along with annoyance at herself. When had she ever cared about a man's movements, as long as they did not jeopardize her home? Perhaps since she had decided to learn the fine arts of seduction, she thought with a wry grimace.

But without her victim's presence, she could only sit back and stew, a very disturbing sensation that made her wonder just how much she was investing in this little plan of hers. It was near sunset, and the holiday revelry was winding to a close as the villeins and freemen who had spent the day at the castle prepared to take their leave.

Stephen was acting the gregarious host, and Joy debated whether to ask him or his brother where their father had gone. While part of her rebelled at seeking out her prey, another part declared such knowledge necessary to the fulfillment of her plan. Racked by the unaccustomed confusion, Joy finished the bush with an impatient gesture.

She looked up, prepared to call a servant over to hang it, only to find Stephen standing in front of her. Too close. There was nowhere to go, and the massive chair was too heavy to slide backward. Besides, it was not in her nature to cede ground to a man, so she simply lifted her chin and gave him a questioning look. To her annoyance, he placed his hands on the table on either side of her, effectively hedging her in as he loomed over her.

"Beautiful, work, my lady. Shall we try it?" he asked, in a low voice, tilting his dark head toward the bush. And before Joy could answer, he lowered his mouth to hers.

The mistletoe that was lodged among the evergreen boughs, ribbons and nuts was supposed to promote the kiss of peace, but this was no friendly brush of the lips. Stephen's was a kiss of seduction, his lips moving expertly over her own, and Joy, a stranger to such things, made the mistake of gasping in surprise. To her astonishment, Stephen seized the opportunity to thrust his tongue into her mouth. He tasted of wine and bitterness. The cold calculation of his movements fueled her outrage, and Joy pulled back at the same time that she lifted her knee.

Although she had little experience in kissing, she knew how to protect herself, and she heard Stephen's yelp of pain as she slipped from his embrace. Watching him warily, she saw him teeter precariously before plunging toward the table. Only the innate de Burgh grace saved him from smashing his handsome face into the worn wood, and Joy spared him no sympathy.

Reynold grunted in amusement, and Stephen turned his head, his handsome face surly, but Joy lifted her chin, meeting his glare with her own until he shoved away from the table. His easy smile returning, he bowed his head toward her. "Touché, lady," he said softly, before turning to go.

"Coddled whelp," Joy murmured, but she held her ground until he disappeared up the stairs, then she sank back down into her chair with a sigh at the vagaries of fate. She did not want the son's attention, but the father's! It was only after her gaze fell upon the abandoned kissing bush that Joy realized she ought to thank the errant de Burgh, and a slow smile crept over her face.

Stephen had given her what Roesia would not—a clue to the art of seduction—and Joy seized upon the tempting idea, hoping that her efforts went far better than Stephen's. As the plan took root she ignored her own trepidation and rose to her feet, walking toward the servant who was removing the last cups of ale from the trestle tables.

"Wilda?" Joy asked. At the woman's wary nod, she smiled. "I wondered if you knew where Lord Campion might be."

"Taking a bath, I gather, though why the men of this family feel such a need to be clean I will never know. Why, it's not natural!" the servant confided, before realizing that she might have said too much. She glanced away, her eyes downcast as she reached for another cup. "Probably something he read in those foreign books of his," she muttered.

"Or a man's sport," Joy said dryly. She knew that oftentimes male bathers had women attendants, which could lead to more than washing.

Wilda immediately shook her head at the implication. "Oh, you won't find anything of that here, my lady!'' she declared. "His lordship and all the boys are good men. Oh, Stephen's a bit of a rogue, but how can he help it when all the females adore him?''

Joy could have argued with that, but she was relieved to learn that the earl was as honorable as she had judged him.

"Lord Campion ought to be back down soon, for he likes to keep an eye on his hall, to make sure the celebrating doesn't go on all night," Wilda noted with a grin.

"I see," Joy answered. "Thank you. I think I will wait to...speak with him."

"You do that, my lady!" Wilda said, returning to her work. Turning, Joy walked slowly back to the high table, where she idly fingered the kissing bush. Around her the festivities were coming to an end, servants cleaning away debris and dousing candles so that soon the massive vaulted space was in shadow. Taking a seat in Campion's chair, Joy watched Reynold usher out a few straggling knights before he sought his own rest. Then some of the servants began making up pallets on the other side of the room, so far away that they disappeared into darkness.

Night was coming at last to Campion. Where was the earl? Joy knew an odd sensation that she ascribed to anticipation, not to overwrought nerves. But when, at last, she heard footsteps, she flinched, suddenly regretting her impulsive decision. Turning, she saw Campion standing on the stairs, surveying his domain, and the very sight of him flooded her with warmth.

Any doubts she had entertained fled swiftly as she rose to her feet.

"Campion." It felt wonderful to speak his name, but Joy knew a possessive need to discover his first name, his true name, and whisper it to him in the dark of his chamber. She shivered.

"Lady Warwick. I am surprised to find you here so late," the earl said. Concern colored his voice, and Joy wanted to be rid of it—and all else that stood between them.

"How do you like it?" she asked, moving aside to reveal her work. Campion looked at her, and for a moment, she saw a glimpse of vulnerability behind those all-knowing eyes, a dazed look of slumbering…something. But then it was gone, replaced by his maddeningly courteous demeanor.

Courtesy be hanged, Joy thought with a mutinous glance. She wanted to scream and shout and drag a reaction from Campion that was more than polite welcome, that was impolite welcome, that was even a small measure of the overwhelming heat she felt in his presence. Instead, she gestured toward the table. "Here. Come see your Christmas bush," she said. "What think you of it?"

Campion stepped forward, his movements fluid, his tall form cast in shadow, and Joy swallowed. As he studied her creation, she inched closer. When he turned his head to find her next to him, he cleared his throat, staring down at her with a certain intensity that gave her hope. "Lovely," he answered.

"Do you think so?" Joy asked, her breath quickening at his nearness. Even in the dim glow of the remaining candles, she could see his broad shoulders, the elegant way in which he held himself. She wanted to reach out and touch him. "Then we must make use of it," she murmured. A surge of power ran through her that she would never have associated with the role of seductress, and she liked it well.

Campion lifted his brows in polite query. Too polite. "A kiss," Joy demanded.

Surprise glinted his eyes. "Certainly," he said, and to Joy's chagrin, he did not look one bit excited by the prospect. He was at his most dignified, the earl, and he bent his head as if to brush her cheek, but a glancing touch of peace was not what Joy wanted. She was blossoming in her new role, and at the last moment, she turned to meet his lips with her own.

They were warm and firm and so very delicious that Joy grabbed onto his tunic to pull herself closer. She tried to remember just how Stephen had managed to get inside her mouth, but it was awfully hard to keep her mind on her task when she felt so odd, all fiery and alive. Campion went still and for a moment, Joy thought he would push her away, just as she had done to his son. She made a low sound of protest, but then his mouth opened over hers, his arms came around her and his breath mingled with hers in exquisite union.

Joy moved against him, her arms circling his broad chest as his tongue meshed with hers, for Campion took the kiss beyond Stephen's calculated efforts. No cool display of expertise was this, but a passion that rivaled her own. One of his hands moved behind her head, as if to hold her in place, while the other stroked her back, lower and lower still, until it closed around her buttocks and lifted her. Joy felt the hot, hard length of him rub her stomach, and she wiggled against it, wanting more. It was shocking and primitive and so exciting that she cried out in glorious surrender.

And then it was over. Just as suddenly as it had been unleashed, Campion's potent ardor was restrained once more. Joy, whimpering a protest, realized that he was setting her away, gently but firmly. She had but a glimpse of his stricken expression before he turned his head away.

"Forgive me. I had no right, no call to—" He broke off, and when he swiveled toward her, she saw that he had assumed his usual dignity. "You must seek your chamber. It is late, and you are without your attendant."

That is the idea! Joy wanted to scream. "But—"

"There is no excuse for my behavior."

"But—"

Someone moved at the entrance to the kitchens, and Campion, with seemingly preternatural recognition, called softly, "Wilda, would you please escort Lady Warwick to her chamber?"

"Yes, my lord," came the reply, and Joy wanted to shriek in frustration. So much for her seduction attempt! But what could she do? Tell Wilda to mind her own business? Press the earl back upon the high table and force him to appease her desires? The very notion grated and, lifting her chin, Joy went, chagrined at her rejection.

But even as she stalked away, she knew that for one precious moment she had felt the earth move, and she had moved Campion, too, whether he willed it or not.

Campion arose early after a uneasy night filled with images of his guest which, while enthralling, left him feeling guilty and ashamed. Even in the broad light of dawn, the memory of their embrace plagued him, and he groaned. What had possessed him? He could not recall ever acting so impulsively, so *wildly*. It was simply not his nature. Perhaps he was growing old. Old and mad!

He stayed in his chamber, unwilling to face the frantic revelry of the season, at least until the feasting began again, but he found himself pacing the length of the room with a restlessness he had not known in years. It was in this state that Reynold found him, and his son's innocent inquiry after his health suddenly annoyed him beyond endurance.

"I am fine," Campion muttered. *A fully functioning man,* he felt like adding. *A man who realizes what he has been missing and now must fight the craving for what he cannot have.* He stood at the window, hands clasped behind his back, and stared out at the bleak landscape below, enjoying the chill wind upon his face. *Mayhap it would cool his hot blood.*

Behind him he heard Reynold take a seat on the settle near the hearth. "'Tis looking more like Christmas in the hall," his son said.

"Yes," Campion answered. *Thanks to his bargain with the guest he had treated so poorly last evening!*

"Already the knights have made use of the kissing bush."

At Reynold's mention of the greenery that held the mistletoe, Campion felt a flash of heat scald his cheekbones. The memory of Lady Warwick in his arms, his hand buried in her thick hair, made him clear his throat.

"That is as it should be, as long as the revelry does not get out of hand," Campion said. He was a fine one to talk, he thought, for, as lord, it was up to him to set an example for his subjects. Last night he had set a poor one, should anyone have seen him with Lady Warwick in the shadows, and the knowledge that his actions may have injured his visitor's reputation made them doubly regretful.

"Stephen tried it out first," Reynold said in a deceptively careless tone that made Campion turn to look at him. "With the lady herself."

Campion stiffened. "Lady Warwick?"

Reynold nodded. "You know Stephen, always one for the ladies, whether they want him or not."

Campion held his tongue for a good long moment as he tried to divine Reynold's meaning. "Are you

saying that Stephen *forced* himself upon our guest?''
His fury mixed with his own shame, for had he not
done the same?

"Well, he didn't hurt her. In fact, she hurt him.
First, she drove a knee into his groin, and then she
practically knocked him face-first into the high table.
It was quite amusing, although I suspect his pride was
injured more than anything else,'' Reynold said.

Campion was glad he had not been present, for it
had been a long time since he had brawled with one
of his own sons, and right now he had an overpow-
ering urge to thrash Stephen. "Where is he?"

Reynold shrugged. "Off with someone who is not
so immune to his charms.''

"When he reappears, I will have him apologize,''
Campion said, more to himself than Reynold. Then,
remembering Reynold's presence, the earl eyed his
son carefully, wondering at his motives. The boys had
always held together, keeping each other's mischief
from their sire. Why had Stephen's actions suddenly
compelled Reynold to speak? "Thank you for telling
me,'' Campion said.

Reynold shrugged and rose to his feet. "Lady Warwick seems well able to take care of herself, but I
thought you should know that she came away from
the encounter looking as if she had just tasted some
rancid meat.'' Reynold grunted in amusement and
turned to go, leaving Campion staring after him.

Had Lady Warwick looked the same after she left
him last night? No, he could still hear her low cry of

pleasure, feel her pressing against him. Or was that only what he wished to recall? With a frown, Campion knew he owed his guest an apology, not just for his son, but for himself. What must she think of the de Burghs? he wondered with a shudder.

Campion found her in the solar with her attendant, sewing small figures, presumably for the kissing bush, and he felt guilty for their bargain, especially considering what had come of her handiwork. Standing in the doorway unobserved, he took a moment to admire the guest who had wrought so much havoc among the de Burghs.

Although young and beautiful, Joy looked far too somber to arouse such passions, making Campion wish that he could remove the line that blotted her brow and the tension in her mouth. What mysteries lay behind her serious demeanor? He would ease her cares, if only she would confide in him, but she kept her own counsel, and with such fierce independence that he would not presume to intrude.

Then, as if his perusal alerted her to his presence, she glanced up to see him, and Campion was rewarded with a smile that struck him so forcefully he hardly noticed her nod of dismissal to her attendant. "No, Lady, you need not send Roesia away," he protested as the woman passed him, leaving him alone with Lady Warwick in the cozy room.

Unnerved, Campion drew upon his dignity and approached his guest, bowing his head in greeting.

"Lady, I have just had some grievous news," he said. At her startled expression, he moved forward to halt in front of her.

"Nay, nothing tragic," he said gently. "But, nonetheless, it is disturbing. I heard that Stephen treated you ill last night, and of course, my own actions were inexcusable. I want you to know that Stephen will apologize and that our family is usually not so poorly behaved. As a guest in my home, you should be inviolate, safe and secure from any sort of imposition, and I assure you that nothing of the kind will happen again during your stay."

Instead of thanking him tearfully, Joy shrugged off his words. "I am becoming accustomed to the childish antics of your sons, but I will be pleased to hear Stephen's repentance," she said. Campion was nonplussed, but then when had this woman ever behaved in a predictable fashion? As if to prove his theory, she stood, giving him a smile that he could only describe as roguish. "As for you, I will accept no apology."

Campion felt stricken until she stepped closer. "But I will take another kiss." To his astonishment, she lifted her hand to reveal a small sprig of mistletoe, which she dangled above them. He stiffened in dismay. Surely this lovely young woman did not mean she wanted him to... He was most puzzled, for why would she reject Stephen in one breath and tease him in the next? She waited expectantly while Campion struggled for a polite reply.

"My dear lady, I am most..." *What?* Flattered? Surprised? For once, he was at a loss for words. "Tempted. However, after last night, I think you will agree that it would be wiser to refrain from these holiday rituals with Stephen or myself."

"I am not interested in Stephen," she said.

She spoke in that direct way of hers, her violet gaze challenging, and if Campion didn't know better he would think she was proclaiming her interest in... himself. "Lady," he said, chiding her gently. "You cannot know what you are about. You are a young and vibrant woman, while I...I have sons older than those you have met, seven sons in all, and grandchildren!"

"Ah, so that means you are no longer interested in women?" she asked, her lips tilting in an echo of his own chiding expression.

Campion frowned. "Of course not. I find you most attractive." Intriguing, *arousing*. "But surely you would prefer someone your own age, like Reynold or Stephen." Although Campion nearly choked on their names, unwilling to urge the lady toward either son, he was determined to be sensible and to make his guest see reason.

At the mention of his sons, she dropped all pretense of teasing, granting him the direct gaze he so admired. "Stephen and Reynold are still boys, despite their ages, and we both know it," she said, before turning to move gracefully toward the hearth. Stunned, Campion felt he ought to defend his sons, but he suspected she was all too right in her assessment. Although full-grown knights, in some ways, those two were like children, neither one mature enough to stand on his own.

Silently Campion watched her circle the room, each step charming and assured, until she paused before the window. "I've had a boy, and I find I'm more interested in a man," she said, turning her head toward him, and Campion's mouth went dry.

Never before had he been treated to such bold speech. Oh, there had been ladies at court, with their subtle and not-so-subtle pursuits, but most of their intrigues had left him cold. Lady Warwick spoke with a forthrightness that left no doubt as to her intent, yet somehow her words were not brazen, nor were her actions. He could not imagine that she did this with any degree of regularity, and that knowledge was even more daunting.

Already Campion felt his body respond to the desire implicit in her words, and he took a deep breath in an effort to control it. As the man, elder and more experienced, it was up to him to put a stop to this nonsense. Surely she was too young, too unworldly, to know what she was doing.

"Lady—"

"Joy. Please call me Joy."

"Joy." Her name slid far too easily off of his tongue, for he had swiftly come to think of her as bringing joy to his holiday, along with other more complex emotions. Although she seemed at once too serious and too willful for so frivolous a title, Campion thought the name suited her. *Joy.*

"And you are called?"

Campion stilled, stunned for a moment at her request. When he spoke, he did so automatically, without pausing to consider the wisdom of granting her such an intimacy. "Fawke," he said slowly.

"Fawke." She echoed his name in a low voice that skittered along his nerve endings to rouse both his lower body and the heart he had thought better schooled after all these years. How long had it been since someone had called him by his right name? Standing there, watching the slight figure who stood at his solar window, Campion had the sudden, eerie sensation that he was meeting his fate, and all that he might do would simply delay the inevitable. He shook the feeling aside and cleared his throat, striving to regain his reason.

"Joy, you can hardly be serious about this…" *Infatuation? Dalliance? Simple kiss?* Again Campion was at a loss for words.

"And why not?" she asked, over her shoulder. Campion watched the gentle sway of her black curls and felt his body tighten treasonously. "I was wed at age sixteen, an arrangement to keep property in the family. He was thirteen." Her tone was flat, but Campion sensed her resentment and added his own. Although such alliances were not uncommon, he did not approve of marriages involving children of either gender.

"Not a year later, he was gored by a wild boar, and I've been a widow ever since. During all that time, I have never had any desire to remarry, nor any desire to dally with a man." As the startling revelation of her words struck him, Campion found that she had turned to face him once more, her chin lifted in the familiar expression of defiance. "So don't tell me what I want or don't want. I'm a grown woman. I know my own mind."

What Joy would have done or said next, Campion didn't know, for at that point his steward entered, anxiously wishing to consult with her about some petty detail of the feast. Something about candles? Effortlessly sliding into the role of chatelaine that had been assigned her, she moved toward the man, her soft replies barely discernible to Campion, whose mind was still focused on something else entirely. As if aware of his thoughts, Joy gave him a nod and a smile before following his steward from the room with a grace, confidence and allure unequaled.

Campion stood there staring after her, feeling as if his mouth were hanging open from their encounter. Joy wanted *him?* Joy *wanted* him. He drew a deep breath, tamping down the elation that swept through him and replacing it with a more appropriate response.

He had not held his earldom by succumbing to impulse or irrational behavior, no matter how tempting. Unlike his son Stephen, Campion did not engage in brief liaisons, and despite the admiration and attraction he felt for his Christmas guest, he had nothing else to offer her.

The truth was that he had no intention of taking another wife and, even if he did, Joy was too young. Too beautiful. Too alive. Too stubborn. Too *everything*.

Chapter Five

After what happened in the solar, Campion kept a careful, if cordial, distance from his guest. Despite her protestations otherwise, Joy was a headstrong young woman who could not be expected to make the best judgment, and in this case, she was simply not thinking clearly. Campion had a wealth of experience with avoiding temptation, and he knew better.

But he could still enjoy her visit, and he did, delighting in her company. He had decided that Joy was too somber, and in keeping with their skating lesson, he was determined that she learn to enjoy herself while visiting his demesne. Just yesterday, he had encouraged her to join in the games that were part of the Christmas celebration, and tonight, having learned that she did not play chess, he was taking great pleasure in teaching her.

And Joy was an adept pupil. Already, during their second game, she was evincing a remarkable talent for the strategy necessary to win. Really, she was a fascinating creature, Campion mused as they sat before the hearth, the chess table between them. Concentrating on her next move, her dainty fingers hovering over the pieces, she was more beautiful than anyone he had ever seen.

Campion knew that "fair" was used to describe women with blond tresses, but surely not one of those ladies could rival Joy with her dark locks hanging loose and heavy. His son Dunstan's wife had fuzzy brown curls, but Joy's were black as night, the sleek long locks seeming to possess a life of their own as they fell clear to her waist.

For all the delicacy of her features, she was a strong-willed, capable woman. And despite her bold speech, there was a subtle air of innocence about her that Campion found very attractive, as if she had missed out on so much of life, including the activities she deemed frivolous. Had she suffered a hard existence? Her clothes were fine enough, her train well manned. Joy was a puzzle, and one he would enjoy unraveling, if he had the time.

And therein lay the cause of Campion's unease, for already it was the fifth day of Christmas, with only seven remaining. Although Joy seemed to enjoy their play well enough, what would happen when she left? Would she return to a life of toil? Campion found his thoughts more and more occupied with her departure and the future that would follow.

Of course, it was only natural that he be concerned with the welfare of one of his guests, but Joy was not the sort of woman who would answer questions about her situation. She was intensely private, another trait he admired, yet he found himself wanting to penetrate that privacy, to establish an intimacy with her that no one else could claim. In a paternal sort of way, Campion told himself, even as his gaze followed the brush of her slender fingers against her bishop.

"Very good!" he said, when he saw her placement of the piece. "You are an excellent student."

Her answering smile nearly stole his breath, and Campion swiftly moved his own piece and tilted back, putting some distance between them. But Joy only leaned closer, her voice so low that he had to bend near to hear her.

"It occurs to me that if you are so determined that I learn all these games of which you are so fond, perhaps there is another manner of play you can teach me, that would be even more pleasurable, for us both," she said, her violet eyes like pools under those thick lashes. Her husky whisper caused an immediate reaction in Campion's body, but he cleared his throat, ignoring the provocative suggestion.

"Watch your queen," he advised hoarsely without daring to look at her. Despite his best efforts, Campion was plagued by unseemly urges when Joy was present, and inappropriate thoughts when she was not. Her teasing comments did not help, and he was becoming thoroughly exasperated with himself.

He had loved both of his wives. He had been very young when he wed the first time, more mature when he married Anne, and yet he could not recall feeling this…unsettled by a female. His wives had both been gentle souls, but Joy, for all her fragility, was not. Her look of cool composure hid a fiery spirit with a core of steel. A fit wife for any man, Campion thought, before catching himself.

Obviously he had been without a woman too long. Indeed, there had been no one since his last visit to court, for he did not believe in the misuse of women and would provide an example for his sons. Yet there was something about Joy that affected him like no other. He began to feel like a randy boy, more true to Stephen's nature than his own! He did not believe in allowing passions to rule one's life and so had long ago suppressed such yearnings, yet now, it was as if his dormant desires wished to make up for the years of celibacy as soon as possible. With Joy.

It was aggravating…and vaguely exhilarating.

"Check," she said, warning of her intent to capture, and Campion looked up in surprise to see her sly smile. She was referring to the chessboard, of course. Then why did he have the impression she meant something else entirely?

Stephen glanced at the cozy scene by the hearth and frowned at his brother Reynold. "She has him rattled," he muttered.

"Who? Father?" Reynold let out a rough sound that was the closest he came to laughter. "Campion is never rattled."

"Yes, he is," Stephen argued. Reynold was too young to recall his mother's death and Campion's long vigil in her chamber, but Stephen remembered it as a chilling time when even his all-wise father seemed to be lost. He shrugged off the memory and took a drink. "I've seen it before, but I never thought to see it again. He hasn't been shaken from his usual stoicism for years. Until now. Until *her*."

Reynold snorted. "You're just piqued that the lady won't notice you."

"Well, I have to admit that there's something wrong when a beautiful young woman pays more attention to my father than me," Stephen said, with a nod toward the duo by the fire. "I wonder what she's up to."

"Nothing," Reynold scoffed. "Do you think that any woman who is interested in Father must have an ulterior motive? You're daft!"

"He's a powerful man," Stephen mused. "While I'm nothing but a younger son with no prospects."

Reynold snorted. "If you would get your head out of your wine cup long enough—"

"Don't start on me, when you should look to yourself," Stephen snapped.

Reynold grunted but did not rise to the bait. "Father is still a handsome fellow to the ladies. Haven't you heard Marion coo about him enough to know that? Just because he's lived like a monk these past years doesn't mean he is one."

"A scary thought," Stephen commented. "Surely

you cannot be suggesting that the almighty Campion might have needs like the rest of us mere mortals?''

Reynold muttered a low oath. "Can't you see *anything* around you except yourself?" His gaze swung toward the hearth and then back to Stephen. "He's lonely, and she's good for him. Leave them be."

With a black look, Reynold shook his head and left the table, much to Stephen's disappointment. He never would admit as much to a soul, but he found himself missing Simon, who could always be counted upon for a good quarrel until he fell for a sword-wielding Amazon in the Forest of Dean. Reynold, who did not suffer an excess of bile, was simply not as much fun.

And as for his insinuation that Campion felt the same as less exalted beings, Stephen doubted it. He glanced toward the fire and shook his head before lifting his cup to drink. Still she had the earl rattled, there was no doubt of it.

It was the sixth day of Christmas, and Joy's frustration was mounting. Although she sensed that Campion was not indifferent to her, he maintained a strict decorum that left her no opportunity to test his remarkable restraint. She had hoped for another cozy game of chess, but tonight he had talked her into playing hoodman's bluff, and so she was standing in the midst of the hall, blindfolded, while the other players turned her around several times.

Laughing at a momentary dizziness, Joy felt her

tension ease. Although she could not imagine engaging in such nonsense at home, here at Campion everything, even the most foolish of pastimes took on a magical glow, whether from the season or the castle. Or Campion. At the thought of the stubborn earl, Joy smiled. The object of this game was to find and identify someone without the aid of sight, and she knew just whom she would seek.

Ignoring the loud encouragement of those close by, Joy moved away from the crowd, for she knew Campion would be on the periphery, watching quietly with those enigmatic eyes. He would not be jostling others or frantically hopping about for attention. Campion would be still, his power leashed with dignity.

"You're heading for the kitchens, lady!" someone called, and indeed, Joy recognized the odor of food drifting toward her. Her outstretched fingers brushed against something, a man's chest, but the softness of it made her turn away. There was no softness about the earl, except inside him, where goodness and honor and gentleness dwelt. Much laughter and teasing ensued when she passed by the man, and her hand next found the wooden screen that stood at the end of the hall near the entrance to the buttery and the kitchens.

There she stopped as a faint whiff of something else caught her attention, and suddenly the game and its noisy participants all faded away. In the darkness there was only herself and the man she had sought, whose scent she recognized as well as her own. She could sense his presence, his strength, and smell the familiar flavors of him: clean clothing, the spicy soap that he used and that which was his alone. She had known it before in the darkness of the hall by the kissing bush, and now she reached unerringly out to it again.

Joy was aware of the sound of the crowd, but only as an irritating rumble, for she was focused solely on the earl. One more step and she felt his heat, her hands lifting to rest upon his broad chest, and she stood there, wishing that she could remain where she was always, that he would draw her into his arms and hold her. Keep her.

Someone pulled off the hood, but Joy stayed in front of Campion, and amid shrieks and cheers, the game continued, moving away from the dim area at the end of the hall. Drawing him with her, Joy backed behind the carved screen that would hide them from prying eyes.

There, in the sheltered shadows, Joy tried her hand at a new game, one far more dear to her, as her fingers slid up Campion's chest into the sleek softness of his dark hair. She stroked it with wonder, despite his stillness and the intense regard of his brown eyes.

Along with the usual warmth that came with his nearness, Joy felt something more, a sweetness that seemed to fill her, pressing behind her eyes until she wanted to weep with the pleasure of touching him. Roesia's warning came back to her, but she wondered if it was not too late to heed her attendant, for she already had come to care for this man.

Recklessly Joy raised herself up on her toes and touched her mouth to his, and it was even more wonderful than she remembered. The kiss was an exploration, a greeting well met that nonetheless sent heat surging through her, and her arms slipped around his waist, anchoring her to his strength.

After a moment's hesitation, Campion kissed the corner of her mouth, her eyelashes, her brows and the line of her jaw, murmuring her name in a tone that she had never heard before. It was a whisper that spoke of awe and desire, and Joy responded with abandon, pressing her body against his and welcoming his lips with her own. She recognized now the hard ridge of his manhood against her stomach, and she wanted nothing more than to feel all of him, around her, inside her, as part of her.

"Let us go to your chamber," she urged breathlessly against his cheek, but he stiffened even as she spoke. Joy could sense the withdrawal of his passion, and she whimpered in protest. Still he set her away. Even in the shadows, she could see the glint of his eyes, shining with wisdom and ardor withheld.

"It would not be right," he said.

"But I want you. I...I care for you," Joy said. At her faltering confession, his expression softened, and he reached out to stroke her hair in a gesture of comfort that only made her need more.

"Nay. 'Tis but a passing thing, and I would be a rogue indeed if I were to take advantage of it," he said.

His words made Joy bristle, and she shrugged off his hand. "Do not speak to me as if I were a child, Fawke, for I am not! I am a woman full grown, a widow who has maintained a holding for years! Why do you not credit my decision? Do you think I'm a fool?"

"No, of course not," he said in gentle placation that only made Joy angrier.

"Then why do you dispute me? Why can't I know my own mind? If I chose Reynold, would you fault me?" Joy saw the flicker of emotion that crossed his face, and was well glad of it. She wanted to hurt him, to punish him for denying her.

"No," he said softly, then he turned away, releasing a heavy sigh into the shadows. "The problem, as you've divined, bright lady that you are, is with me. I loved my wives, but after I buried Anne, I vowed never to put myself in such a position again."

Stunned by his admission, Joy came up behind him, placing a palm against his broad back. She had glimpsed a vulnerability in this strong man, but she had never imagined that he had forsaken women to avoid the pain of another's death. How could she argue against such emotion? She slid her arms around his waist and rested her cheek against him.

"Foolish man, you are always complaining about my age," she muttered into his tunic. "Now see how it can only be to your advantage, for I will surely outlive you anyway!"

Campion stiffened, then turned toward her, and Joy

was afraid her audacious response had been too much. But he only shook his head and started laughing, a deep rumble of merriment that gladdened her heart. It seemed the perfect opportunity for a kiss or more, to lay claim to this man and convince him to join her in bed, but his admission gave her pause.

She might care for him, but Joy was still intent upon leaving, and although it was hardly the same as dying, she wondered if Campion would be hurt by her defection. He valued loyalty and honor, as did she, so why did she feel that her plans to go were both disloyal and dishonorable?

And so when their moment of quiet intimacy was disturbed by servants bringing the wassail from the kitchens, Joy said nothing, caught in a coil of her own making as surely as Roesia had predicted.

Jostled to his senses by the wassailers, Campion held out his hand to Joy, whose sudden, stricken expression made him rue his words. He should never have talked about his grief for Anne! It was an ill-mannered man who spoke to one woman of another, and yet, his wives were a part of him and Joy should know it. Perhaps it would remind her of the differences between them.

But even as he tried to hold on to them, Campion felt his objections slipping away. Other men his age took young wives, oftentimes to give them heirs, and although he had plenty of those already, Campion knew no one would fault him for marrying a woman of Joy's years. It was more difficult to rid himself of his refusal to love again, but already she had somehow slipped beneath his reserve to nudge at his heart—and elsewhere.

As his fingers closed over hers, Campion felt the surge of arousal that came simply from touching her. Would that he could lead her upstairs to his chamber! She had offered herself up to him, and his body clamored to accept, but he held firm to his honor.

It would not be right. There was too much standing between them, even more yet unknown, and Campion couldn't shake his feeling that she was keeping something from him. Nor could he completely dismiss his initial impression that Joy was not the best judge of what was best for her.

So, instead of taking her to his bed, Campion escorted her to the chair beside his own, where the rousing game of hoodman's bluff was coming to an end. A glance over the table told him that the revelers were growing weary and that Stephen, slumped in one of the chairs, was drunk. It was not surprising these days, especially with the added festivities, but Campion saw the reckless gleam in his eye and frowned.

He had reason to be proud of all his sons, Stephen included, but right now his patience with the boy's antics was running low. And, along with the exasperation, he felt a familiar guilt that he had somehow failed his son. Perhaps if there had been more of a woman's presence in the household, he thought, and his eyes traveled, unbidden, to Joy.

She spoke of wanting him, but for how long? Barring more ill weather, in only a few more days she would be gone, and they had not talked about extending her visit. Although he ought to be relieved to see the end of his temptation, all he felt was a wrenching despair, as if the lady represented his last chance for her namesake. Joy.

Campion realized that his own perusal had drawn Stephen's, and he felt a sudden, unreasoning proprietorship. *His Joy,* he thought, even as he recognized the reaction as rather barbaric. He had told her often enough to choose another, and now he wanted to deny it, to shout his possession to the world. Only great force of will kept him in his seat.

One of the wassailers stopped by his chair, wishing him prosperity in the coming year, and although Campion turned and smiled, his thoughts remained with those at the high table. He wondered from whence came his passion, for he could not recall ever feeling so deeply, so violently.

"You're going about it the wrong way, you know," Stephen drawled, making Campion wonder what his son was up to now.

"What?" Joy's soft reply followed, and Campion listened intently even as he nodded at the fellow raising his cup in song before him.

"You'll never lure Campion into marriage by pursuing him." Stephen's snide comment made the earl jerk his head toward his son, the wassailer forgotten.

"I have no interest in marrying the earl," Joy replied, and the rebuke that Campion was forming for his son died on his lips. *She didn't want to marry him?*

Stephen continued just as if Joy had not spoken. "He's too noble to marry a pretty young thing like you. Now, if you were in desperate straits, in need of a husband to protect you, then you can be sure the honorable earl would do the right thing, no matter what his personal feelings," Stephen said, sneering.

Both stunned and appalled by his son's words, Campion nonetheless recognized the truth of them. If Joy needed him in some way, he would gladly seize the excuse to make her his, and the knowledge did not sit well upon his shoulders.

"Why not plead your case, Lady Warwick?" Stephen said, inclining his head toward Campion. "Why not tell him the truth?" he asked, his mobile mouth moving into a hard line. "Why not explain that you left your home, rushing into a snowstorm, in order to avoid the arrival of your uncle, who has been pressing you to marry again. Another cousin of his, perhaps? Someone you liked no better than your first husband?"

Campion's gaze swiveled toward Joy. Did Stephen speak the truth of things? Few monied widows were allowed to remain so for long, if they had male relatives or liege lords who would benefit from their remarriage. A widow with no children and a decent holding would be worth a nice settlement, and Campion had wondered at Joy's freedom, but her strength and assurance had fooled him. He had thought her wholly independent, not a woman under siege.

No wonder she had turned to him.

Campion felt a stir of disappointment. He had thought Joy's desire for him was genuine, if misguided, but now he saw her overtures for what they were: the actions of an intelligent woman trying to save herself from another bad marriage. He could hardly blame her, nor did she lose his respect, but for a long moment, he knew a sharp pain, a prick of more than his pride. But it was swiftly overwhelmed by his sense of honor. Here was a lady in distress, a lovely, educated, capable woman who sought his protection. And he had denied her.

"Was it just happenstance that led you here, or were you hunting better game?" Stephen drawled. "Perhaps someone who wouldn't care that you might be barren?"

Surprised at the rage that rose within him at Stephen's taunt, Campion surged to his feet and laid his hands on the table. "That's enough." It was all he trusted himself to say.

Stephen swung his gaze around, as if he had all but forgotten his sire's presence, and was even more stunned by the rebuke. Their gazes locked for a long moment until finally, with a low grunt, Stephen picked up his cup and drank. Around them, the silence was deafening, and Campion gestured for the wassailers to begin anew. When they did, he once more took his seat and turned his attention to the woman beside him.

"Is it true?" he asked gently. Joy's head was bent, her face obscured by her luxurious midnight hair, and Campion had the horrible suspicion that she was weeping.

She quickly disabused him of that notion, lifting her chin to reveal a fierce expression. "Perhaps. But what if it is?" she asked, as if in challenge. "'Tis not the first time Hobart has harried me to take a husband, and I'm sure it will not be the last. But do you see me wed? Nay."

She rose to her feet, magnificent in her controlled fury, and whirled toward Stephen. "Since 'tis my business and not yours, Stephen de Burgh, I will keep my own counsel, but let me assure you that I am fully able of handling my uncle and have done so for years. Dare you imagine otherwise?"

The look she gave Stephen made him squirm in his seat, a feat few could manage, and without waiting for a reply, she turned on her heel and stalked from the room with a dignity that stole Campion's breath. He had been right all along. Not only had she kept something from him, but she was too much for him. Too beautiful, too willful, too independent and too passionate—for him to resist.

He knew what he must do.

Chapter Six

Campion awoke on the eve of the new year with new purpose. He had learned long ago that choosing one's moment was vital, and so he had not pursued Joy when she left the hall the night before. She was a stubborn woman, more so when angry, and he gave her time to recover from her outrage in the hope that she would be better able to see reason, come the new day.

As for himself, Campion had made his own decision, for in the face of Joy's dilemma, his resolve not to marry again had fallen by the wayside. He told himself he was doing the honorable thing, but it was the threat of another taking his place that spurred him to action. The mere thought of Joy going to someone else's bed, of marrying a man of her uncle's choosing, was enough to rouse his blood to a fever pitch. *His Joy.*

No longer startled by such violent sentiments in connection with his guest, Campion did his best to wrestle them into submission, cloaking his passion in dignity. He had prepared his arguments and, confident of his success, he sought her out.

She was in the solar with her attendant, and Campion took a moment to admire her beauty before he was discovered. Roesia immediately rose to leave, and Joy, eyeing him with something akin to alarm, voiced her protest. But it went unheeded, and soon he was alone with the woman who would be his wife.

The rebellious look she gave him boded ill, and Campion knew a sudden, swift disappointment, for he missed the welcome he had once seen in her expression. Had it been an illusion, as Stephen claimed? Campion only knew he wanted to bring it back, fool that he was. When she pursued him, he had decried it, but now he missed his bold seductress. *His Joy.*

"I apologize once more for any distress that my family has caused you," he said softly, cursing both Stephen and himself. But Joy only shrugged and turned away, a movement that struck Campion painfully, and he moved to sit before her upon a low stool.

"Why did you not confide in me?" he asked, without accusation.

"Do all who tarry here share their most personal problems with the lord of the land?" Joy answered with a bitterness that dismayed him.

"Nay, but neither do they offer themselves to me, a far more personal act, wouldn't you say?" Campion replied.

She flushed and frowned. "I have spent long years

holding on to that which is mine against the encroachment of men, so you will pardon me if I was wary of trusting you at first sight. What if you were the kind who would send for Hobart?''

Campion shook his head, understanding her reluctance and yet smarting from it. ''But now, surely, you must know I would do nothing to hurt you,'' he said.

She laughed at his words, an unhappy sound that made Campion flinch. Had he hurt her? How? Surely not with his rebuffs? ''Joy, I...I was just trying to do what was best for you,'' he explained.

Her chin lifted, and her violet eyes flashed. ''And how could you be certain what is right for me? You may have ruled wisely and well for a lifetime, but you are not omnipotent, my lord. You cannot possibly know everything!''

Campion stilled, astounded, not for the first time, by her perception. She was right, of course. Years of making decisions, of running his demesne, of ruling over the disputes of his people and the well-being of his family had left him all too accustomed to proffering answers whenever questions were presented to him. Had he become pompous and all-knowing? Campion made a low sound of apology as the realization struck him that this time, perhaps, he had been wrong.

He reached out to take her hand, to tell her so, but all the fine arguments he had prepared vanished in a swell of foreboding. ''Marry me,'' he said, the words released hurriedly as emotions buffeted him. He needed time to think upon her words, to take a good, long look at himself, yet his blood was beating out a demand that he do something now, before it was too late.

But it was already too late. As Joy shook her head in denial, Campion knew he had rejected her once too often, sealing his fate, along with her own. She pulled her hand from his and stood, as if to dismiss him.

Lifting her chin in the familiar gesture of defiance, she faced him, and Campion could see that her anger was barely controlled. "I want no proposal born of pity," she said. "I have already suffered one marriage arranged for reasons other than affection, and I will not be a party to another, thank you very much."

"'Tis not an offer born of pity, nor one I make lightly," Campion answered grimly, but she shook her head, backing toward the door, and he felt the situation slipping away from him. For the first time in years beyond count, he was not in control.

"And what of your uncle?" he asked, desperate to stay her.

"I'll evade him. It's a game we play and none of your concern." The look of contempt she gave him made him surge to his feet.

"And what about your feelings for me? Are they so easily forgotten? What of that which you asked of me? Were you going to share my bed and then leave, without so much as a word?" Campion asked, risking his pride with the question.

Joy's eyes widened, her expression stricken, but

she nodded. "Yes," she whispered, and before he could respond, she hurried through the doorway, as if she could no longer bear his presence.

Her answer so shocked him that Campion made no move to follow. Instead, he sank back down upon the stool in unaccustomed confusion, mind and body in a turmoil such as he had little known in his life. Anger and hurt and disbelief warred together as he stared after her, unwilling to accept what had just occurred. He had ruled his demesne long and well, there being little over the years that was beyond the reach of his will.

It was a humbling experience to be so thoroughly thwarted, and yet Campion's only regret was the loss of what might have been. *But what of me?* he thought in the stillness of the solar. *What of my joy?*

The Earl of Campion could not remember ever being so uncertain. Deeming it best to let the passions that had flared in the solar cool before he spoke again with Joy, he had retired to his chamber, where he hoped to bring his jumbled thoughts and emotions to order. But when one of the villeins reported a block of ice had broken off, threatening to dam the river, he was glad for a chance to go out and tackle a task with which he was familiar.

He would speak again with Joy when he was finished. Meanwhile, he took pleasure in riding his favorite destrier and directing the movements of the men who were breaking up the frozen water. He even got down and lent a hand, despite Reynold's protests, for if his son could aid them without complaining about his bad leg, then Campion would do well to work, too.

He was wet and cold and feeling his age when at last they returned to the castle, his thoughts firmly fixed upon a hot bath. It was only after he was clean and dry and fortified by a hot cup that his thoughts turned once more toward Joy.

Obviously Stephen was wrong, and Joy was not after his money, else she would have agreed to marry him eagerly. Why, then, had she pursued him so diligently? No matter what her bold speech, Campion sensed that she was not a woman to make free with her favors. She had too much the air of innocence about her for that.

Then why? Campion could come up with only one conclusion. Joy truly had wanted him and cared for him. The knowledge settled like a warm ember around his heart, firing his blood and rousing him to action. Surely all the disagreements between them could be resolved somehow, for didn't he return that regard?

No, he thought ruefully, *regard* was too mild a name for what he felt for Joy, and he was determined to tell her so, to persuade her by any means possible that she belonged at Campion, by his side. And with new resolve he went below to look for her.

Down in the hall he found Stephen still at the high table, for he had not gone to the river, dismissing the need with a clever remark. Obviously the boy was still sulking. As Joy must be, Campion decided, for she was not among the revelers, nor in the solar. "Have you seen Lady Warwick?" he asked, glancing about curiously.

"She's gone," Stephen replied.

"Gone?" Campion echoed, uncertain he had heard his son correctly.

"She left before the meal, soon after you went out to break up the ice."

Joy was gone? Campion ignored the rapid pounding of his heart as he tried to make sense of his son's speech. "But where did she go?"

Stephen shrugged carelessly. "I know not. Perhaps back home to face her uncle or on to another demesne to work her wiles on a new lord."

Campion stiffened. "You mean, she has packed her things and taken to the roads, with her train?" At Stephen's nod, the earl leaned forward, palms spread upon the table in an effort to control the emotions that swept through him. "Why didn't you send word to me?"

Stephen shrugged again. "I knew not where you were along the river or that you would even care to be notified. And far be it from me to involve myself in the affairs of the lady, who warned me well to stay out of her business," he added with a sneer.

"But why? Why would she leave so suddenly?" Campion asked in astonishment, throwing up his hands. Joy was a strong woman, not the sort to cringe and sneak away like a thief in the night. What had driven her to flee?

"She probably didn't like being found out," Stephen drawled.

His son's taunt drew Campion up short, and he leaned upon the table once more. Staring long and hard at the son who so sorely tried his patience, he realized that it was time he spoke. "Aren't you too old to sulk like a boy just because a pretty woman doesn't fancy you?" he asked.

Stephen's head came up swiftly, his eyes glittering. "And aren't you too old to be chasing after a skirt?"

A long moment of silence passed between them until finally Campion answered calmly. "No. I am no doddering invalid. I am a man. What of you, Stephen? What do you call yourself?"

At the question, Campion saw his son's hand tighten around the ever-present cup of wine until the knuckles grew white. Then, without a word, Stephen knocked it aside and swung to his feet. He stalked away, leaving Campion alone at the high table with Reynold, who watched Stephen go with a somber expression.

"He is angry because you bested him in a contest for the lady's affections. It wounds him, for he is well proud of his way with women. 'Tis all he has," Reynold murmured.

"No. You're wrong," Campion said, as he too stared after his errant son. "'Tis not all he has, but 'tis a pity he thinks so." Although it pained him,

Campion knew there was nothing he could do for Stephen until the boy decided for himself that he was more than a careless charmer.

With a sigh, Campion swung his gaze toward the window. Outside, the sky was clear, but the shadows were lengthening. Although the snow had begun to melt with the recent warmth, the roads would still be half-frozen and muddy and difficult. Was she all right? Immediately, the knowledge returned to him with the force of a blow.

Joy was gone.

And for all his wealth and power, there was nothing he could do about it. She was a grown woman with no ties to Campion, a guest who was free to leave as she might will, and he had to accept her decision. But she had come into his life like a force of nature, stirring up his safe and staid existence until he felt so good that he wanted to reach out and grasp life in his hands. *And he didn't want to let go.*

Campion had thought to make her see reason, to talk her into taking him as her husband, but wisdom and reason were what had made him refuse her in the first place. They were no use to him. Nor were all his vows to honor and protect a lady in distress. He saw them now for what they were: convenient excuses to have what he wanted without any of the attendant guilt.

To have *Joy.* And now that she was gone, Campion saw too well his mistake. He had been thinking with his mind, patiently deliberating when he ought to have listened to the rest of himself, to the heart that was thundering a protest in his chest, to the desire that she had stoked to a fevered pitch. Joy was a fire in his blood, and now it ran cold with the want of her. How long ago had she left? he wondered as he whirled around.

Reynold met his panicked gaze and spoke haltingly. "Mayhap she wanted to be married for her own sake, not any other reason," he said, and the stark look in his eyes made Campion pause. Reynold disdained romantic love, and yet, his words held a yearning for someone to see beyond the limp that loomed so large in his own mind.

As Campion should have seen beyond his own image of himself as too dignified, too powerful to succumb to the charms of a beautiful young woman. Dignity be damned! It was time he admitted that he lusted after Joy in a shockingly primitive manner, that he not only admired her but loved her with a frightening and powerful strength, the like of which he had never known before.

But he had pushed her away. Would she believe him now when he admitted his feelings? Shoving aside the doubts of his mind, Campion seized upon the determination of his heart. It was time for action. He strode for the door, calling for his sword and his steed.

"Where are you going?" he heard Reynold ask from behind him.

"I'm going after her!" he shouted over his shoulder. And, he was coming back with her, Campion decided, a smile beginning to curve his lips. It had been a long time since life had thrown him a challenge, and now he found himself taking up the gauntlet with relish.

For Joy.

Campion flung open the doors to his great hall with a stubborn willfulness that even the woman squirming in his arms could not match. He had found her still upon his lands and, without stopping to argue, he had lifted Joy from her horse to his own. When they reached the entrance to the hall, she had balked, and so Campion had simply thrown her over his shoulder.

"Campion! Have you lost your senses?" she cried from behind him, but he dismissed her shouts and the pummeling of her small fists against his back with a grunt of enjoyment. He felt more alive than he had in years. He barely noticed the cheers from the servants, whether delighted at his retrieval of Joy or anticipating the First Foot of the new year as a harbinger of good luck to come.

Campion needed no such omen. He knew that his life had taken a turn that would provide him with joy aplenty, for he held it in his arms. And despite his wiggling burden, he climbed up the stairs with an effortless stride to stalk straight into the great chamber.

He suspected that he ought to kick the door shut, but that seemed a little too violent for his taste, so he carried his prize to the bed, tossing her onto the wide expanse before returning to close and bolt the heavy oak entrance. When he faced her once more, Campion smiled at the sight of Joy, here in his room, alone with him. Since the night of her arrival, he had pictured her in his bed, and he knew a soul-stirring satisfaction to finally have her there.

She was a tangle of cloak and skirts, her mass of heavy black curls falling over her shoulders to her waist, and Campion had a tantalizing glimpse of one slender ankle. As he watched in silence, she struggled up on her knees and lifted her small pale hands to push back her unruly mane. Campion stiffened at the thought of those delicate fingers running through his hair, touching his body. *Soon.* He felt an exhilaration such as he had never known before, as if she alone had tapped some wildness he had long held in check.

"What are you doing?" she demanded, and Campion girded his loins for a pitched battle.

"I'm taking the matter out of your hands," he replied, smiling at his own words.

Her mouth formed an O of astonishment that made him feel absurdly pleased before she managed to recover her usual poise. "See here, Fawke, if this primitive display is fueled by some misguided sense of honor—"

Campion felt his grin widen, and he reached down to unclasp his sword. "Oh, I guarantee you that honor has nothing to do with it," he said. His gaze never left her as he dropped the weapon and moved forward, and he thoroughly enjoyed the shocked expression that came over her face. Joy had always been the aggressor, trying his control with her guileless attempts at seduction, but now it was his turn, and when he kicked off his boots and approached the bed with deliberate purpose, her violet eyes widened in surprise.

He reached her and lifted his hand to test one long, dark lock between his fingers while delighting in Joy's speechless, breathless stare. "I'm afraid you were under a mistaken impression when you left here in such a cowardly manner," he murmured, his gaze never leaving hers. The words made her lift her chin, as he intended, and her eyes flashed.

"Cowardly? I—"

"Don't ever run from me again," Campion said. It was not a threat or a plea, only a statement of fact, but, being Joy, she opened her mouth to argue. He didn't let her, distracting her with his movements as he leaned over her to slip her cloak off and away.

"Because you are mine, Joy," he said, answering any unspoken questions. "*My Joy*. Whether you will it or not. You started this between us, and now I've a mind to finish it," he said, his voice a low rumble as he lowered his mouth to take hers, *to make her his wife*.

She tasted as rich and ardent as he remembered, more so, in fact, for this time they were both unfettered by restraint. He pressed her back into his bed, losing himself in the hot pleasure of her kisses, his hands in the thick heaviness of her hair, his body in the soft embrace of hers.

He had been right about Joy's passionate nature, for she quickly displayed her eagerness, fumbling delightfully as she tried to remove his tunic, and stroking his chest in wonder, just as if she had never touched a man before. Her movements excited him beyond measure, and Campion, too, felt as if all were new to him.

Although he had loved both his wives, he recalled his nights with them with a gentle warmth that little resembled this frantic heat. Joy was bold in her demands, pulling at his clothes, stroking his skin, rubbing her breasts against his chest, as she moaned her pleasure in a manner that drove his own passions to a fevered pitch. He could not get enough of her, and nearly tore her gown in his haste to have her naked beneath him.

Just a few days ago, Campion might have been horrified by his actions, but his blood was running too fierce, too freely, to hesitate. Joy was not satisfied with tender caresses and suddenly he wasn't, either. She had unleashed something inside him that made him mad for her, a certain madness that would not be eased by sweet kisses and light touches, but that craved a deeper, unbridled union.

In the throes of this blessed madness, Campion kissed her throat, her breasts, her stomach, while his hands roved over her smooth skin, exploring every curve and hollow. When at last he nudged her thighs open, Joy cried out in welcome. And when he cupped her there, he felt her teeth rasp against his shoulder in response.

Campion groaned, seizing her hips in his grasp, his fear of hurting her the only thing that kept him from taking her with a wildness he had never imagined. But as he waited, poised above her, his body shuddering with the force of his restraint, he realized that Joy was no gentle virgin, but a widow. Relief swamped him, sweeping away the last vestiges of his control, and with a lusty cry, Campion drove himself into her body.

Too late he felt the give of her maiden's barrier and her jerk of pain, for he was already buried deep inside her. And his pleasure was lost in his shame at this rough handling. Lifting his head, he looked down at her flushed face. "Joy?" he whispered.

She gazed up at him, her violet eyes wide but holding no rebuke. "I suppose now would be as good a time as any to tell you that my marriage was never consummated."

With a groan, Campion rested his forehead against hers, trying to think of something to say to soothe her, to apologize, but his usual eloquence deserted him, for the rest of his body clamored for something other than words. And then he heard the soft sound of her laugh.

He lifted his head once more. "Forgive me," he murmured, just as she said the same, and Campion felt his own rumble of laughter, a robust release that made him marvel at lovemaking where humor and ardor could exist together. Joy might be the virgin, but he felt she was teaching him afresh. And there was still so much to share with her, he realized, as his body suddenly reminded him of its position inside hers.

He kissed her hair and her ear and her throat, reveling in the taste of her salty skin, while she made soft sounds of delight, her laughter fading away when he rolled onto his back, so that she rested along his length. "Better?" he whispered.

"What?" She lifted her head, an expression of disbelief on her delicate features. "I'll die if it gets any better," she answered breathlessly, and suddenly all amusement left him as he moved, joining her in that sentiment. His efforts at long, slow thrusts were hampered by her impatient movements and her low moans of encouragement, until finally he gave in, burying himself inside her with uncontrolled passion, giving himself up to his joy until her guttural cry brought on his own shout of pleasure.

In the relative quiet of the aftermath, Campion left her resting upon him, her slight weight negligible, and he held her close as exhaustion claimed him. His new bride would either be the death of him or revitalize him beyond his wildest dreams, he thought with delight, but when her silence lengthened, his mood shifted.

"There is something else I forgot to tell you," she murmured, and Campion stiffened as she lifted her face to meet his gaze, her black hair an inky curtain around them. What now? he wondered, with no little alarm, but then she gave him a shy smile endearingly at odds with her former wantonness. "I love you."

Campion sucked in a breath as the strength of his own feelings threatened to overwhelm him. "And I love you, as I have never loved before," he whispered, knowing it was true.

Joy's violet eyes were wide and soft, and she leaned to press a kiss upon his mouth. When she pulled back, however, she tipped up her chin, and Campion nearly groaned at the sight that surely boded ill.

"I must say that as much as I enjoyed your rather barbaric efforts to win me, don't think that I'll stand for such tactics very often," she warned.

Campion frowned. "You'll marry me, Joy," he said, using his most regal tone.

"Yes," she murmured.

"Good," he said, sighing with relief. "Then there won't be any more primitive displays."

"Except in the bedchamber," Joy noted with a sly smile that roused his blood once more. Campion groaned.

"And there is one more thing," she said. Her dainty fingers played with the hair on his chest in a way that made it difficult to concentrate on her words. "You might have guessed that the rumors about my being barren are a little premature."

Startled from his contemplation of the feelings she

was inducing in his body, Campion lifted his head and laughed aloud. Everything about Joy was a joy, he thought, his arms tightening around her. But she was not yet ready for more love play.

"I hope you are not set against more children, just in case," she said, a hint of vulnerability showing in her violet eyes.

"Oh, I would welcome more babies," Campion said in all truth. He knew a sudden exhilaration at the notion and laughed again. "But is the world ready for more de Burghs?"

Epilogue

New Year's Day dawned clear and shiny as a piece of silver, just as if the Earl of Campion himself had decreed it, and Joy wondered for a moment if the man had dominion over the weather itself, causing it to strand her here to serve his purpose. The thought was not quite as improbable as it might seem, for had he not won dominion over her, a feat seemingly as impossible as ordering the snow and ice?

Yet as she stood in the great hall, watching the preparations for the feast to follow her wedding, Joy could summon no regrets. Roesia had been right. There was no stopping love and, having known it, she would sacrifice all for it. But Joy did not feel she was forfeiting anything in exchange.

Indeed, she was not giving up her independence so much as she was gaining a partner, joining forces with Campion in a union that would not stifle, but enrich her. Suddenly her world was bright with promise, not only of sharing a bed and a life with an incredible man, but of children of her own, a dream she had long ago dismissed as impossible.

For the first time in her life, she was part of a family, and what a family it was! Around her the hall was humming with the congratulations of the servants, genuinely happy at the news of the betrothal. Even Stephen seemed resigned if not enthused about the marriage.

"I suppose there's no help for it," he had said with a shrug, and lifted his cup in salute. "But I refuse to call you mother."

And Joy had laughed, her heart too full to argue as she waited for the priest and the guests to arrive. Although word had gone out, inviting all within the bounds of Campion's lands to attend, none had yet entered the hall, as if they were awaiting some sign. When Joy had asked why, Wilda informed her that none dared to be the First Foot of New Year's Day. Apparently the first person over the threshold was responsible for the whole year in some way that Joy did not full comprehend. And since she and Campion had arrived before midnight, all were watching the doors for the first official entrant.

Just as Joy grew impatient with such nonsense, there was a great commotion outside, as if the approach of many horses, while someone shouted about a party at the gate. Wedding guests? Remembering her own unforeseen appearance, Joy did not know what to expect, and she found herself watching nearly as breathlessly as Wilda. Although she cared little enough for superstition, this was her home now, and all who entered here would affect her.

A hush fell over the hall while each servant stopped to look, and then the great doors were flung open, and in strode a huge knight, followed by several others, and Joy knew a moment's fright. Frozen in place, she watched him doff his helm and shake out his dark hair—oddly familiar dark hair—and then a cheer rose up around her as all greeted the man's appearance as a good omen of the year to come.

And then Campion was hurrying forward to embrace the massive creature amid the cries of his people. "My lord Wessex!" they shouted. Wessex? Was this Campion's eldest son, Dunstan? But even as Joy tried to identify the man, she was surrounded by others until she felt buffeted by a sea of humanity: tall, dark-haired men, a variety of ladies in elegant costume, squalling infants, servants and outriders, all talking excitedly while the dogs barked their own loud greetings. It was an impossible din, and yet Joy could not help smiling.

It was Campion's family, and never had she seen such a wonderful, happy reunion. She tried to hang back amid all the poignant greetings, but to her astonishment, she too was embraced, by a petite, brown-haired lady. "Hello! I'm Marion, Dunstan's wife," she said, and promptly gave Joy the most beautiful smile she had ever seen, complete with two dimples. Joy smiled back, uncertain how to respond until she felt a familiar arm pull her close and the warm solidarity of Campion's body.

She leaned against it, no longer deeming herself weak for taking the comfort it offered, for this family was a bit overwhelming, in size, clamor and its sheer physicality. Joy would have felt dwarfed by them all, but for the woman called Marion, who, despite her stature, seemed as impressive as the rest of them.

And then, just as suddenly as it had started, the noise faded away to low murmurs, and all eyes turned toward Campion. How did he gain their attention so easily? Joy wondered, with pride and just a touch of awe. He smiled, and Joy could see how much he was affected by the presence of these people. "Welcome, my sons, but why would you brave such weather?" he asked.

"We were all at Wessex!" someone answered.

"Aye. They've been there for weeks, eating up my stores," the big one, called Dunstan, grumbled. "But we were loath to travel the last miles to Campion until the snow stopped."

Campion laughed with pleasure. "Then I shall not scold you for your trip, but welcome you gladly. You're just in time for the wedding!"

"A wedding! You haven't even met my wife yet!" a tall, rather grim looking fellow groused, acting annoyed. "Who is it? I suppose it's you!" he said, glaring at Stephen as if the brother had long been his nemesis.

Stephen made a low sound of disgust. "It's not me,

nor will it ever be me, for I have more sense than the rest of you!" he said.

All the dark heads surrounding them swiveled toward Reynold. "Don't look at me," he said with a grunt.

"Who then?" Dunstan growled.

Reynold tilted his head toward their father.

"Father?" Dunstan stared at his sire with a blank expression of astonishment that made Joy smile.

"Oh, how wonderful!" Marion rushed forward to embrace him and then hugged Joy once more. "Oh, I knew you were someone special," she whispered.

Joy was grateful for the welcome and the support implicit when Marion moved to stand beside her, for she faced seven strapping knights, two rather ferocious looking females and a variety of attendants, holding at least two babies. She swallowed, feeling distinctly uncomfortable under their regard, and she lifted her chin.

"This is Joy, soon to be Lady Campion," Campion said, and the glance he sent her was so filled with pride and love that Joy's anxiety eased. "At first she refused to marry me, but finally I managed to convince her, so please make her welcome, as I don't want to have to harry off after her again to bring her home."

Low laughter filled the hall, and Joy heard a voice call out, "Sounds like he got himself a stubborn wench!"

Although her face flamed, she could not help but

smile when three of the massive knights turned a sympathetic expression toward their father. The grim one was heard to mutter, "Aye. Join the rest of us."

Joy laughed aloud when a lovely blond lady beside him elbowed him in the ribs so hard that he grunted. And then the woman stepped forward, and suddenly Joy was surrounded not by dark knights but by beautiful ladies.

"Ignore them," said a slender, ginger-haired woman, directing a fierce frown toward the de Burghs.

"Yes! You are the one who has our sympathy," the blond one said. "I'm Bethia, and I know 'tis not every woman who can handle the men of this family."

"Well, I did not want to give up my independence," Joy said, seeking to explain the reluctance Campion had mentioned. And to her surprise all three of the women nodded in earnest agreement.

"Neither did we," Bethia said.

Joy blinked in confusion. "Then why did you wed?"

All three women glanced at each other before eyeing Joy with what could only be called wicked grins. Then Bethia leaned close, with a meaningful nod toward the men who stood not far away. "'Tis obvious enough," she said.

"As I'm sure you've discovered, these de Burghs can be most persuasive!"

Joy felt herself flush once more as she remembered

the manner in which Campion had convinced her to be his bride. Had similar skills in the bedchamber done much to win each of these singular women? Feeling a giddy kind of kinship with them, Joy loosed an answering smile much to their delight. The women immediately dissolved into laughter, making the men turn their heads with varying degrees of suspicion, and Joy realized that she would never be able to look at Campion's sons in quite the same way again.

Considering the pleased expressions of these ladies, the de Burghs were very persuasive indeed.

*   *   *   *   *

*If you enjoyed
"THE UNEXPECTED GUEST,"
be sure to look for Deborah Simmons'
upcoming Harlequin Historical,
THE GENTLEMAN THIEF, which will be
available in January 2000. Set in England
during the Regency period, it's the delightful
tale of a beautiful brain who stirs up trouble
during a season at Bath when she investigates
a jewel theft. Her "assistant," quite
remarkably, is the handsome and much
sought-after Marquis of Ashdowne....*

Start the year right with
Harlequin Historicals' first
multi-author miniseries,

KNIGHTS OF
THE BLACK ROSE

Three warriors bound by one event,
each destined to find true love....

THE CHAMPION, by **Suzanne Barclay**
On sale December 1999

THE ROGUE, by **Ana Seymour**
On sale February 2000

THE CONQUEROR, by **Shari Anton**
On sale April 2000

Available at your favorite retail outlet.

HARLEQUIN®
Makes any time special ™

Visit us at www.romance.net   HHKOTBR

Looking For More Romance?

Visit Romance.net

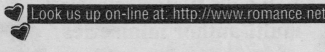
Look us up on-line at: http://www.romance.net

Check in daily for these and other exciting features:

Hot off the press

View all current titles, and purchase them on-line.

What do the stars have in store for you?

Horoscope

Hot deals

Exclusive offers available only at Romance.net

Plus, don't miss our interactive quizzes, contests and bonus gifts.

PWEB

Coming in December 1999
Two award-winning authors invite
you home for the holidays!

'TIS THE
Season
by
DEBBIE
MACOMBER and
LISA JACKSON

CHRISTMAS MASQUERADE by Debbie Macomber

He'd stolen a kiss in the crowd—and taken her heart with it.
Then she met him again, engaged to another! Jo Marie
dreamed about uncovering the truth behind the engagement
and claiming Andrew for her own groom!

SNOWBOUND by Lisa Jackson

All Bethany Mills wanted for Christmas was peace and quiet.
But sexy investigator Brett Hanson stirred up the past and
then whisked her away to his mountain cabin for safety—but
from whom did she need protecting…?

Available December 1999 at your favorite retail outlet.

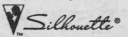

Silhouette®

Visit us at www.romance.net

PSBR21299

Temperatures rise and hearts sizzle in

TEXAS HEAT by MARY LYNN BAXTER

Bestselling author **Mary Lynn Baxter**
brings you three tempting stories about the
power of mutual attraction.

Passions ignite when three fiery women meet
the Western heroes they've always dreamed of.
But will true love be found?

Find out in **TEXAS HEAT**,
on sale November 1999
at your favorite retail outlet.

Silhouette®

Visit us at www.romance.net

PSBR31299

HEART OF THE WEST

Every Man Has His Price!

Lost Springs Ranch was famous for turning young mavericks into good men. So word that the ranch was in financial trouble sent a herd of loyal bachelors stampeding back to Wyoming to put themselves on the auction block!

July 1999	*Husband for Hire* Susan Wiggs	January 2000	*The Rancher and the Rich Girl* Heather MacAllister
August	*Courting Callie* Lynn Erickson	February	*Shane's Last Stand* Ruth Jean Dale
September	*Bachelor Father* Vicki Lewis Thompson	March	*A Baby by Chance* Cathy Gillen Thacker
October	*His Bodyguard* Muriel Jensen	April	*The Perfect Solution* Day Leclaire
November	*It Takes a Cowboy* Gina Wilkins	May	*Rent-a-Dad* Judy Christenberry
December	*Hitched by Christmas* Jule McBride	June	*Best Man in Wyoming* Margot Dalton

HARLEQUIN®
Makes any time special ™

Visit us at www.romance.net

PHHOWGEN

Come escape with Harlequin's new

Series Sampler

Four great full-length Harlequin novels bound together in one fabulous volume and at an unbelievable price.

Be transported back in time with a Harlequin Historical® novel, get caught up in a mystery with Intrigue®, be tempted by a hot, sizzling romance with Harlequin Temptation®, or just enjoy a down-home all-American read with American Romance®.

You won't be able to put this collection down!

On sale February 2000 at your favorite retail outlet.

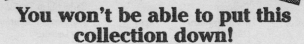

HARLEQUIN®
Makes any time special ™

Visit us at www.romance.net   PHESC